FROM THE EARTH

TO THE MOON

JULES VERNE,

TRANSLATED BY

EDWARD ROTH.

———

THE BALTIMORE GUN CLUB

*

THE INTERIOR OF THE PROJECTILE.

FROM THE EARTH

TO THE MOON

FROM THE FRENCH OF
JULES VERNE

FREELY TRANSLATED BY
EDWARD ROTH

(THE BALTIMORE GUN CLUB)

ÆONIAN PRESS
MATTITUCK

Republished 1976

Library of Congress Cataloging in Publication Data

Verne, Jules, 1828-1905.
  From the earth to the moon = The Baltimore gun club.

  Translation of De la terre à la lune.
  Reprint of the ed. published by King & Baird, Philadelphia.
  I. Roth, Edward, 1826-1911. II. Title. III. Title:
The Baltimore gun club.
PZ3.V594 Fro34   [PQ2469]   843'.8   76-26161
ISBN 0-88411-901-7

AEONIAN PRESS, INC.
Box 1200
Mattituck, New York 11952

Manufactured in the United States of America

TO

JOHN J. M^CELHONE, Esq.,

OF WASHINGTON,

A GENTLEMAN WHOM I AM PROUD TO CALL

MY FRIEND,

THIS ENGLISH EDITION OF

JULES VERNE'S WORKS,

IS GRATEFULLY DEDICATED BY

EDWARD ROTH.

PHILADELPHIA, MAY, 1874.

PREFACE.

Six years ago Verne's wonderful stories, among others his *De la Terre à la Lune*, fairly fascinated me. The boldness of the conceptions, the naturalness of the incidents, the details founded on the strictest practical knowledge, the liveliness of the narrative, the clearness of the thought—all revealing a mind that had sounded the depths of many an intricate scientific problem—were indeed a new revelation. Not only that. The elements usually considered indispensable in the ordinary novel, were totally absent. There was no killing, no betraying, no persecution, no heart breaking, no courtly pageantry, no metaphysical speculations, no mystery, no complicated plot, no thrilling descriptions, no fine writing, no photographic sketches of real life, no turning the human heart inside out, no apotheosis of nastiness—and still the story was profoundly and absorbingly interesting! An ideal story, pure as a sunbeam, less elaborately constructed than Poe's, but like them appealing altogether to the intellect of the reader and his innate love of the marvellous.

Surely, I thought, Verne's are just the books for our clear-brained, quick witted, inquisitive, restless, reality loving Young America, so different from his brothers in Europe, whether plodding Teuton or visionary Celt.

Our boys, I said, devour dime novels by the millions, for want of something better. They read English reprints, written for a lower order of minds, and therefore sure to deprave their tastes if not to corrupt their hearts. They blind

(3)

themselves, physically and morally, over books intended for older readers of more vigorous stamina, and therefore less liable to irreparable injury. Their school books are irksome and apparently useless, having so little in common with the volumes they find lying about at home.

Would not Verne's stories, I asked, suit them exactly? They treat on healthy manly subjects ; they give the intellect an exciting but not an enervating stimulus ; they are more suggestive of a breezy walk over sunlit mountains than the painted gorgeousness of a theatre or the sickening perfumes of a ball room ; they present pictures that invest studies in geography, chemistry, geology, history, and mathematics and physics generally, with a charm that is nevei discovered in school books. They inculcate earnestness, steadiness, thoughtfulness. When a bright eyed, pure hearted boy asks his teacher what book he can recommend, he may be answered at once, without any hemming or hawing.

Therefore, I fondly concluded, Verne's books are going to be immediately translated by enterprising American publishers, and scattered by tens of thousands all over the land.

How I reckoned without my host!

For five or six years not a single work of Jules Verne issued from the American press, except " Five Weeks in a Balloon," which, though in the main a good translation, contains so many geographical mistakes that it must have been done in a hurry.

Whence proceeded this indifference of American publishers to the Daniel Defoe of the nineteenth century? Was there some radical defect in his stories so great as to counterbalance his innumerable merits? No doubt some thought so. Cool heads might consider his conceptions rather extravagant, the incidents impossible, his science now too profound, now hard to separate from mere fancy, his local coloring distortion rather than exaggeration, his humor too thin to bear translation, his men machines rather than human beings, his sentiments odd, his English names harsh and even absurd, and his whole book, in fact, intended for a cast of mind essentially different from that of the ordinary American reader.

Charges of this nature, whether well or ill founded, seem to have completely blinded American publishers for several years, with regard to the merits of Jules Verne.

How little they knew the American public!

In spite of the alleged drawbacks, hasty translations of Verne's works by English hands, in which, either through ignorance, incapacity or prejudice, his errors—sometimes merely typographical—were uncorrected, his defects exaggerated, and even some of his best passages omitted—these translations, reprinted by American publishers, spread like wild fire last year over the country and were everywhere hailed with the greatest delight by both young and old.

Then my resolution was taken. It was to make an original translation, the best I could, of works of such undeniably inherent merit, a translation which, while strictly following the spirit of the author—this it could not do if slavishly bald and literal—would try to make the most of his strong points, throw the weak ones into shade, soften off extravagances, give the names a familiar sound, correct palpable errors—unless where radical, and then say nothing about them—simplify crabbed science, explain difficulties, amplify local coloring, clear up unknown allusions, put a little more blood and heart into the human beings—in short, a translation which should aim as far as possible at that natural, clear, familiar, idiomatic style which Verne himself would have used if addressing himself in English to an American audience.

Such services rendered to Jules Verne's stories, if done honestly, unobtrusively, and with even tolerable success, could hardly fail to be of decided advantage to the American public.

The present volume is my first instalment. In it the reader has Jules Verne done into real English, corrected, edited, annotated, revised—

Improved?

Well—I only hope the public may kindly think so.

E. R.

BROAD STREET ACADEMY,
        PHILADELPHIA, *April*, 1874.

CONTENTS.

ILLUSTRATIONS.

———◆———

CHAPTER I.

THE ARTILLERISTS.

It was during the great Civil War of the United States, that a new and very influential club started in Baltimore, Maryland. Every body knows the astonishing energy with which the military instinct suddenly developed itself in that ship-building, engineering, and commercial nation. Shop keepers who had hardly ever heard of West Point, jumped from their counters into the position of captains, colonels and even generals. Their knowledge of the art of war soon almost equalled that of the great masters of the old world, and, like them too, they won victories by enormous discharges of bullets, men, and "greenbacks."

But in gunnery especially the Americans even surpassed their brethren in Europe. Not that their arms ever reached a higher degree of precision; but they were constructed on a scale of such extraordinary dimensions that ranges were soon attained that had never before been known. As far indeed as regards plunging fire, flank fire, horizontal fire, oblique fire, raking fire, or reverse fire, the English, the French, the Prussians, had very little to learn; but even to-day the best European cannons, howitzers, and mortars are only mere pocket pistols in comparison to the formidable engines of the American artillery.

This is not surprising. The Yankees, the best mechanics on earth, are natural born engineers, as the Italians are natural born musicians, and the Germans are natural born philosophers. It is therefore the most natural thing in the world to see them bring their daring ingenuity to bear on the art of gunnery. Hence their colossal cannons, far less useful, indeed, than their sewing machines, but quite as astonishing and much more bewildering. The huge monsters devised by Parrot, Dahlgren, Rodman, are well known. And the Armstrongs, the Pallisers, the Whitworths, the Treville de Beaulieus, the Krupps, had nothing for it but to surrender gracefully to their American rivals.

Accordingly, during the terrible struggle between the North and the South, artillery ruled the roast in America; every day the Union journals chronicled enthusiastically the new inventions; in every country store, in every bar room throughout the land, the air resounded with "rifled cannon," "columbiads," "swamp angels;" and nearly every green grocer's clerk went crazy from calculating difficult problems about "the long range."

The moment an American conceives an idea, he gets another American to share it with. If they are three, they elect a president and two secretaries; if four, they nominate a vice president, and the society takes action; if five, they call a stated meeting and the club is established. That is exactly what happened at Baltimore. The first inventor of a new cannon associated himself with the first man who cast it and with the first man who bored it. Such was the nucleus of the Gun Club. A month after its formation, its register contained the names of 1,800 effective, and 30,575 corresponding, members.

It was an imperative condition on every one wishing to join this club, an absolute *sine qua non*, that he should have invented or at least improved a cannon—or if not a cannon, a fire arm of some kind. Still the inventors of 15 shooters, of revolving carabines, or of sabre pistols and such small fry, enjoyed but slight consideration among the members of the Gun Club. Here, as throughout the nation at large, the artillery men overshadowed every body else.

"The reputation they obtain" as a learned orator of the Club said one day, "is in proportion to the masses of their cannon, and in exact ratio with the square of the distance reached by their projectiles." A comical application of Newton's law of terrestrial gravitation.

The Gun Club once founded, you can easily figure to yourself the results soon reached by the inventive genius of the Americans. The new war engines assumed proportions still more colossal, so that the shells they discharged often killed people who were quietly engaged at their occupations miles beyond the target. Such inventions naturally soon left far behind them the timid instruments of European artillery. Just figure it out a little for yourself.

Once, "in the good old times," it was thought to be a pretty respectable performance, if a 36 pounder, at a distance of 300 feet, pierced, by a flank shot, 36 horses and 68 men. That was only the art in its infancy. It has made some progress since. The Rodman cannon threw a ball weighing half a ton a distance of seven miles, and could have easily stretched 500 horses and 300 men. For a time the Gun Club seriously entertained the idea of convincing the world of such tremendous energy by a grand ocular demonstration. But though the horses might possibly be brought together, unfortunately the men upon whom it was proposed to operate objected so decidedly that the idea was unwillingly abandoned; so this great scientific question is left unsettled to the present day.

One thing, however, is quite certain : the effect of these cannons was very destructive. At every discharge, the combatants fell before them like grass before the mowing machine. In comparison with such projectiles what was the famous ball that, at Coutras in 1587, in the wars of Henry IV., put 25 men *hors de combat*? Or that other which, at Zorndorff in 1758, when Frederic II. was fighting the Russians, killed 40 men? or the one thrown by the Austrian cannon at Kesselsdorf in 1745, which at every discharge made seventy enemies bite the sod? What were even those wonderful guns of Jena and Austerlitz that had so often decided the day? These terrible engines of death would be considered mere children's playthings in the Federal War! At the battle of Gettysburg, a conical projectile, shot by a rifled cannon, struck down 173 Confederates, and in the retreat across the Potomac, a Rodman ball sent 215 Southerners out of this wicked world without giving them even time to bless themselves. We must here likewise make mention of a formidable mortar invented by J. T. Marston, a most distinguished member and the Honorary Secretary of the Gun Club. This mammoth piece of ordnance at first excited universal enthusiasm, but its results by no means gratified the general expectation, for it burst at its first public trial, and killed a large number of the spectators, men, women, and children—337 all told.

These eloquent figures speak sufficiently for themselves. Nothing we can say could add to their effect. Accordingly we shall conclude this part of the subject by giving the following result, obtained after much calculation by W. G. Pitcairn, Esq., the statistician of the Gun Club. By dividing the number of victims who had fallen beneath bullets and balls, by the number of the active members of the Gun Club, he found that each one of the latter had killed, on an average, 2,375⅙ men. Even a hasty glance at the number must convince the disinterested reader that the only avowed objects of this learned society were: 1st, the annihilation of the human race—of course on grounds strictly philanthropical—and 2d, the improvement of cannon as the best instruments of civilization. The Gun Club

was in fact a Society of Exterminating Angels—
though at heart they were, no doubt, the very
best fellows in the world.

It is hardly necessary to add that these
Americans, brave as fire, by no means confined
their speculations to theory ; they tested them
by frequent practical experience. You could find
in the Club Register officers of every grade,
lieutenants and generals ; soldiers of every age,
blushing debutants in the career of arms and
grizzly veterans still standing solid at their posts.
Many had fallen in the battle field, and their
names were all carefully recorded on the Roll
of Honor. And many who had returned still
bore on their persons the marks of their un-
questioned intrepidity. Crutches, wooden legs,
artificial arms, iron hands, gutta percha jaws,
silver sculls, platina noses, false teeth—nothing
was wanting to the collection ; and W. J. Pitcairn, the statistician already mentioned, calculated that in the Gun Club, on an average,
there was only one arm for every four men,
and one pair of legs for every six.

But such trifling considerations never disturbed
the equanimity of these valiant artillery men,
and their bosoms swelled with proper pride, and
they congratulated each other with justifiable

emotion whenever the *New York Herald's* battle bulletin announced that the number of the slain was ten times greater than that of all the bullets, balls, and shells counted together.

One day, however, a sad and miserable day, peace was signed by the survivors of the war; the roaring of the artillery ceased; the mortars grew dumb; howitzers tightly muzzled, and cannons with their heads hanging downwards, were dragged off to the arsenals; the balls were piled into pretty pyramids; the bloody tracks of war began to fade away; the cotton plants grew to an enormous size on the richly manured fields; mourning garments began to disappear from the streets; and the Gun Club remained plunged in a lethargy profound, exanimate, and hopeless.

A few irrepressible workers, to be sure, unremitting drudges, would still keep on figuring at ballistic calculations and dreaming of gigantic shells and cyclopean howitzers. But, without practice, wherefore such vain theories? Accordingly the club rooms became gradually deserted; the waiters dozed in the antechambers; the newspapers, unread, grew mouldy on the files; the dark corners resounded with mournful snores; and the members of the Gun Club, once so bustling, so noisy, so exuberant, now reduced to silence by a disastrous peace, sulkily dawdled away their days and nights in reveries of platonic artillery!

"This is abominable," exclaimed Tom Hunter, one evening, wearily stretching his wooden legs, a splendid pair of Palmer's best. "Nothing to do! Nothing to hope for! What a miserable existence! Where is the grand old time when the cannon from Federal Hill woke us up every morning with its joyous detonations?"

"Those happy days are gone," sang Billsby the brave, jolly as ever, though one of his eyes was only glass. "That *was* a time to live in! You invented your cannon; it was hardly cast before you could try it on the enemy. Then on your return to the camp you got a shake hands from Little Mac, or an encouraging nod from Sherman. But now the generals are all back at their counters, sanding their sugar, watering their whiskey, and making the women believe that cotton is wool. Ah! the melancholy days are come indeed, and Othello's occupation is gone!"

"It's a fact, Billsby!" cried old Colonel Bloomsbury, quite energetically. "Our fate has been pretty rough. Take myself for instance! I gave up the oyster packing business forever,

2

to go to the war. I went to the war, I learned how to fight, I took my share in everything going, for nearly five years. A life of excitement and adventure became a second nature to me. Where am I now? Here, a shattered hulk, stranded high and dry, with nothing to do but put my hands in my pockets!"

The gallant old Colonel must have desired himself to be understood figuratively. Never again, poor fellow, could *he* put his hands in his pockets. The pockets indeed were plentiful enough, but what had become of the hands nobody ever knew—they had been blown off—arms and all—on the Fourth of July, 1864, by the bursting of a columbiad in the works before Petersburg. The Colonel had offered a liberal reward for their recovery, but it had never been claimed.

"And not a thing likely to turn up!" cried J. T. Marston, scratching with his iron fingers a part of his head where the skull had been replaced by gutta percha. "Not a shadow of a cloud in the political horizon! At a time, too, when so much has been left undone in the science of artillery! Even this very morning, I, the individual now talking to you, completed the drawing, with plan, section, elevation and all, of a mortar destined to work a revolution in the annals of warfare !"

"You don't say so ?" asked Tom Hunter, somewhat hurriedly, thinking perhaps of Marston's last experiment.

"Yes, it is all finished," replied the latter. "But what will be the good of so many studies mastered, of so many difficulties vanquished ? Isn't it working for nothing and finding yourself ? We Yankees seem determined to live in peace for the next hundred years, so that even Greeley is alarmed, and in this morning's *Tribune* comes out in an article showing that we shall increase so fast before the century is out that we shall be obliged to eat each other up for want of room."

"Still, Marston," replied the Colonel, "they are always fighting in Europe for something or other."

"Well ? what of it ?"

"Why, we might see what we could do over there, and if our services were accepted——"

"What are you thinking of, Colonel ?" exclaimed Billsby, even his artificial eye flashing with horror. "Study ballistics for the benefit of our natural enemies !"

"Better do even that than do nothing at all," retorted the Colonel.

"You're right, Colonel," said Marston. "Still we must not think of such a thing."

"Why not?" asked the Colonel.

"Because," replied Marston, "the folks of the old world entertain ideas regarding promotion singularly unconformable with our American notions. These people think that you should never become commander in chief without having commenced as lieutenant! That's as much as to say you should never point a gun without having commenced by casting it! Now I call all that——"

"Absurd nonsense!" cried Hunter. "But I know it is useless to argue with such people, and now I don't see anything else left for us to do except to raise tobacco in Virginia, or dig oil wells in Pennsylvania."

"What's that?" exclaimed Marston, in a voice that rang like a trumpet on the morning of a battle. "Do we so soon forget the grand and lofty aims for which our club was called into existence? Are we not most solemnly pledged to devote the remaining years of our lives to the improvement of all kinds of fire arms? Do you imagine that no opportunity will ever occur again for trying the range of our projectiles? That the atmosphere will never again flash with

the fire of our red artillery ? That no inter-
national difficulty will ever occur again which
will allow us to declare war on some trans-
atlantic power ? Will the French never run
down one of our steamers ? Will the English
be very anxious to settle the Alabama claims ?
Will the Spaniards never fire at our flag, mis-
taking us for fillibusters ?''

"I'm afraid not, Marston," answered Bloomsbury. "The incidents to which you refer are
too good to be likely to occur soon. And
even if they did take place, we should never
profit by them ! France, England and Spain may
bully us to their hearts' content ! Let them
bully ! We have made up our minds to have
peace for a hundred years, and peace we shall
have ! Thin-skinned Americans are getting out
of date. The conscription and the taxes have
so much disgusted us with war, that we are all
fast becoming a nation of women !''

"Humiliating thought !" cried Billsby.

"Degrading thought !" repeated Hunter.

"Both humiliating and degrading, if true !"
cried Marston, vehemently. "And true I am
afraid it is ! There are a thousand reasons cut
and dry for fighting, and yet fight we shall not !
We economise legs and arms for people who

hardly use them !—Hold on ! Did **n**ot America once belong to the British ?"

" So they say, at least," answered Hunter, curious to know what Marston was driving at.

" Well then, should not Great Britain in her turn belong to the Americans ?" asked Marston with a triumphant air.

" That would be only justice," exclaimed Billsby.

" Well, you go and propose that to President Grant ; how will he receive you ?"

" He would send us off with a flea in our ear," mumbled Billsby, between the only four teeth the war had left him.

" I shall never vote for him again," cried Marston.

" Never shall Grant obtain a vote from me !" cried all these invalid warriors with one voice.

" And now to conclude ;" resumed Marston ; " my new mortar is designed, and if I am not furnished pretty soon with the opportunity of testing it on a real battle field, I shall first send in my resignation as member of the Gun Club ; then I will buy a ticket and travel as far west as the Pacific Railroad will take me— never to return !"

"And we shall all follow you—never to return!" unanimously replied all his hearers.

In fact, things by this time had come to such a pass that the club was threatened with immediate dissolution, when all at once an unexpected event prevented the occurrence of a catastrophe so much to be regretted.

The very morning after the conversation detailed above, each member of the club received a circular worded as follows:

"BALTIMORE, MD.
"*October* 3, 186–.

"The President of the Gun Club has the honor to announce to his associates that at the stated meeting of the 5th instant, he will lay before them a communication calculated to interest them profoundly. Accordingly, he entreats them not to fail being present on said important occasion.

"Their devoted colleague,
"J. P. BARBICAN,
"*P. G. C.*"

CHAPTER II.

At eight o'clock on the evening of October 5th, the rooms of the Gun Club, 24 Monument Square, were crowded to suffocation. All the members residing in Baltimore or the neighborhood had been on hand almost since midday. As to the corresponding members, the trains had been landing them at all hours, and even at eight o'clock the cry was "still they come." The immense hall could not hold half of them. The neighboring rooms were closely packed: the passages were jammed: there was not a square inch of room to spare even on the grand staircase that ornamented the front of the building. All the streets in the neighborhood were so thronged, that the city cars stopped running for six hours. It had leaked out somehow that the President of the Gun Club had a very strange communication to make that evening, and every one in Baltimore, rich and poor, white and colored, was intensely curious to know its nature. In spite of the vast numbers, how-

(24)

ever, it was not a noisy crowd; the most exciting, contradictory and absurd rumors passed
from mouth to mouth, but only in whispers;
fear of losing anything by loud talking kept
them all comparatively still; though, of course,
they bustled and jostled, crushed and pushed,
and elbowed and shouldered, with all that liberty of action peculiar to a people accustomed
to self government, and never backward in ex-
ercising its privileges.

That evening, in Baltimore, no amount of
money could purchase a ticket of admission into
the grand hall; it was reserved exclusively for
the most distinguished members, resident or correspondent: even the ladies had to stay outside:
the Mayor and the City Council fared no better,
having to stand in the passages, where they
could see nothing, and with outstretched ear
trying to catch as well as they could all that
was going on.

The hall itself presented a spectacle at once
startling and interesting. The decorations of the
vast apartment were wonderfully appropriate.
Tall pillars, formed of cannons fitted to each
other in fishing rod style, stout mortars serving as
the bases, sustained the light, airy, lace-like cast-
iron trusses of the roof. Trophies, made of blun-

derbusses, arquebusses, linstocks, carabines, match-
locks, all kinds of fire arms, ancient and modern,
were grouped in picturesque array along the lofty
walls. Gas blazed forth from chandeliers made
of thousands of glittering revolvers, whilst giran-
doles of pistols and candelabras of guns piled
in circles, completed the splendid illumination.
Models of cannons, specimens of gun metal,
breech-sights riddled with bullets, target plates
pierced by the balls of the Gun Club, rammers
and sponges in varied assortment, shells strung
like pearls, grape shot twisted into necklaces,
fire balls formed into garlands,—in a word—an
endless variety of an artillery man's complete
stock of tools and materials surprised and pleased
the eye by their symmetrical arrangement, and
almost made you think that their object was
decoration rather than destruction.

In a most conspicuous position could be seen,
carefully protected from the dust by a magnificent glass shade, a shapeless mass of iron, rent
and twisted by the action of powder—the precious remains of J. T. Marston's giant cannon.

At the extremity of the hall, the President,
attended by four secretaries, occupied an elevated
platform. His seat, supported by a sculptured
gun carriage, affected the form of a 32-inch

mortar; it was pointed at an angle of 86° and suspended by the trunnions, so that the President could swing himself at pleasure as in a rocking chair, a convenience sometimes very desirable on account of the great heat. On the desk, which was a large wrought-iron plate supported by six carronades, lay an ink bottle of exquisite taste, made of a beautiful Biscayan rifle splendidly carved; beside it stood a detonating bell, which, on touching the button, went off with a report as loud as a pistol shot. Many a time, during the stormy debates, the ringing crack of this new fashioned bell, sharp and stunning as it was on ordinary occasions, altogether failed to make itself heard above the stentorian voices of the excited disputants.

In front of the desk, benches arranged in zigzag, like the circumvallations of an entrench-ment, formed a succession of bastions and cur-tains where the members of the Gun Club took their seats, and this evening indeed it could be said with truth that

"Warriors thronged the rampart heights."

They knew the President's nature well enough to be certain that he would not have called them together unless for some very grave reason.

J. P. Barbican was about fifty years of age,

calm, cold, austere, remarkably serious, and of all men perhaps the most taciturn and reserved; punctual as a chronometer, of a temper that nothing could ruffle, and of a resolution that nothing could shake. With no pretensions to chivalry, he rather courted dangerous—even rash—adventures, but he went into them coolly, and with a head full of practical ideas. He was rather an extreme specimen of the New Englander, the Northern settler, the descendant of Cromwell's Ironsides, and, therefore, the implacable foe of all cavaliers, whether they showed themselves as royalists in the old world, or republicans in the new. In a word, he was a cast-iron Yankee.

A native of the State of Maine, he had made an immense fortune in the lumber trade and shipbuilding; in the early part of the war he had equipped and sent to the field a whole regiment almost entirely at his own expense. His extraordinary genius for gunnery was soon known and highly appreciated, and though his name seldom appeared in the papers, his was the master hand that directed most of the great artillery operations by land and water. Fertile in expedients, bold to rashness in his ideas, he contributed powerfully to the progress of this branch of the service, and gave experimental researches an extraordinary impulse.

He was of about middle size and—rare exception in the Gun Club—his limbs were whole. His strongly marked features singularly resembled those given to Uncle Sam by the illustrated papers, only without their humor or grotesqueness. Severe, perhaps even harsh, they seemed to have been drawn with a square and ruler.   If, as it is said, you can tell a man's real disposition by looking at his profile, Barbican must have possessed energy, audacity, and imperturbability, each in an extreme degree.

At this moment he was resting motionless in his seat, silent, absorbed, concentrated, his face almost concealed by one of those tall "stove pipe" hats which seem to be screwed on to American craniums.

His associates chatted noisily around him, but he hardly seemed conscious of their presence; they asked questions, they ventured answers, they launched into regions of the wildest speculation, keeping a close eye in the meantime on the slightest movement of their President : it was all in vain : they were still as far as ever from getting at the difficult x of his inexcitable placidity.

But the moment the last stroke of eight o'clock

had been struck by the fulminating time-piece of the great hall, the president rose to his feet as suddenly as if he had been shot up by a spring; in an instant all noise ceased; the vast assembly was still as death, as the orator, in a slightly emphatic tone, commenced his long-expected speech:

" GENTLEMEN:

" Too long, as you well know, has a barren peace been steeping the members of the Gun Club in the mire of a listless inactivity. After a most exciting and eventful, but unhappily too brief, period of a few years, we have been compelled to abandon our labors and come to a complete stand still on the path of progress. I do not hesitate to say aloud, and I care not who hears me, that another war coming from any quarter whatsoever, got up under any pretence whatsoever, if it only once more put arms in our hands, I should hail with delight——"

" Certainly !" cried the excitable Marston. " We must get up another war !"

" Hear ! hear !" broke in the assembly on all sides, intensely interested.

" But war," continued the President, " at present is impossible, and, whatever may be the expectations of the honorable gentleman who has just interrupted me, it is my well founded opinion that many a year must elapse before we shall again hear our cannons roaring on a battle field. We must therefore make the best of our bad fortune, and look around in search of some other outlet for the restless energy that consumes us, and, if not legitimately employed, must soon destroy us!"

Redoubled attention on the part of the audience. The President was evidently coming to the point.

"For the last few months, gentlemen," resumed the speaker, "I have been asking myself if, whilst strictly confining ourselves to our speciality, we could not undertake some grand experiment worthy of the nineteenth century, and if the progress we have already made in ballistics did not afford reasonable grounds for its tolerable success. Therefore, I have been trying, devising, calculating, and the result of my labors has been my certain conviction that we are bound to succeed in an enterprise, which in any other country would not only be impossible, but actually ridiculous from its apparent absurdity. This great project, long and carefully elaborated, is to be the object of my present communication. I need hardly say that I consider it worthy of you, worthy of the honorable Gun Club, and that it cannot fail to make a noise in the world at large !"

"A great noise ?" demanded an excited gunner.

"A very great noise in every sense of the word," replied the President.

"Order ! order !" cried some of the members.

"No interruptions !" cried others.

"Therefore, gentlemen," resumed the President, "I bespeak your most earnest attention."

A thrill of new interest pervaded the assembly, as was particularly shown by eager cries of "louder ! louder !" from some old gentlemen listening outside in the passages, who were rather hard of hearing.

The President went on:

"There is no one among you, gentlemen, who has not gazed long and carefully on the Moon, or at least who has not heard of those that have. Do not be surprised if I have to say a few words to-night regarding the Queen of the starry sky. For us is perhaps reserved the glory of being the Columbuses of another new world. Have confidence in me, and second me by all the means in your power, and I shall guide you to her State or Territory, which we shall annex to all the other States and Territories that form the totality of our glorious Union !"

" Three cheers for the Moon !" cried the Club in an ecstacy of excitement, and the wild hurrahs almost blew the roof off.

" The Moon has been carefully observed and studied ;" resumed Barbican, " her mass, her density, her weight, her volume, her composition, her movements, her distance, her part in the solar system has been perfectly determined. Maps of the Moon have been constructed of a perfection pretty nearly equalling, if not surpassing, that of the best maps of the earth. Photography has taken incomparably beautiful charts of the surface of our terrestrial satellite.* In a word, we know regarding the Moon everything that the mathematical sciences, astronomy, geology and optics are capable of discovering : but to this day no direct communication has been established with her."

A violent expression of interest and surprise welcomed this assertion.

" Permit me, gentlemen," continued the orator, " to remind you in a few words that certain

---

* For instance, the splendid photographs obtained by De la Rue, Rutherford and others.

3

eager spirits, embarked on imaginary voyages,
pretended to have penetrated the secrets of our
satellite. In the sixteenth century a certain
David Fabricius, the discoverer of spots on the
sun, claimed to have seen with his own eyes
the inhabitants of the Moon. In 1649, a Frenchman, named Jean Baudoin, published a work
entitled *A Journey to the Moon, by Domingo
Gonzalez, a Spanish adventurer.* About the same
time Cyrano de Bergerac gave the world his
*Comic history of the States and Empires of the
Moon,* so much relished by the French even of
the present day, and the work from which
Dean Swift conceived the idea of writing *Gulli-
ver's Travels.* Somewhat later, another Frenchman—the French take great interest in the
Moon—the illustrious Fontenelle, wrote the *Plu-
rality of Worlds,* the master piece of the age.
But science in her onward march crushes even
master pieces ! About thirty years ago, a pamphlet, reprinted from the *New York Sun,* related
how Sir John Herschel, sent to the Cape of Good
Hope by the British government to prosecute
his astronomical observations, had constructed a
telescope internally illuminated and of such
wonderful power, that he had brought the Moon
within a range of eighty yards. Of course, at

such a short distance it was easy to perceive the dark caverns inhabited by hippopotamuses, the green mountains fringed with golden lace, the ivory-horned sheep, the snow white deer, the inhabitants themselves, 'man-bats,' winged creatures half bird half human being. This pamphlet, professing to be the advanced sheets of an article written for the *Edinburgh Journal of Science* by Sir John himself, was really the work of a countryman of our own named Richard Adams Locke, as I need hardly remind many of you, and it created for a time a profound sensation. It was translated into every language and had extraordinary success in all countries. In France particularly the excitement was intense. But it was soon discovered to be a hoax of the purest water, and the French themselves were the first to laugh at it.''

"A Frenchman to laugh at an American!" exclaimed Marston, "a *casus belli*, if there ever was one!"

"Keep cool, my worthy friend; the French, before laughing, had been completely duped by our clever countryman. But now, to end this rapid sketch, I must add that a certain *Hans Pfaal* of Rotterdam, quitting the earth in a balloon filled with a gas extracted from nitrogen, and thirty-seven times lighter than hydrogen, reached the Moon after a passage of nineteen days. This trip, however, I need hardly say, was like all the preceding, simply imaginary, but it was the work of another American, of strange, erratic, but transcendent, genius. There is no necessity to say that I allude to our famous townsman, the brilliant Edgar Allen Poe!"

"Hurrah for Poe!" cried the electrified assembly.

"I have now done" resumed the President, "with attempts purely literary and evidently insufficient to establish any serious relations between our earth and the queen of the nightly host. However, I must add that a few geniuses of a practical turn of mind, have endeavored to put us into serious communication with her. A few years ago, a German geometrician proposed sending a commission of savants to the steppes of Siberia. There, on the vast plains, thousands of miles in extent, they should erect structures in the shape of immense geometrical figures, among others, for instance, the square of the hypothenuse. These figures, strongly illuminated by reflected lights, every intelligent being could easily understand the meaning of. The inhabitants of the Moon, seeing them, would reply by a corres-

ponding figure, and communication once established, it would be the easiest thing in the world
to create an alphabet wherewith we could maintain
a regular conversation with our lunar brethren.
This was the German geometrician's ingenious
idea, but his project, for some reason or other,
was never put into execution, and to this day
no direct connection exists between the earth and
her satellite. But, gentlemen, it · is reserved for
the practical genius of Americans to establish this
connection. The means of doing so is at once
simple, easy, certain, infallible, as you will all
readily admit in a very few moments."

A hurricane, no, a cyclone of applause interrupted these words. Even the listeners outside
on the steps had caught an idea of what was
going on, and gave vent to the wildest expressions of excitement. But the people in the streets
kept still as death.

"Order! order! silence! shut up!" soon resounded sharply and imperiously from all quarters.

When the general agitation was a little calmed,
Barbican resumed his discourse in still graver
tones.

"You know, gentlemen, what progress the
science of gunnery has made within a few years,
and to what degree of perfection fire arms would

have attained, if the war had lasted a little longer. You are also well aware that, speaking in a general manner, the resisting power of cannons and the expansive power of gun powder may be considered actually illimitable. Therefore, grounding myself firmly on this principle to start with, I have asked myself if, by means of suitable apparatus constructed with reference to well determined laws of resistance, it would not be possible to send a ball to the Moon!"

Language cannot describe the mighty cry that rang from the vast assembly at these words. It was the concentrated expression of surprise, joy, pride, enthusiasm, all raised to the highest pitch of intensity. Then there was a calm like the hush preceding the earthquake shock. Then the storm burst forth in all its grandeur : a storm of yelling, shouting, screaming, stamping, beating the floor with sticks, and waving umbrellas in the air. The whole building shook with the reverberations. It was a tremendous scene. The ordinary American crowd is pretty quiet, and when under excitement rather undemonstrative than otherwise. But even in America, scientific men are exceptions to the general rule of humanity. In vain did the President try to restore order. He touched off the detonating bell.   He roared till he was black in the face.   His arms played around his head like the sails of a wind mill, until they dropped from sheer fatigue.   Fully ten minutes had elapsed before the storm had spent its rage so far that he could succeed in making himself heard.   " Let me finish, won't you ?" he cried in husky tones, " I have faced this great question in all its aspects, I have over-hauled it in all its phases, I have scrutinized it in all its relations, and figures` impossible to gainsay have convinced me that any projectile starting with an initial velocity of 12,000 yards a second, and shot in the. direction of the Moon, must surely and necessarily reach her. This grand experiment, gentlemen, I have now the honor of proposing to you for a trial !"

CHAPTER III.

THE EFFECT.

It would be useless to attempt giving even a faint description of the effect produced by the President's last words. The tempest broke forth with greater fury then ever. The yellings, screamings, stampings, batterings, wavings, etc., were repeated with an energy that seemed to have paused only to take fresh breath. If all the arms in the hall, not excepting the columbiads, had been fired off at once, they would not have made half such a din: or, to speak learnedly, they would not have set the vibrating sound-waves in half such tremendous commotion. But this, after all, is not so surprising. When we come to think of it, we know plenty of cannoniers who are far noisier than their cannons.

The President alone remained standing, calm and collected in the midst of this wild storm of enthusiasm; probably he wished to say a few more words on the subject, for his arms made desperate, but ineffectual, signals for silence, and the fulminating bell pealed volleys of detonations in vain. Very soon he was laid hold of by violent but friendly hands, and carried out in triumph to the balcony in front of the Club House, where his appearance was the signal for new demonstrations of the wildest applause from the vast multitudes.

They had all comprehended the idea in an instant, and saw no real difficulty in it. An American sees no real difficulty in anything. Whoever said that the word "impossible" is not French, was certainly wrong: he mistook the dictionary. In America everything is easy, everything is simple, from throwing off 50,000 printed impressions in an hour, to moving monster hotels, guests and all, to any quarter of the city at pleasure. In America, engineering difficulties seem to be all still-born. Between Barbican's project and its complete realization, no true American could see the shadow of a difficulty. To *say* it, meant to *do* it.

A grand torchlight procession was extemporized on the spot. Every one took part in it. The foreign element of the Baltimore population was quite as much excited as the natives. Irishmen, Germans, Frenchmen, Scotchmen, Englishmen, all national prejudice completely effaced, fell into line in a few moments, every man equipped with a blazing torch, though where they had got them at such short notice, I am sure I can't tell. In the enthusiasm of the moment, every one gave vent to his excitement in words of his own language, so that a strange jargon of sounds soon saluted the startled ear. " *Cead mille Failthe !*" " *Bully for you !*" " *Vive la lune !*" " *Hip, hip, hurrah !*" " *Hoch lebe der Mond !*" " *Three cheers for the Moon !*" " *Ti-gar-r !*"—not to mention the Ethiopian exclamations, which I would give you if I knew them—formed another tumultuary tower of Babel, of which the reader, if of a very active imagination, may possibly form to himself a picture. Strange to say, while this was going on, the Moon, as if aware that it was all done in her honor, came out from behind the fleecy clouds, glittering with a serene brilliancy that soon made the torches " pale their ineffectual fires." All eyes were turned towards her radiant disc ; some saluted her with the hand ; others called her pet names ; some measured her apparent size by separate finger and thumb ; others shook their heads and fists threateningly at her. An optician on Calvert street, who had nearly ruined himself by importing an immense stock of army telescopes before the close of the war, next morning found himself one of the richest men in Baltimore. The Moon was inspected as closely and as curiously as some fine lady in her opera-box on a fashionable night, or rather with the vivid interest which a man betrays for the horse that he contemplates purchasing. These daring Americans looked on her already as part and parcel of their glorious Union. To effect this, nothing more need he done than fire a cannon at her, a rather rude mode of courtship, no doubt, but one very much in favor among the most civilized nations. Annexations, from India to Alsace, are seldom accomplished in any other way.

The Cathedral bell tolled midnight, but the enthusiasm showed no signs of diminution; it seemed to have equally pervaded all ranks. The mayor, the stevedore; the city councilman, the hod carrier; the judge, the newsboy; the professor, the bootblack; the lawyer, the chimney sweep; the merchant, the sailor; the doctor, the policeman;—all felt themselves glowing with patriotic emotion; the national honor was intimately bound up with the success of the enterprise; accordingly, "Old Town" and "New Town," the wharves on the Patapsco and those on the Basin, Mount Clare and Canton, all parts of the city overflowed with crowds full of joy, noise, and whiskey. Everybody talked, speechified, discussed, disputed, applauded, contradicted—from the gentleman treating his numerous guests to champagne in the aristocratic mansions of Washington Square to the boat hand poisoning himself with "bug juice" in the dens of Fell's Point.

But as everything human must come to an end, the excitement at last began by degrees to die away. Barbican reached Barnum's Hotel in a dreadful state, his clothes all torn, and his body all black and blue. A Hercules could hardly have encountered such enthusiasm and lived. As the hours advanced, the streets become more and more deserted. The four great railroads converging at Baltimore, the Philadelphia and Wilmington, the Northern Central, the Baltimore and Ohio, and the Baltimore and Washington, had a busy time of it all that night and next day in whirling off the strangers to their homes in various quarters of the Union.

You must not, however, suppose that, during this memorable evening, Baltimore alone was the prey of such absorbing emotion. All the other great cities, New York, Philadelphia, Boston,

Albany, Chicago, Washington, Richmond, St. Louis, Charleston, and New Orleans, even San Francisco, from the Lakes to the Gulf, and from the Atlantic to the Pacific, all shared in the universal intoxication of intense curiosity. The 30,000 corresponding members of the Gun Club had each received the President's circular, and all those that could not go to Baltimore had been waiting with feverish impatience for the famous communication of the fifth of October. Accordingly, that very evening, as the words fell from the lips of the orator, they flew over the wires to all parts of the Union, at the rate of 20,000 miles a second. The assertion, therefore, may be safely risked without much fear of contradiction, that the whole United States of America, ten times the size of France, joined together in one tremendous in-stantaneous hurrah! and that forty millions of hearts, swelling with joy and pride, fluttered at the very same instant with the very same pulsation.

In "less than no time," as they say in Ireland, the question was grappled by the 574 daily papers,* by the tri-weeklies, the semi-weeklies, the

---

* Census of 1870.

weeklies, and by all the magazines, semi-monthly, monthly, bi-monthly and quarterly, 5,871 in all. They attacked it under every aspect, physical, meteorological, economical, moral, and whether viewed from the stand point of politics or of civilization. They asked themselves if the Moon was a world already arrived at perfection, or was it still undergoing some important transformation? Did it resemble the Earth at the time before our atmosphere had commenced to exist? What spectacle would be presented by that face of hers which always remains invisible to us terrestrians? Although at present the all-important point was to send a projectile to the starry queen, everybody could see plainly that this would be only the first of a series of experiments. It was expected confidently that the day was not far off when America would sound the profoundest depth of yon mysterious disc, and even some long-headed politicians fancied that they already saw therein the beginning of the breaking up of the European balance of power.

The question having been once set squarely before the public eye, not a single paper entertained the least doubt of its ultimate and complete realization. It was as certain as the "Centennial." The project everywhere met the warmest popular favor. Even the serious papers issued by the societies—scientific, literary, and religious—were quite enthusiastic on the subject, and published long eloquent articles conclusively proving that the millenium of happiness would dawn on mankind, and that all our sufferings, physical, mental, and moral, should instantly cease the moment intimate relations were established between the Earth and the Moon. In particular, the "*Historical Society*" of Boston, the "*American Society*" of Albany, the "*Geographical Society*" of New York, the "*Society of the Natural Sciences*" of Philadelphia, the "*Young Gentlemen's Christian Association*" of Chicago, and the "*Smithsonian Institute*" of Washington, wrote thousands of letters, congratulating the Gun Club, and offering every assistance in their power, whether money, advice, or active co-operation.

Never, we can truly say, did project receive such an immense number of adherents; of hesitation, doubt, uneasiness, there was not the glimpse of a shadow. As to malicious jokes, caricatures, or songs, which in Europe generally, but in France particularly, would have covered with ridicule the idea of sending a ball to the Moon—woe to the wit that would make them, to the artist that would draw them, and to the paper that would publish them! Even in America the caricaturists have to be careful in choosing subjects for excoriation. There, of course, as elsewhere, it is always pretty safe to make fun of the weak, to strike the man that is down. But even journals of civilization know better than to ridicule the party, the sect, or the idea that may, for the moment, be playing the predominant part in the eyes of the nation.

No wonder, therefore, if, for the time being, J. P. Barbican became all at once the most distinguished man of any age or country, a scientific GEORGE WASHINGTON, the popular idol whom it was absolute suicide to gainsay. One little anecdote, among many others of the same kind, will show how far "one man worship" may be carried even in the United States.

A few evenings after the famous meeting of the Gun Club, Mr. Marshall, the lessee of the Holliday Street Theatre, announced his intention of bringing out before the Baltimore public at an early date Shakespeare's famous play of *Much ado about Nothing*, with new dresses and scenery and an admirable cast of characters. But a crowd of those roughs called "*Plug Uglies*," and "*Blood Tubs*," seeing in the title of the play an offensive allusion to Barbican's project, broke into the theatre, tore up the seats, and threatened to set fire to the building, if the lessee did not immediately change his programme. Mr. Marshall, bowing before the storm of popular indignation, promptly withdrew the unlucky piece, replacing it by another of Shakespeare's plays, *As you like it*, which for several weeks had an immense run, the theatre being packed every night, as the *Baltimore Public Ledger* pithily expressed it, "from pit to dome," and "thousands being turned away, unable to obtain admission."

4

CHAPTER IV

All such triumphs had very little effect on Barbican's incessant activity. Without losing an instant, his first care was to call another meeting of the Gun Club. There, after slight discussion, it was unanimously resolved, first to consult the astronomers regarding the astronomical part of the enterprise; then, on the receipt of their reply, to decide on the most approved mechanical means of securing the success of the magnificent experiment.

Accordingly, a letter worded in the most precise terms, and demanding information on the most important points, was sent off that very evening to the Director of the University Observatory, Cambridge, Mass. This university, the first founded in the United States, it is hardly necessary to say, enjoys a world-wide fame, particularly for its astronomical department. Here are to be found united the most watchful of observers and the most daring of theorists; here Peirce has written his *Moon-Culminations*, Bond has

(50)

resolved the nebula of Andromeda into discrete points of light—a problem that had so far baffled all other astronomers—and Clarke has discovered a satellite to Sirius. Here, therefore, could the Gun Club, most confidently expect the latest and most reliable information on everything terrestrial and celestial, whether lunar, solar, or planetary.

In three days the answer punctually arrived, and you may conceive with what interest Barbican was listened to as he read its contents.

> "CAMBRIDGE OBSERVATORY, MASS.
> *October* 8, 186–.

"To the President and the other Members
of the Gun Club, Baltimore, Md.:

"GENTLEMEN:

"On receipt of your esteemed favor of the 6th inst., addressed to the Director of the Cambridge Observatory by the Gun Club of Baltimore, I have the honor to state that the members of our astronomical staff were immediately called together, and the several questions having been successively laid before them, the following respective replies were unanimously resolved upon:

"1. To question first: *Is it possible to send a projectile to the Moon?* we answer:

"Yes, quite possible, if you only endow your projectile with an initial velocity of twelve thousand (12,000) yards a second. A simple calculation shows such a velocity to be quite sufficient. As the force of terrestrial gravity decreases according to the square of the distance from the earth, the weight of the ball must rapidly diminish, and it will be reduced to zero the instant the attraction of the Moon becomes equal to that of the earth—that is to say, when the projectile has made the $\frac{47}{52}$ of the transit. At that moment it will have lost all its gravity, and, once that it clears this point, as a matter of course, it must fly directly to the Moon in obedience to the law of lunar attraction. The theoretic *possibility* of the success of the experiment being therefore rigidly demonstrated, its *certainty* clearly depends altogether on the force of the engine employed to discharge the projectile.

"2. To the second question: *What is the exact distance between the Moon and the Earth?* we reply:

" As the Moon's track around the Earth, is not a *circle*, but an *ellipse*, of which our globe occupies one of the *foci*, it follows that the Moon must be nearer to the Earth at some points than at others. The difference between her maximum and minimum distance is quite considerable. In her *apogee*, or greatest distance from us, she is 252,958 miles away; in her *perigee*, or nearest point to us, she is 221,593 miles away; which makes a difference of 31,000 miles between the two points, or more than a ninth of the whole distance. It is on our distance, therefore, from this *perigean* point of the Moon, that we must base our calculations.

" 3. To the third question : *How long would it take a projectile to travel this minimum distance, provided it had received sufficient initial velocity ; and, consequently, at what moment should it be discharged so that it might hit the Moon at a pre-determined point ?* we reply :

" Supposing the bullet to maintain all through its initial velocity of 12,000 yards a second, it would take only about nine hours to arrive at its destination; but, as this initial velocity must gradually diminish, it has been found, by some careful calculation, that the projectile would take $83\frac{1}{3}$ hours to reach the point where the terrestrial and the lunar attractions neutralize each other, and that from this point it would take 13 hours, 53 minutes and 20 seconds more to reach the Moon. In order to hit the Moon, therefore, at a pre-determined point, the projectile should be discharged 97 hours 13 minutes and 20 seconds before her arrival there.

" 4. To the fourth question: *At what precise moment will the Moon present herself in the most favorable position to be hit by the projectile ?* we reply :

" According to observations already presented, it will evidently be necessary not only to select the time when the Moon is in her *perigee*, but also, if possible, the precise moment when she is in the *zenith*, as that would be an additional shortening of the transit, by nearly 4,000 miles, the length of the earth's radius. Now, though the Moon is in her *perigee* once a month, it is only very seldom that she is in the *zenith* at the same moment, long intervals often elapsing before the two conditions are fulfilled. Evidently, therefore, you must wait for the coincidence of the *perigee* with the *zenith*. Fortunately, in the present instance, you will not have long to wait. On December 4th of next year, the Moon will present the two following conditions: at midnight she will be in her nearest point to the earth, and at precisely the same moment she will have reached her highest point in the sky.

" 5. To the fifth question: *At what point in the heavens should the cannon discharging the projectile, be aimed?* we answer:

" The preceding observations being once admitted, the cannon should be aimed vertically, so that, the line of motion being perpendicular to the plane of the horizon, the projectile may the more rapidly rid itself of the effects of terrestrial gravitation. And, as the Moon never departs further than 28° north or south of the equator, it is evident that the cannon must be placed in some spot comprised within these latitudes. Anywhere else the shot should necessarily have an oblique direction—a condition highly injurious, if not fatal, to the success of the experiment.

" 6. To the sixth question: *What point should the Moon occupy in the sky the instant the projectile is discharged?* we answer:

" Several considerations must here be taken into account: 1st, the velocity of the Moon; 2d, the velocity of the projectile; 3d, the effect of the earth's motion in deflecting the course of the latter. Omitting the

third consideration for a moment, it is clear that, as
the Moon moves in her orbit at the rate of 13° 10'
35" every twenty-four hours, she should be at a point
east of the zenith and four times that distance from it,
at the moment of the discharge; because as the
bullet takes four days to make the transit, at the end
of that time the Moon and the projectile should necessarily come together. But as we must also take into
consideration the amount of deviation imparted to the
bullet by the two fold motion of the earth, and as
we have ascertained this to amount to 11 degrees on
the Moon's orbit, we must evidently add these 11 degrees to the 52° 42' 20" already obtained, so that we shall
have a total of, say, 64 degrees in round numbers.
Therefore if, at the moment of the discharge, a line
from the Moon's centre makes with the vertical an
angle of 64 degrees, and *if all goes well*, the projectile and the Moon will infallibly come together in four
days, one hour, thirteen minutes and twenty seconds, a
few seconds more or less being allowed for the unavoid-
able imperfection of our instruments.

" To sum up :

" 1. The station for the cannon must be in some
country lying between 28° north and 28° south of the
equator.

" 2. The cannon must be aimed directly at the zenith
of the station.

" 3. The projectile must possess an initial velocity of
12,000 yards per second.

"4. It must be discharged on the first of December, next year, at one hour, thirteen minutes and twenty seconds before midnight.

"5. It will meet the Moon four days after, at midnight precisely, the very moment she reaches the zenith.

"The members of the Gun Club should therefore commence without delay all the necessary labors, so as to be ready at the appointed time, for if they let slip the favorable conjuncture presented at midnight between the fourth and the fifth of December, they will have to wait 18 years and 11 days before a similar opportunity occurs again.

"In conclusion: the professors composing the staff of the Cambridge Observatory unite in assuring the members of the Gun Club, that they will be always exceedingly happy to answer, as far as in their power, all further questions in theoretic astronomy; and they cordially join with the rest of our great Union in desiring the Club's complete success in practically solving the grandest scientific problem of the day.

"With highest regard,

(*Signed,*)   "J. M. BELFAST,

"*Director of the Cambridge Observatory.*"

CHAPTER V.

THE ROMANCE OF THE MOON.

Laplace, the Newton of the 18th century, surprised at finding the planetary orbits all nearly in the same plane, and the planets themselves not only rotating on their axes, but also revolving around the sun, in the same general direction, undertook to account for such phenomena by what has since been called the "*Nebular Hypothesis.*" This theory, though far from tenable on more grounds than one, is too stimulative of reflection, and too important in other respects, to be overlooked by the young astronomer. We consider the present a most favorable moment for alluding to its chief features, by way of an introduction to our Romance of the Moon.

Millions of ages ago, an observer, endowed with an eye of supernatural penetration and placed in the centre of our mighty universe, might have seen himself surrounded on all sides by endless myriads of atoms shooting incessantly in all directions, but by degrees more and more disposed to move around each other and to combine together, in obedience to the great immutable laws of attraction and chemical affinity which the omnipotent Creator of all things had established from the beginning. As the atoms coalesced, the observer could behold the particles growing larger and larger, and gradually assuming the nature of those nebulous clusters that we see at present faintly glittering like misty clouds in the dark depths of the midnight sky. The larger the masses grew, the rapider became their motion around a central point, where, as the whirling matter became more and more condensed, a bright central sun, the nucleus of the *nebula*, was the final result. What took place in his immediate neighborhood, the observer could see everywhere repeated around him, even into the regions of infinite distance. At the present day, astronomers count actually nearly 5,000 nebulas separate and distinct, and among them one, called by us the Milky Way, which contains at least 18 millions of stars, each the centre of a great solar system.

If our observer had watched one of these stars, and that by no means the largest or the brightest, he would have seen our SUN undergoing all the successive developments to which

every individuality in the Universe is subject.
He would have seen it, while still in a gaseous
state, and composed of ever restless molecules,
turning on its axis to complete its work of
concentration. He would have seen this motion,
in obedience to mechanical laws, become accelerated more and more with the increasing diminution of volume, until, at last, the time would
come when the centrifugal, or centre-flying, would
get the better of the centripetal, or centre-seek-
ing, force.

Then another phenomenon would take place
before the eyes of our observer. The molecules
lying in the plane of the equator would fly off
at a tangent, like a stone from a sling when
the cord snaps, and would form around the Sun
several concentric rings, resembling those of
Saturn. These rings, composed of cosmical matter, while spinning round the central mass, would
break up in their turn and decompose themselves
into secondary nebulas, that is to say, *planets*.
These planets, if attentively watched by our observer, would be seen to comport themselves
exactly like the Sun their parent, throwing off,
as he had done, one or more cosmical rings,
the origin of those secondary planets called
moons or *satellites*.

Counting back then from the satellite to the planet, from the planet to the Sun, from the Sun to the central star, from the central star to the nebula, from the nebula to the *nebulosity* (a shapeless mass of nebulous matter), from the nebulosity to the molecule, and from the molecule to the atom, we have all the transformations undergone by the various celestial bodies since the beginning of Creation.

So much for the *Nebular Hypothesis*.

The Sun, a small star belonging to the nebula called the Milky Way, insignificant as he appears in the immensities of the starry universe, is in reality of enormous size, his bulk being more than a million and a quarter times greater than that of our Earth. Around him gravitate eight planets, sprung, as has been conjectured, from his viscera, but how many ages ago nobody can say. These planets are in order: Mercury, Venus, the Earth, Mars, Jupiter, Saturn, Uranus, and Neptune. Besides these, in the space between Mars and Jupiter, are circulating the Asteroids, more than 110 of them being discovered so far; they are probably the pieces of a shattered ring or planet, though Leverrier has shown that their combined mass can hardly exceed the one-fourth of that of our Earth.

The planets are kept in their orbits around the Sun by the great law of gravitation, and some of them in their turn are attended by satellites of their own, Saturn having eight; Uranus, eight; Jupiter, four; Neptune, perhaps three; and the Earth, one. It was this latter one, called the *Moon*, the least important of all the heavenly bodies, that our daring Americans had now determined to conquer.

This beauteous queen of the night, relatively so near us, and so regular in the variety of her phases, must from the very beginning have shared with the Sun the interested attention of man. For the Sun, with all his power and majesty, is too dazzling to the eye to be contemplated with pleasure, whereas the gentle Phœbe, gracious and more humane, attracts the delighted gaze of all by the sweetness and modesty of her demeanor. With all her demureness, however, she sometimes takes the liberty of eclipsing her mighty brother, completely shearing the radiant Apollo of his golden beams. The regularity of the period of her revolution around the earth, nearly 30 days, being probably the first astronomical observation ever made by man, she has given her name to the early division of time called the *Month*, and even to this day among the Mahometans, the *lunar month* is the regular and the only one.

The ancients held the chaste goddess in especial esteem, and paid her divine worship; the Egyptians calling her Isis; the Phœnicians, Astarte; the Greeks, Artemis; the Romans, Diana; but in the early ages, even the philosophers appear to have known very little of her constitution or size, and the laws which regulated her movements. The Arcadians held that their ancestors had inhabited their country before the very existence of the Moon; Simplicius considered her to be motionless and fixed in a crystal sphere; Tatius looked on her as a detached fragment of the solar disc; Clearchus made her a polished mirror, reflecting the surface of the oceans; while others saw in her nothing but a revolving globe half ice, half fire, or .even a condensed mass of vapors exhaled from the earth.

Still, some of the sagacious ones, by dint of careful observations, every now and then got a glimpse of the true state of things. Thales, born at Miletus about 640 years before Christ, said that the Moon was illuminated by the Sun, and predicted an eclipse. Aristarchus of Samos, gave a correct explanation of her phases. Berosus, of Chaldea, who lived in the time of Alexander the Great, discovered that the period of her rotation round her axis was equal to that of her revolution around the earth, and that, therefore, she should always present to us the same face. Hipparchus of Rhodes, 150 years before Christ, discovered inequalities in her movements, which were confirmed, 150 years after Christ, by Ptolemy of Egypt. Further investigations, successfully prosecuted by Abou l'Wafa, of Bagdad, in the tenth century, were at last completed by Copernicus, the famous priest of Thorn, in the fifteenth century, and by Tycho Brahé, of Denmark, in the sixteenth, who at last pretty nigh exhausted every difficulty in the great problem of the lunar movements.

Then Galileo of Florence took up that of her physical constitution, and, by means of shadows cast upon her surface, calculated some of her mountains to be about 27,000 feet high, almost equal to the Himalayahs. This altitude Hevelius of Dantzic reduced to 15,000 feet, about the height of Mont Blanc, but Riccioli, the Jesuit professor at Bologna, calculated some of the mountains in the Moon to be at least 42,000 feet high. Sir John Herschel, the illustrious discoverer of Uranus, by means of his gigantic forty foot telescope erected at Slough, near Windsor, about 90 years ago, reduced these altitudes even below that given by Hevelius. But Herschel himself was wrong, and the long and patient studies of many eminent astronomers, more particularly those of Messrs. Beer and Mädler, and of many others before them whose names it would now be tedious to enumerate, were still required before the question was finally decided. Thanks to such labors, the height of the mountains of the Moon is now well known. Professor Mädler, till 1866 the Director of the famous Observatory of Dorpat in Russia, in conjunction with his intimate friend Wilhelm Beer, brother of the celebrated composer Meyerbeer, has published a map of the Moon, giving the locality and height of 1,095 mountains, of which twenty-two are ascertained to be above 14,000 feet high, six to be above 15,000, while the highest peak lifts it summit nearly 29,000 feet above the surface of the lunar disc. Galileo, therefore, and especially Hevelius were very nearly right, and it is worthy of remark that the height of the great mountains of the Moon was known long before that of those of the Earth.

The surface of the Moon was also subjected

to the closest examination; it appeared to be riddled with craters, and every observation confirmed its volcanic character. From the fact that the planets eclipsed by her underwent no refraction at the moments of occultation, it was argued that she must be absolutely without an atmosphere. Absence of air necessitated an absence of water, so that the Selenites (the inhabitants of the Moon), if there were any, must evidently possess an organization of a very special nature and totally different from ours.

By means of their improved instruments, the astronomers, leaving no part of the Moon's surface unexplored, went on confirming or disproving old discoveries and making new ones. They ascertained her diameter to be 2,159.6 miles, somewhat more than the quarter of our Earth's; her surface to be about 14½ millions of square miles, bearing the proportion to that of our globe as 1 to 13; and her volume to be about forty-nine times smaller than that of our terrestrial abode. They further remarked that the Moon, at her full, showed certain portions of her disc streaked with white lines, which, at her phases changed into corresponding black ones. These strange phenomena they puzzled over long and carefully, without coming to any satisfactory

5

conclusion as to their nature or origin. They were long narrow furrows, with parallel sides, ending generally in the neighborhood of craters, their average width being less than a mile, while their length varied from ten to a hundred miles. The Germans called them *Rillen;* the French, *rainures;* the English, *grooves* or *clefts;* but that was all they had for it. Whether they were immense cracks produced by the cooling of the surface, or streams of lava, or dried up beds of ancient torrents, nobody could say with any certainty.

Of this great geological curiosity, the Amercans were now fully bent on determining the nature. They also reserved to themselves the task of investigating the *famous series of parallel ramparts or earth works,* claimed to be discovered on the Moon's surface by Professor Gruithuysen of Munich, who looked on them as a system of gigantic fortifications erected by the Selenite military engineers. Such points, and many others still involved in hopeless obscurity, could evidently be finally settled only by direct communication with the Moon.

As to the relative intensity of her light, the Club knew that they had not much to learn. Zöllner's tables had satisfied them that the Sun gave more light than half a million full Moons scattered together all over the sky like stars, if there would be room for them. Her heat—as Lord Rosse's experiments with his mirror, reflecting the most minute deflections of an exceedingly delicate galvanometer, had informed them—was of no practical account, as it exerted no effect deserving appreciation; and as to the *ashy light* by means of which we see the phenomenon of " *The old Moon in the young Moon's arms,*" they already knew it to be due to the *earth-shine*, or the sun-light reflected to the Moon from the Earth's surface.

This was about the total amount of positive knowledge to which the world had arrived regarding the nature of its satellite, when the members of the Gun Club set themselves to work to complete it in every point of view, whether cosmographical, geological, physical, political, or moral.

The young reader who finds the preceding chapter somewhat dull, might mend matters considerably by going over it again with redoubled care and attention. Doing so would certainly enable him to enter with greater relish on the recital of the tremendous difficulties that the enthusiastic Baltimorians were preparing to encounter.

CHAPTER VI.

WHICH LADY READERS ARE REQUESTED TO SKIP.

The immediate effect of Barbican's proposal was to make every body brush up whatever astronomical knowledge he had ever acquired regarding the Moon. All books on the subject were in immediate and universal demand. You would think it was the first time she had ever appeared in the sky. Nobody could see enough of her. She became the rage, and I must say that, for a "star," she behaved herself with remarkable modesty. The newspapers were full of paragraphs learned, brilliant and sentimental, and sometimes very much otherwise, on the inexhaustible subject. The humorists filled their almanacks with jokes about her: when the lecturers announced her as their subject, the audience had not sufficient standing room: in short, all America, as the *New York Herald* wittily phrased it, had "Moon on the brain."

No wonder then if the monthlies and the quarterlies soon teemed with heavy articles on "*Nodes,*" "*Librations,*" and "*Synodical revolu-*

(68)

tions," or if the *New York Weekly Bulletin,*
with its circulation of 420,000, escaped immediate destruction only by interrupting its great
story of " *Grim Dick, the one-eyed Robber,*" in
its 75th chapter, to make room for a series of
articles on the "*Lunar Parallax,*" by an eminent professor of Yale College. In a word, a
flood of science overwhelmed the land, and from
one end of it to the other there was no true
born Yankee to be found, man or woman, who
was not ready to seize you by the button, and
tell you in five minutes more about the Moon,
than you had perhaps ever learned before in all
the days of your life.

For instance, if you had forgotten how the
distance from the Earth to the Moon is calculated, they told you it was easily got by measuring the Lunar parallax, that by this method
the mean distance was ascertained to be a little
less than 240 thousand miles, and that, if you
had any doubt on the subject, they could convince you by the simplest laws of trigonometry
that the astronomer's greatest possible error could
not amount to more than 70 miles at the utmost. Thereupon, they told you, whether you
desired the information or not, that the Moon
has two separate and distinct motions, one

around her own axis, and the other around the
Earth, both being accomplished in exactly the
same time, about 27⅓ days, the period of the
sidereal revolution. At this should you unfortunately, through mistaken politeness, feign an
interest you were far from feeling, they took
advantage of the opportunity to assure you that
the rotation of the Moon around her axis
caused her days and her nights to be of equal
length, each a half month long. The face
turned towards the Earth, however, they hastened
to inform you, did not suffer as much as might
be expected from a night of such unconsciona-
ble duration, as all that time the Earth illuminated it with an intensity equal to that of
thirteen full moons. As for the other face,
"ne'er of human eye beheld," for fourteen
mortal days its night lasted of absolute darkness, dense and dismal, unless it was tempered
by the

"Gloomy splendor of the pallid stars."

Supposing that you were of too practical a turn
to relish poetry, and accordingly asked how it
could happen that the Moon, whilst revolving
on her axis, invariably kept the same face
turned towards the Earth, they were down on
you like lightning with a reply prosaic enough.

"Go into your dining room," they cried; "walk round your dining table in such a way as to keep your eyes always fixed on its centre. When you have turned around it once, you will have turned around yourself also, since you will have faced every point of the room in succession. Well! the room is the sky, the table is the Sun, and you are the Moon yourself!" In their delight, however, at the aptness of the comparison, they never forgot to add that, speaking with rigid exactness, in consequence of a certain vibratory movement of the Moon termed "libration," she shows somewhat more than the half of her disc, about 57 per cent. on an average.

Though they had by this time crammed you with as much knowledge regarding the rotation of the Moon on her axis as could be conveniently held even by the Director of the Cambridge University, they had no notion whatever of letting you off without enlightening you further on the nature of her motion around the Earth. This time they compared the "starry firmament on high" to a vast dial plate upon which the Moon marks the days of the lunar month by her varying phases; observing that she is *full* when the Moon and the Sun are in opposition, that is, in opposite parts of the heavens; that she is *new* when they are in conjunction, that is, nearly together; and that she is in her *first* or *last quarter*, when lines from the Sun and the Moon, meeting in the earth, there form a right angle.

A suppressed yawn accompanied by a gentle hint that you had read something like this long ago in your school books, would have very little effect. Alarmed lest you had forgotten all about the theory of eclipses, they hastened to remind you that in *conjunction* the Moon could eclipse the Sun, in *opposition* the Earth could eclipse the Moon, and that if these eclipses did not take place twice a month, it was all owing to the fact that the Sun and the Moon do not follow exactly the same path in the heavens.

This remark, of course, brought on another as to what path the Moon *does* follow. The Cambridge letter had been sufficiently explicit on this point, but the temptation to *spread himself* would be too great for your informant to resist. " As the Moon," he would say, " never comes further north than 28 degrees from the equator, and never goes further south than a corresponding distance, it is evident that the grand experiment can be made only in countries lying within those parallels. Baltimore, being in 39°, Philadelphia, in 40°, and New York, in 41° north latitude, these cities can never be taken as the scene of operation. A projectile shot perpendicularly from either of these localities could not possibly reach the Moon, her path lying too far south. A projectile shot obliquely would be too much clogged at the start by the earth's attraction ever to reach its destination. No, no, my dear sir, the success of the experiment imperatively demands that the cannon shall be placed in a spot over which the Moon comes *exactly vertical.* In such a spot alone, sir, the thing has got to be done, but where that spot is, I am not just now quite prepared to say."

Here your informant, very probably the intelligent proprietor of a cigar store, or, still more likely, an enthusiastic Lady Teacher of the Public Schools, seeing the physical impossibility of detaining you any longer, would at last let you off with a parting shot: "As for the line described by the Moon around the earth, every child attending a primary school knows that it is, not a *circle,* but an *ellipse,* as by the laws of mechanics it is bound to be. Now, as the Earth occupies one of the *foci* of this ellipse, it is clear as the noonday Sun, that the Moon must be much nearer to us at her *perigee* than at her *apogee*—excuse me for talking so scientifically—I mean, at one portion of the month than at the other."

Then you made off, staggering under your load of knowledge.

In spite, however, of the universal enlightenment on every subject connected with the Moon, some excentric spirits entertained notions of their own, which, either from an affectation of singularity or a love of contradiction, they would freely ventilate on every possible occasion. One, for instance, would gravely tell you that the Moon was nothing but an old burned out comet, " played out " was his exact expression, and he triumphantly pointed to her volcanic aspect in proof of his assertion. It was useless to tell him that a fatal objection to his theory lay in the fact that the Moon has no atmosphere, whereas comets always have one. This reply might " shut him up " for the moment, but at the very next scientific discussion, his pet theory was enunciated with all the solemnity due to a profound truth when first revealed to mankind.

Another genius, of the timid and self-tormenting order, a graduate of the Philadelphia High School, with a laudable thirst for self-improvement regarding the great question of the day, had taken to reading Proctor's various astronomical works, and the result may be readily guessed. In his honest efforts to understand the various diagrams illustrative of *sidereal revolution, syzygy, annual equation, oscillatory variation, parallactic inequality*, and similar abstrusities, his poor brain had completely given way, and he now remained a hopeless idiot with one fixed idea in his head to the utter exclusion of everything else. This was, that as the velocity of the Moon's motion around the earth was constantly accelerating, the distance between the two bodies should therefore be constantly diminishing, and that consequently the day was fast approaching when the Moon should pop down on us and crush us all to pieces. This alarming notion he seemed to entertain with positive delight, and he took care to propagate it everywhere. "What a capital joke" he would exclaim, rubbing his hands and chuckling gleefully, "for those fellows of the Gun Club to try to get to the Moon! Let them only wait a while, and they will make her acquaintance a little too soon for their

comfort ! Yes, soon and sudden she will come
it with a rush, and knock every mother's son
of us into a cocked hat !'' Everybody, of course,
knew that all this had been often said before,
and that Laplace had settled the matter conclusively by showing how the Moon's acceleration
is self-compensating, or, if not quite so, that
millions of years must elapse before the slightest
collision can ensue. But you might quote Laplace to our alarmist till you were black in the
face. He would pit Adams against him as later
and therefore better authority, and really the
crazy fellow had altogether such a method in
his madness, that he terrified many even of
those heretics hardened enough to make open
profession of disbelief in the oracles of " Old
Probabilities.''

The most numerous of all the dissenters were
the ignorant and superstitious classes, abundant
enough in other countries, and not yet altogether
suppressed in the United States. These worthies
despised all books, observations, and calculations
whatsoever, and took a pride in denouncing
them as all stuff and humbug. They even pretended to thank heaven for their ignorance,
and heaven knows they had quite enough to
be thankful for. Their self sufficiency, however,

did not prevent them from believing firmly in "Mediums," "Clairvoyants," and "Astrologers." They saw in every change of the Moon a warning of *something* that was going to happen very soon, a revolution, an earthquake, a murder, a marriage, a robbery, a railway accident, the breaking up of a "Ring," the birth of a boy, the birth of a girl, a fire, or the failure of a great financial house that plunged thousands of families into ruin. No matter what happened, "Hadn't they told you so?" The worst of it was that they never "told you so" until the thing had become the common talk, and every body else knew everything about it.

But all opponents put together, whether paradoxists, or alarmists, or invincibly ignorants, were a mere drop in the bucket, when compared with the numbers that ranged themselves solid and determined around the great enterprise undertaken by the Gun Club. Ninety-nine out of every hundred were thoroughly "sound on the goose," to use the expression employed by an enthusiastic Philadelphia deputation; and from this time forward the leading and all-absorbing idea of the country was to annex as soon as possible the beautiful Queen of the Night to the territory of the United

States, and to plant the glorious flag of the
Stars and Stripes on the summit of her loftiest
mountain.

CHAPTER VII.

THE MATERIAL OF THE BULLET.

The astronomical side of the question being settled, the mechanical remained. This, of course, was the real trouble, and in any other country the enormous practical difficulties it presented would have been insurmountable. In America it was rather play than work to conquer them.

The indefatigable Barbican without losing an instant had nominated an executive Committee, which, in three separate sessions, was to decide on the three great points of interest: the gun, the projectile, and the powder. The members of this committee were four in number: Barbican himself; General Morgan, the hero of Fort Walker; Major Elphinstone, the inventor of the *Elphinstone Torpedo;* and Mr. J. T. Marston, already well known to us as the inventor of the great cannon-mortar that had burst, and blown up a whole street in Baltimore. They met on the evening of October 9th, at Barbican's residence, 137 North Hanover Street. As it was important that the inner man should not suffer during what promised to be a lengthy discussion, a box of very fine *Partagas* lay on the table, and, by touching a bell, hot coffee and rolls were immediately furnished by a dúmb waiter, in a corner of the room, without any intervention whatever of servants.

Barbican, as President, opened the meeting.

" The question before us this evening, gentlemen," he commenced, " is to resolve one of the most difficult problems presented by Ballistics, that great and fascinating science to the especial study of which we have devotedly consecrated so much of our thought and so much of our time."

" Hear ! Hear !" cried Marston.

" Should it meet your approbation," continued the President, " I propose that, instead of beginning with the cannon,——."

"Oh ! the cannon first, by all means !" cried General Morgan.

" Instead of beginning with the cannon," continued Barbican, not heeding the interruption, " I propose that we commence first with the bullet, since it is evidently upon the dimensions of the projectile that those of the cannon depend."

"I wish to make a few remarks on this subject, gentlemen," said Marston, suddenly starting up; "I want to say a few words on the bullet in a moral point of view. I now leave altogether out of the question the physical bullet, the killing bullet, the terrible element of destruction. We are done with that now, and probably forever. I mean the scientific bullet, the mathematical bullet, the moral bullet, the bullet we shall send to the Moon, the bullet that is to be our ambassador to the celestial spheres! In this bullet I see the most sublime instance of human power. In it, I see that in which man has brought himself nearest to his Creator!"

"Hurrah!" cried the audience.

"Yes!" continued the orator, warming up; "God has made the stars, and the suns, and the planets; and man has made the bullet, a star, a sun, a planet in itself, though, I admit, on a very small scale. To our Creator the glory of the velocity of light, of electricity, of the stars, of the comets, of the planets, of the satellites, of the plunging cataract, of the roaring hurricane! But to us, gentlemen, the glory of the velocity of the *bullet*, a hundred times faster than the fleetest steed that ever spurned earth with flying hoof, a hundred times swifter

6

than the rapidest train that ever skimmed over the glassy surface of a steel railroad !"

The orator had now lifted himself up to the full dignity of his subject, and his words flowed on with the impetuosity of a noble river.

"Do you want proofs of what I advance ?" he continued. "You shall have them, in figures that never lie! in figures of burning eloquence! Take a simple twenty-four-pounder. It moves, it is true, 800 thousand times slower than electricity, 640 thousand times slower than light, 76 times slower than the Earth in her orbit, still, at the moment that it leaves the cannon, its velocity exceeds that of sound—once you hear the report your life is safe—it travels 1200 feet in a second, 12,000 feet in ten seconds, 14 miles in a minute, 840 miles in an hour, more than 20 thousand miles in a day—almost equal to the equatorial rotation of the Earth—and nearly seven and a half millions of miles in a year. It would, therefore, take only eleven days to reach the Moon, twelve years to hit the Sun, and 360 years to arrive at Neptune on the extreme verge of our solar system. That is what our modest twenty-four-pounder can easily do. But what should I say of it, if, increasing its velocity thirty fold, we discharge it with a rapidity of seven miles in a single second! Oh noble bullet, glorious projectile! I love to think on the honors that await thee in yonder luminary, who shall embrace thee with delight, as the lordly ambassador of her sister sphere!"

Warm applause greeted the orator as he sat down wiping his forehead after this eloquent burst, but the President cut it somewhat short by observing dryly:

"From beautiful poetry we must now descend to humble prose. The question before us is how we are to impart to a projectile a velocity of 12,000 yards, or seven miles a second. I have reason to think that we can do it. First, however, it may help matters to see what are the greatest velocities hitherto attained. General Morgan may be able to enlighten us a little on the subject."

"Yes," replied the General, "being on the Experiment Committee during the War, I had many opportunities to get thoroughly posted on the subject. I shall begin by stating that the Dahlgren hundred-pounder threw a ball a distance of nearly three miles with an initial velocity of 500 yards to the second."

"Very well. And the Rodman Columbiad?" asked the President.

" The Rodman Columbiad, tested at Fort Hamilton, near New York, threw a ball weighing a thousand pounds a distance of six miles, with an initial force of 800 yards to the second, a result never attained either by Armstrong or Palliser in England."

" And not likely to be either !" exclaimed Marston. " Johnny Bull is too clumsy with fire arms not to be afraid of blowing himself up !"

" So then," resumed Barbican, " 800 yards a second is the highest initial velocity attained up to the present time ?"

" Correct," nodded Morgan.

" Ah !" exclaimed Marston, " if that mortar of mine had not burst——."

" But it *did* burst, you know," replied Barbican, waiving further discussion by a kindly gesture. " Let us take then for our starting point this initial velocity of 800 yards. This must be increased at least 15 times, and reserving for another sitting the discussion of the means capable of producing such a velocity, we shall now consider, my friends, what are the dimensions required by our bullet. Of course, it is clear that mere 1,000-pounders are not worth wasting breath on."

" Why not ?" asked the Major.

" Because," cut in Marston, " the bullet must be big enough to attract the attention of the Lunarians, if there be any."

" Exactly," resumed the President, " and for another reason perhaps still more important. Sending off a bullet and giving ourselves no further trouble about it, would be making the whole thing end in a bottle of smoke. No, we must make a bullet big enough for us to follow its track until it reaches its object."

" How !" cried the Major, beginning to feel a little mystified. " Follow its track ! Why, you must contemplate a bullet of the most inordinate and stupendous dimensions !"

" Not at all," replied the President calmly. " Just listen a moment. Optical instruments, you are aware, have reached a very high degree of perfection. With certain telescopes a power of 6,000 has been obtained, and, consequently, the Moon has been brought, so to speak, within forty miles of us. Now at that distance objects measuring sixty feet each way are pefectly visible. If the defining power of telescopes has not been further advanced, it is because what is gained in power is lost in clearness, as the Moon's light is too feeble to struggle through the atmospheric undulations with sufficient intensity."

" What do you propose doing then ?" asked
the General. " Would you give your bullet a
diameter of sixty feet ?"

" Oh, no !"

" Will you undertake to give the Moon's
light more intensity ?"

" Exactly so."

" Oh, come down !" laughed Marston.
" That's too good !"

" Nothing simpler," replied Barbican. " If
I diminish the density of our atmosphere,
shall I not render the Moon's light more intense ?"

" Of course."

" Well, to do so, I shall simply carry
my telescope to the top of some high mountain."

" By Jove, that's so !" cried Marston. " Barbican, you are a trump."

" I give up gracefully," said the Major.
" But—let us see—what power do you expect to
gain by doing so ?"

" A power of 48,000, which will bring the
Moon within the short distance of five miles.
At this distance it is easy to distinguish objects
of nine feet in diameter."

" Splendid !" cried Marston. " Our bullet

then should be *only* nine feet in diameter !
Go it while you're young !''

" Nine feet in diameter," said Barbican, sen-
tentiously.

" Oh ! come, Barbican," cried Elphinstone, " a
bullet of such dimensions should weigh——.''

" Before discussing its weight, Major," interrupted Barbican, " allow me to remind you a
little of what our forefathers have done in this
line. Though I'm far from denying that gunnery
has made some progress, it is no harm to
know that in the Middle Ages results were obtained which even in the nineteenth century
would be very surprising.''

" For instance ?" demanded the audience, incredulously.

" For instance ;" continued Barbican. " At
the siege of Constantinople, in 1453, by Mahomet
II., stone bullets were discharged, weighing as
much as 1,900 pounds. In 1565, at the siege
of Malta by the Sultan Solyman, a cannon from
Fort St. Elmo is said to have thrown at the
Turks projectiles weighing 2,500 pounds. A
French historian says that, in the reign of Louis
XI., about 1470, a shell weighing 500 pounds
was shot from the Bastille to Charenton, a distance of nearly three miles. What have we got

since that time ? Armstrong's best, his ' *Big Will* ' discharged a ball weighing only 510 pounds, and Rodman's famous 20-inch bore fired a solid shot of little more than double that weight. Our projectiles, therefore, seem to have lost in weight what they have gained in range. What *we* have to do, then, and what would seem only reasonable enough to expect with the progress of science, is simply to increase ten fold, the weight of the bullets discharged by Mahomet II., and by the Knights of Malta.''

'' That's clear enough,'' said the Major; ''but what metal do you intend using for the projectile ?''

'' Plain cast iron, I should think, would be good enough,'' observed the General.

'' Plain cast iron !'' exclaimed Marston; ''can't we send something better than that to the Moon ?''

'' Plain cast iron is good enough for any bullet, my worthy friend,'' said the General; '' only a ball of such dimensions as nine feet in diameter must have an enormous weight.''

'' Yes, if it is solid,'' said Barbican; '' but not, if it is hollow.''

"Hollow ? Would you think of sending a shell ?"

"Why not ?" broke in Marston. "A shell containing newspapers, the President's message, and specimens of our cotton, sugar and tobacco, would make Europe howl with envy !"

"Yes, a shell," replied Barbican. "Nothing else would do. A solid shot would weigh more than 200 thousand pounds, a weight not to be entertained for a moment ; however, as the projectile must possess a certain stability, I propose giving it a weight of about 10 tons."

"What is to be the thickness of its sides ?" asked the Major.

"According to the ordinary rule in such cases," replied the General, "a diameter of nine feet requires a wall or side a least two feet thick."

"Oh, that is by far too much," observed Barbican. "Remember, the question is not about a bullet intended to pierce iron clads ; it will be quite enough if the sides are sufficiently thick to resist the pressure exerted by the powder at the discharge. Here, then, is the whole thing in a nut shell. What must be the thickness of a cast iron shell, nine feet in diameter, to weigh about 20 thousand pounds ?

Our friend Marston, the lightning calculator, can tell us in a few moments."

"Certainly," said Marston, scribbling down some figures, and evidently going through a very easy calculation. "The sides of such a shell must not be more than two inches thick."

"Will that be sufficient?" asked the Major doubtingly.

"No, certainly not," said Barbican.

"What is to be done then?" resumed the Major, rather embarrassed.

"Give up iron, use another metal," said Barbican.

"Copper?" asked Morgan.

"Still too heavy," said the President: "I know something better than either iron or copper."

"Let us have it," said the Major.

"Aluminium," replied Barbican.

"Aluminium!" exclaimed his three colleagues in one breath.

"Aluminium, no less, my friends," Barbican went on. "You are no doubt aware, that, in 1854, Sainte Claire De Ville, a distinguished French Chemist, succeeded in obtaining this precious metal in pure masses. Now, aluminium is at once as white as silver, as incorrodible as gold, as tenacious as iron, as fusible as copper, and as light as glass. It is easily worked ; it is widely spread in nature, alumina forming the bases of most rocks ; it is three times lighter than iron ; in short, it seems to have been created expressly to furnish material for our projectile !"

" Good for aluminium !" cried the excitable Marston.

" But, President," asked the Major, " is not aluminium rather expensive ?"

" It was, once," answered Barbican. " When first discovered, it cost about 270 dollars a pound ; then it fell to 27 dollars, and to-day a pound of aluminium is worth about 9 dollars."

" Still, nine dollars a pound," remonstrated the Major, " I consider an enormous price."

" Enormous, I admit, my dear Major ; but that it is beyond our means, I deny."

" Have you any idea of the weight of such a projectile ?" asked General Morgan.

" Oh, yes," replied Barbican, holding up a paper covered with figures : " a shell nine feet in diameter, and one foot thick, if cast iron, would weigh 67,440 pounds ; if made of aluminium, its weight would be reduced to 19,250 pounds."

"Almost 3½ times lighter!" cried Marston delighted.

"Very satisfactory, indeed," observed the Major, "but still 19,250 pounds at nine dollars a pound——."

"Will cost exactly $173,250;" interrupted Barbican. "A pretty round sum, I grant. But don't be alarmed, my friends. *Nil desperandum*—never give up the ship! Our enterprise shall not fail for want of funds, depend upon it."

"Funds!" echoed Marston. "We shall be deluged with money!"

"Then, gentlemen," asked the President, before taking his seat, "what do you think of aluminium?"

"The idea is a good one," said the General.

"It is unanimously adopted!" cried the two others with one voice.

The committee then broke up, having resolved the question for the first session in a highly satisfactory manner. The material of the bullet was to be aluminium, its nature and weight were decided on; and the kind of cannon proper to discharge it, was to be settled at the next session.

CHAPTER VIII.

THE CANNON.

The minutes of the Executive Committee's first session, when read next day in the Club Rooms, produced a feeling of great surprise strongly dashed with alarm, particularly among the older members of the Standing Committee. "What! A ball weighing twenty thousand pounds! Preposterous! What kind of cannon could be devised capable of imparting the necessary velocity to such an enormous mass?" To this and sundry questions of similar import, the proceedings of the second session were to furnish a triumphant reply.

The four members met punctually next evening, and business commenced without preamble.

"Gentlemen," said Barbican, after calling them to order, "this evening we have to consider the nature of our cannon, its length, shape, arrangement, and weight. Its dimensions will probably be gigantic, but I think I can take it on myself to say, that we shall not be frightened at the difficulties that may be pre-

(93)

sented by its construction. I bespeak your best attention to the few remarks I am going to make, and I hope you will have no hesitation in stating your objections. For, candidly speaking, I think I can answer them."

An approving murmur greeted these words.

"Taking up the question," resumed the President, "at the point where we left off last evening, the problem we have now to solve may be presented in the following words : '*How to impart an initial velocity of* 12,000 *yards a second to a shell nine feet in diameter, and* 20,000 *pounds in weight ?*' "

"That's exactly what we have got to do !" observed Marston.

"Now," resumed the President, "let us consider what happens as soon as a projectile is launched into space. It is acted upon by three independent forces at once : the resistance of the medium through which it passes, the attraction of the Earth, and the impelling force that has set it in motion. Let us examine them separately. The resistance offered by the medium, that is the air, is of very little importance. In fact, it may be considered almost insignificant when we reflect that, the atmosphere being no where more than about 50 miles in thickness, the projectile would get through it in six or seven seconds. Let us now pass on to the second resisting force—the attraction of the Earth. This, we know, diminishes according to the square of the distance; and we further know that a body, unsupported, falls to the earth at the rate of 16 feet the first second. A little calculation readily tells us that this same body, if transferred to the same distance from us as the Moon, would fall only about the $\frac{1}{20}$ of an inch in the same time."

" Right, President," cried Marston, rapidly figuring with paper and pencil. " Sixteen feet divided by the square of the Moon's distance, brings us so near $\frac{1}{20}$ of an inch that the difference is not worth speaking of."

" This motion of $\frac{1}{20}$ of an inch in a second of time," continued Barbican, " is almost equivalent to a state of immobility. The question, then, is to conquer this force of gravity. How to do it? Simply by augmenting the impelling power."

" Yes, but that's the rub," observed the Major.

" It is indeed the rub, but not an invincible rub," replied Barbican. " For we can obtain all the impelling power that is necessary, by increasing the length of the cannon and the strength of the powder, as the quantity of the latter is evidently limited only by the engine's capacity of resistance. Now this power of resistance we can increase to almost any extent, since the cannon, as it is not to be handled, need not be exposed."

" Yes, that is evident," observed General Morgan.

" Up to the present time," Barbican went on, " the largest cannons, our own enormous Columbiads, have never exceeded twenty-five feet in length ; so I think we shall rather astonish folks by the dimensions that we are compelled to adopt."

" Exactly so, Mr. President," cried Marston. " I have been figuring at the thing myself, and have reached results, which, last night, I acknowledge, I should be the first to laugh at. But you opened my eyes both to the grandeur of our undertaking, and to the consequent grandeur of the means to be employed. My conviction is that we shall want a cannon half a mile long."

" Half a mile long !" exclaimed the Major and the General with one voice.

" That, at least," cried Marston, " and even then I'm afraid it would not be half long enough."

MARSTON'S FIRST DRAFT OF THE GUN.

" Come, come, Marston," remonstrated the Major ; " if this is meant as a joke, I must say it is a capital one, and I enjoy it hugely. Ha ! Ha ! Ha !"

" It's no joke whatever," cried Marston, getting red ; "and allow me to say, Major Elphinstone, you permit yourself to make observations quite uncalled for."

" Marston, that's carrying the joke too far."

" No further than your torpedo carried the *Conshohocken.*"

(During the war the Major had unfortunately mistaken the United States Gunboat *Conshohocken* for a Confederate cruiser, and blown it to pieces with his patent torpedo.)

" Further than your famous cannon, the terror of Baltimore, ever carried a ball !"

" Gentlemen, remember you're not in Congress," exclaimed General Morgan, laughing heartily, for he knew his friends' sore points. " No personalities allowed in the Gun Club ! Besides we are forgetting the respect due to our honored President." The honest artillerymen's ill humor vanished in a moment. They shook hands, made apologies, and humbly begged the President's pardon.

Barbican, so deeply immersed in his calcula-

7

tions as to be hardly aware of what was going on, listened to his colleagues for an instant or two, and then calmly resumed :

" Now, friends, let us reason a little. We evidently require a cannon of great length, since the elastic force of the gases accumulated under the projectile is thereby greatly increased. But beyond certain limits it is absolutely useless to pass."

" Absolutely," chimed in the Major.

" Now, what is the formula prescribed in such cases ? Ordinarily a cannon's length is twenty-five times the diameter of the ball, and its weight is from 235 to 240 times greater."

" That formula doesn't apply here !" cried Marston impetuously.

" Granted, my worthy friend," replied Barbican, " still the formula is not without its utility. Taking the proportions it prescribes for a projectile nine feet in diameter, and 20,000 pounds in weight, our gun would be only 225 feet long, and would weigh no more than about 5 million pounds."

" Fudge !" roared Marston. " Better take a pocket pistol at once !"

" You're right, Mr. Secretary," replied Barbican. " I quite agree with you, and for that reason I propose making our cannon at least four times longer, that is about nine hundred feet in length.''

The Major and the General objected on the one side, and Marston on the other for some time ; but each party supported his own view so warmly, that after a while, the President had little trouble in convincing his colleagues, that his, Barbican's, proposal hit the happy medium ; so a length of nine hundred feet was at last unanimously adopted.

'' Now then,'' asked Elphinstone, '' what is to be the thickness of the metal ?''

'' Six feet,'' replied Barbican.

'' Of course, you don't think of mounting such an enormous weight of metal upon a carriage ?'' asked the Major.

'' Yet the idea is sublime !'' cried Marston.

'' But useless and impracticable,'' replied Barbican. '' No ; I think of casting this cannon in the earth itself. By binding it with thick hoops of forged iron, and surrounding it with a solid piece of masonry, I think we shall succeed in rendering bursting almost impossible. As soon as the piece is cast, the chamber will be measured, smoothed, and polished with great care in order that no loss of gas may occur through windage, and that the whole explosive force of the powder may be employed in impelling the ball.''

'' Hurrah !'' cried Marston. '' We have our cannon !''

'' Not yet, my friend,'' said Barbican. '' Remember we have not yet said a word as to its shape. Shall it be a cannon, a howitzer, or a mortar ?''

'' A cannon !'' cried General Morgan.

'' A howitzer !'' cried Major Elphinstone.

'' A mortar !'' cried Marston.

As each seemed fully impressed with the peculiar advantages of his favorite arm, a new and lengthened discussion seemed imminent, but the President nipped it in the bud.

'' Gentlemen,'' said he, '' you will all agree with each other in a moment if you only listen to what I am going to say. Our Columbiad will unite in itself the properties of all three. It will be a cannon, since its chamber will be of the same diameter as its bore. It will be a howitzer, as it discharges a shell. And it will be a mortar, as it will be pointed at an angle of 90 degrees. Solidly fixed in its unyielding bed, no recoil possible, no waste possible, it will communicate to the projectile the totality of the enormous force accumulated in its interior.''

"Agreed !'' cried his colleagues with one voice.

"One moment,'' added the Major ; "shall our *can-how-mortar* be rifled ?''

"Oh, no ;'' answered Barbican. "We require a tremendous initial velocity, which, as you are well aware, a rifled bore would only diminish.''

"True.''

"Now then we have it, I hope !'' cried Marston.

"Not quite.''

"Why not ?''

"Because we have not said a word about the metal it is to be made of.''

"Propose the question at once then !''

"That is exactly what I am going to do,'' replied Barbican. "Gentlemen, our cannon must unite great tenacity with great hardness ; it must be perfectly proof against heat, oxidation, and the corrosive action of acids.''

"Of that there is no doubt,'' said the Major ; "and as we must employ an immense quantity of metal, I think we are rather limited as to choice.''

" Then," said Morgan, " I propose the best alloy yet known for our purpose : a hundred parts of copper, twelve of tin, and six of brass."

" I agree with you, my dear General," replied the President, "in thinking that this composition has produced very satisfactory results. But, in our case, it would be both too dear and too hard to get. I propose, therefore, taking something good but less expensive, for instance cast iron. What is your opinion, Major ?"

" I am rather inclined to agree with you, Mr. President."

" In fact," resumed Barbican, " while cast iron is ten times cheaper than bronze, it is easily melted, flows readily, and gives very little trouble in working. That is, it saves us both time and money. Besides, it is pretty strong too. I remember myself, when operating with Sherman against Hood, near Atlanta, that some of our cast iron cannons fired as many as a thousand rounds with hardly a pause, day or night, and then seemed very little the worse for it."

" Cast iron is very brittle," observed Morgan.

" Yes, and very stubborn too," said Barbican. " Oh! we shall not burst, if that's what you're afraid of."

" The General is anxious about his reputation," observed the Major.

" He's right too," cried Marston. " Nobody but bank presidents can burst, and be honest men at the same time."

" No bursting is possible in our case," said the President decisively ; " unless you go wrong in your figures, Mr. Secretary, which I think is hardly likely. For instance, can anybody be quicker or more correct than you in calculating the weight of a cannon, nine hundred feet in length, nine feet in bore, and six feet in thickness ?"

In less than a minute Marston had the work done :

" Such a cannon would weigh 68,040 tons."

" And at two cents a pound, this would amount to—— ?"

" It would amount to $2,721,600."

At this announcement, his three colleagues cast a forlorn glance of dismay at their President, but Barbican's smile was bland, and his voice cheery as he replied :

" I only repeat now what I said yesterday : *Nil desperandum*—never give up the ship ! Our enterprise shall not fail for want of funds."

The Committee then broke up their second

session in the best possible spirits, and promised to be punctual in their attendance on the following evening.

CHAPTER IX.

THE POWDER.

The third question to consider was the kind of powder to be employed, and the public at large waited its decision with the keenest interest. The projectile was so enormous, the cannon was so gigantic, the necessary quantity of powder should be of an amount so fabulous, that, in spite of the reckless bravery of the Americans, something like dismay pervaded the popular mind, and people almost shuddered at the results both possible and probable from the employment on such a vast scale of an agent so terrific as gun powder.

All such legends as attribute the invention of powder to Schwartz, the Benedictine monk of Freiburg on the Rhine, in the 14th century, or to Friar Bacon of Oxford on the Thames, in the 13th century, or to the Byzantine monks of the 6th century, whose " *Greek Fire* " gave the Greek Empire a new lease of life for nine hundred years—I say,—all such legends are to be at once discarded.

Nobody knows who invented powder; its use was well understood in China several hundred years before the Christian era. Its employment as a propellant is probably of more recent date. All, however, that it concerns us to know at present, is a little regarding its tremendous mechanical force. A few remarks on the subject may be enough for the general reader.

A pound of powder occupies a certain space, say so many cubic inches. When started into gas, it requires a space 400 times greater; when this gas is acted upon by a heat of about 1300° Fahrenheit, it fills a space ten times greater still. That is, the volume or size of the powder is to the volume of the gas produced by its deflagration as 1 is to 4,000. Judge then of the tremendous explosive action of this gas when confined in a place 4,000 times too small for it.

This fact and hundreds of others of a similar nature, you may be sure, our friends of the Executive Committee had at their fingers ends, when they took their places at the next meeting. Barbican called on the Major, in graceful recognition of the merits of the famous *Elphinstone torpedo*, to open the proceedings. The Major at once complied.

" Gentlemen," he began, " I shall preface my remarks by giving some figures taken from the Report of the Committee on Artillery. The 24-pounder, whose execution our honored Secretary described in such glowing phrases a few evenings ago, is impelled by a charge of only 16 pounds of gun powder. The Armstrong gun requires only 75 pounds for an 800-pound projectile, and the Rodman Columbiad expends only 160 pounds of powder to discharge a ball weighing half a ton.

" A self-evident consequence to be deduced from these figures," proceeded the Major, " is, that the increased weight of the ball does not require a corresponding increase in the charge. For instance, though a 24-pounder requires 16 pounds of gun powder—or two-thirds of its own weight—a ball weighing 1,000 pounds is very far from requiring a charge in the same proportion. In fact, instead of 666 pounds, or two-thirds of its own weight, a charge of 160 pounds has been found to be quite sufficient. In other words, the more rapidly you increase the weight of the projectile, the more rapidly you diminish the proportional weight of the charge."

" Come to the point, Major," interrupted

Barbican, who could be long-winded enough himself sometimes.

"He's coming to it rapidly," cried Marston. "He will convince us presently that, if we only make our projectile heavy enough, we shall end by requiring no powder at all to discharge it."

"I shall consider my friend Marston's knowledge of gunnery almost as poor as his jokes," resumed the Major, "if he forgets that during the war, in the case of our largest guns, we reduced the weight of the powder to the tenth of that of the ball."

"Put that in your pipe and smoke it, Marston," said General Morgan; "the Major is perfectly correct. But before deciding on *how much* powder we are to employ, I think we should first fix on *what kind*."

"We shall employ coarse-grained war powder," replied the Major; "it explodes more rapidly than when pulverized."

"Yes," replied the General, "but it is very hard on the gun, and soon injures the internal surface."

"That may be an objection for cannons generally," replied the Major, "but not for our Columbiad. The powder must ignite instantaneously, if we want to have the mechanical effect complete. Fine powder burns too slowly."

" To render the combustion more rapid," observed Marston, " we might contrive to ignite the powder in several places at the same time."

" We might," said the Major ; " undoubtedly we might, but the operation would be very troublesome. No ; I return to my first idea ; coarse-grained war powder avoids all these difficulties."

" All right," said his colleagues.

" To load his Columbiad," resumed the Major, " Rodman employed a powder in grains as large as chestnuts, made of willow charcoal simply roasted in iron boilers. This powder was hard and lustrous, left no mark on your hand, contained a great proportion of hydrogen and oxygen, caught fire instantly, and though violently explosive, it was not very hard on the fire arms."

" Enough said," observed Marston. " Our choice is made."

So far Barbican had held himself almost entirely aloof from the discussion. He listened, and let them talk, evidently having his own ideas on the matter. At this point he broke silence.

" Now, gentlemen," he asked, " what quantity of powder do you propose ?"

The three Committee men looked at each other for some time. At last General Morgan spoke :

" The weight of the projectile being 20,000 pounds, according to Major Elphinstone's remarks, a quantity of powder one-tenth that weight should be sufficient to discharge it, but since we require the enormous initial velocity of 12,000 yards a second, instead of taking *one-tenth* of the weight of the projectile, we should take *ten times* its weight for our charge. Therefore I propose 200,000 pounds."

" Too little," said the Major ; " I propose 500,000 pounds."

" Still too little," cried Marston. " Both together are too little. I propose 800,000 pounds weight of gun powder to discharge our projectile."

Notwithstanding the enormous power represented by these figures, the work to be done was enormous, almost beyond calculation. Therefore, no one accused Marston of exaggeration this time. A general silence ensued for a few moments, which was finally broken by the President :

" Gentlemen," he said, " I start with the principle that the resistance of a cannon constructed as ours is to be, is almost limitless. I shall, therefore, perhaps, surprise our honorable Secretary by telling him that he has been rather timid in his calculations, and I propose to double his eight hundred thousand pounds of powder.''

" Sixteen hundred thousand pounds !'' exclaimed Marston, bouncing off his chair like an india rubber ball.

" Just that much.''

" Then you will have to fall back on my cannon half a mile long,'' said the Secretary, without, however, showing the least sign of triumph.

" That's clear,'' observed the Major.

" How so ?'' asked the General.

" Clear as daylight !'' cried the Secretary, reading off some figures that he had been scribbling on a piece of paper. " 16 hundred thousand pounds of powder will occupy a space of about 22 thousand cubic feet ; and as our cannon can contain only 54 thousand cubic feet, it will be nearly half filled with the charge alone, and, of course, it will not be long enough for the expansion of the gas necessary to give the projectile sufficient impulsion.''

Against this there was absolutely nothing to

be said. Marston's figures were beyond dispute.
His colleagues looked at Barbican.

"Nevertheless," observed the President, "I
hold fast to my opinion. Just reflect a moment ;
16 hundred thousand pounds of powder will
give rise to not much more than 200 million
cubic feet of gas. Is that too much for our
purpose ?"

"Hardly," said the General.

"What is to do then ?" asked the Major.

"Simply reduce the enormous quantity of
powder," replied Barbican, "without diminishing its mechanical power."

"Yes, that's where the shoe pinches," said
Marston.

"It can't be done," cried the General and
the Major in one voice.

"Excuse me, gentlemen," calmly continued
the President. "It *can* be done, and I am
going to tell you how."

Their eyes devoured him.

"In fact there is nothing easier," he went
on, "than to reduce this powder to a volume
four times less bulky. You are all acquainted
with the curious substance forming the element-
ary tissues of plants, and commonly called *cellu-
lose*. It is obtained in a perfectly pure state

in several bodies, particularly in cotton or
the down covering the seeds of the cotton plant.
Now, cotton steeped for a while in nitric and
sulphuric acid and left to dry, is transformed
into a substance eminently insoluble, eminently
combustible and eminently explosive."

" Oh ! now I understand you !" cried the
General and the Major, simultaneously.

" By Jove, Barbican," roared the delighted
Marston, " you are a right bower !"

" Nearly forty years ago," pursued Barbican,
" in 1832, this substance was discovered by a
French chemist named Braconnot, who called
it *xyloidine.* In 1838 Pelouze, another Frenchman, suggested its application to artillery, and
in 1846 Herr Schönbein, a Basle professor,
announced to the British Association at one of
its meetings that he had rendered cotton as explosive as gun powder."

" Look here, Mr. President," interrupted Marston, " is there no American name connected in
any way with that discovery ?"

" Not exactly with the *discovery* of gun cotton, my dear Marston," replied the President,
" but very closely with one of its most important
applications. I am happy to gratify your patriotic
spirit by stating that a countryman of ours, May-

nard of Boston, when a medical student in
1846, discovered *collodion*, which is simply gun
cotton dissolved in a mixture of ether and alco-
hol. Collodion he highly recommended as likely
to be of vast service in surgery by its power
of preserving wounds from contact with the air.
It has since proved indispensable to photo-
graphers, as it is the well known white film
covering the glass when a negative is taken.
Another French chemist, it is true, also claims
the honor of this great discovery, but of course
we are bound to sustain the glory of our own
countryman.''

" Of course we are and of course we do,''
cried Marston. " Hurrah for Maynard and the
gun cotton !''

" This powerful explosive agent,'' resumed the
President, " is prepared with the greatest ease.
Cotton steeped for ten or twelve minutes in a
mixture of sulphuric and nitric acid, then
thoroughly washed and dried—nothing is simpler than the whole process. But this is only
a trifle when compared with its other advantages.
It is unaffected by moisture—a most valuable
quality, since it will take us a good many days
to load our cannon ; it takes fire readily ; and
its combustion is so rapid that it will flash off

on a pile of gun powder without igniting it.
Besides, its explosive power is at least four times
as great as that of gunpowder, and even this
can be immensely increased by adding to it $\frac{8}{10}$
of its weight of nitrate of potash."

" Will that be necessary ?" asked the Major.

" Hardly," replied the President. " So then
instead of 1600 thousand pounds of gunpowder,
we shall require only 400 thousand pounds of
gun cotton, and, as 500 pounds of cotton
can be easily contained in a space of 27 cubic
feet, the whole charge will occupy only about
180 linear feet in the Columbiad. Consequently," concluded the President in a tone at
once confident and triumphant, " the projectile
will have about 700 feet length of bore to tra-
verse under the impulse of 200 million cubic feet
of gas before it leaves the cannon to wing its
rapid way towards the radiant Queen of Night !"

Marston, in his increasing excitement, had been
latterly growing more and more ungovernable, but
this flowery peroration of the President shot
him off like a rocket. He flung himself head-
foremost into Barbican's arms with a force that
would have certainly punched a hole in his illustrious friend had he not really been, as we
have said before, a cast iron Yankee.

This incident ended the third and last meeting of the Committee. The plan of the campaign being now settled in all its chief features, henceforth nothing more remained to be done than to put it into execution.

And that was "a mere question of time," as Marston said to every man, woman and child that spoke to him on the subject.

CHAPTER X.

AN ENEMY !

It is almost needless to state that the American public took a most absorbing interest in every detail of the great enterprise. The reports of the Committee occupied the best columns of the newspapers and furnished reading matter that grew more and more exciting every day. The enormous figures, at first only faintly comprehended, were read over and over again with renewed wonder, and as the tremendous nature of the difficulties to be overcome slowly dawned on the public mind, the general curiosity to learn more about them became every day more and more intense. Like the silkworm, the more it fed the hungrier it grew. Never even had the war in its palmiest days given the public inquisitiveness so keen a whet. Even in out of the way places, like Dubuque, many an ancient maiden lady protested that the proceedings of the Baltimore Gun Club were ten times more fascinating than even her favorite *New York Ledger*.

And more than a year was to elapse between

the commencement of the undertaking and its final accomplishment. How delightful ! A stock of excitement that was sure to hold out for at least three hundred and sixty-five days longer ! Every morning a new instalment ! The choice of a place for the scene of operations ; the construction of the immense mould ; the casting of the gigantic Columbiad ; the lodgment of the terrific charge ; and then the grand, high-wrought, overwhelming catastrophe ! At this, of course, the interest would reach its culminating point for the public at large. What would become of the projectile after its disappearance, how it would comport itself in space, how it would reach the moon, should evidently be taken on hearsay, and that, from the nature of the case, would be anything but reliable. Accordingly, the chief interest settled upon the preparations for the vast enterprise, and the slightest detail copied from paper to paper, was everywhere welcome, and everywhere commented upon with the keenest gusto.

Great as was the public excitement, it was soon raised to an even higher pitch by an incident worthy of being related in full.

We know already what numberless legions of admiring friends Barbican's daring genius had

rallied around him. But the public idolatry
of which he was the object, was not exactly
unanimous. One man, the only man throughout the length and breadth of the great United
States, was found bold enough to protest against
the project of the Gun Club. He attacked it
with might and main, and on every possible
occasion ; and, as is usual with poor human
nature, Barbican was more sensitive to the opposition of a single man than to the applause
of all the others.

Not that he was not well aware of the motive
of this antipathy, of the source of this isolated
enmity ; he fully understood why this opposition
was of a purely personal nature of ancient date,.
and how jealousy and rivalry had given it birth.

This bitter enemy, Barbican had never yet
laid eyes on—a fortunate circumstance for both,
as bloodshed would have been the probable
consequence. Like Barbican, he was a practical
scientist, and, like many other scientific men,
of a hot temper, a domineering disposition, and
implacable in his resentment. He was a Philadelphian by birth, and, like many of his towns-
men, was descended from that tough-jointed,
clear-headed, stubborn-hearted, close-fisted race
that had emigrated from the north of Ireland, and

settled in Pennsylvania in such numbers, eighty or ninety years ago. Having spent the early years of his youth on board a Mississippi steamer, in the capacity of captain's clerk, he was familiarly known all over Philadelphia as Captain McNicholl, though he was now one of the greatest iron men in the country.

Everybody has heard of the curious contest that existed during the Confederate War between the cannon and the iron clads—the one bent on being irresistible, the other on being impenetrable. The consequence was a radical change in the navy of both continents. The projectile and the iron plate fought each other with unexampled persistency, the one increasing in thickness as fast as the other increased in weight. Vessels armed with tremendous guns, and sheltered by their invulnerable coat of mail, went unharmed under the hottest fire. The *Merrimacs,* the *Monitors,* the *Miantonomahs,* the *Weehawkens,* the *Dictators,* the *Dunderbergs,* were thus enabled to discharge their enormous projectiles almost with perfect impunity. They did unto others what they would not allow others to do unto them—a highly immoral principle, though the whole art of " glorious" war is based on it.

Now if Barbican was a great founder of can-

non, McNicholl was a great forger of iron plates.
The one worked night and day in his great
foundry on the Bel Air Road, Baltimore, the
other worked day and night in his great machine
shop, Broad street, Philadelphia. Each ran directly counter to the other in the course of
his ideas. The moment Barbican invented a
new projectile, McNicholl invented a new shield.
The Baltimorian passed his life in attacking,
the Philadelphian in repelling. Hence a bitter
antagonism between the two, the consciousness
of which neither could shake off. In his dreams
Barbican saw McNicholl in the shape of an
adamantine target against which he was driven
headlong, to be flattened like a leaden bullet;
McNicholl saw Barbican in *his* dreams, in the
shape of a hissing steel-pointed projectile, hurled
against him with resistless force and sure to
sweep him off the face of the earth.

Though they certainly never tried to avoid
each other, fate had so ordained it that, as said
before, as yet they had never met face to face.
When Barbican was seeing to the cannons of the
Army of the Potomac, McNicholl was attending to
the gunboats of the *Army of the Mississippi;*
when McNicholl was Grant's right hand man
before Richmond, Barbican was marching to the

sea with Sherman. Of course their friends who knew the injury the country would sustain in the loss of such valuable citizens, threw every obstacle in the way of a personal rencounter.

It was hard to say which of these inventors got the better of the other; the results left the matter undetermined. The probability was that the plate should succumb to the bullet, though expert judges still had their doubts. At one of the later experiments, Barbican's cylindro-conical projectiles made McNicholl's rolled iron plates look like a pin cushion, but did no further harm. On that day the great Philadelphia iron worker, considering his victory secure, spoke of his rival in terms of lofty contempt; but the tables were turned with a vengeance when Barbican dropped the conical bullets and took six hundred pound steel shells in their place. Though endowed with but a moderate velocity, they pierced, smashed, and broke to pieces armor construc- ted of the very best material.

To this point matters had come: the victory seemed to rest with the bullet, when Lee sur- rendered on the very day that McNicholl had completed his patent target of forged steel! It was a masterpiece of its kind, and defied all the projectiles ever devised. The Captain had

it immediately conveyed to Washington, set it
up on the heights of the Potomac near the Long
Bridge, and immediately sent Barbican a challenge to come and pound at it as long as he
pleased, and with whatever bullets he pleased,
solid, hollow, round or pointed. Peace being
made, Barbican, unwilling to compromise his
last success, respectfully declined. McNicholl,
exasperated at the refusal, tried to tempt him by
giving him his choice of distance. Two hundred yards ? One hundred yards ? No, not
even at seventy-five.

"Take fifty yards then !" wrote McNicholl
in the *Washington Star*, " or even forty yards
from my target, and I shall stand behind it
myself !" But Barbican replied in the *Washington Union* that he would not fire if McNicholl
should stand even before it.

At this, McNicholl's rage exceeded all bounds.
He wrote a long letter in the *New York Herald*
full of personalities. He insinuated that a
coward in one way is a coward in every way ;
that a man refusing to fire a cannon can hardly
be called brave ; that those artillerymen who
fight each other six miles apart, try to substitute mathematical formulas for personal bravery ;
and that *at least* as much courage is shown by

waiting quietly for a bullet behind a target as by discharging it according to all the rules of art.

To such innuendoes Barbican did not vouchsafe the least reply—the probability is that he knew nothing about them, immersed, as he now was, over head and ears in his new project.

When he heard of the famous communication to the Gun Club, the Captain went almost crazy. The cruel stab of envy was rendered more poignant by the consciousness of his utter inability to mend matters. How could he think of inventing anything to surpass a Columbiad nine hundred feet long? What armor could resist a bullet weighing 20,000 pounds? The shot pretty nigh killed him; but he was one of the " die hards;" after the first stunning effect was over, he gradually recovered from the blow; then he picked himself up and registered a great oath that he would smash Barbican's project or perish in the attempt.

He let fly tremendous broadsides at the whole idea in a series of letters, which the papers positively refused to publish, until they found that nobody minded them. He undertook to demonstrate its utter absurdity at first from a scientific point of view, but, war once declared, he drew his arguments from every quarter, and, sooth to say, some of them were poor enough.

He began by attacking the calculations. The Captain covered the paper with *x's* and *y's*, proving Barbican's utter ignorance of the first principles of Ballistics. For instance, it was a physical impossibility to impart to any projectile an initial velocity of 12,000 yards, and even if it were imparted, he demonstrated by an algebraic formula within a schoolboy's comprehension, that no bullet of such a weight could ever get beyond the limits of the terrestrial atmosphere. It would not go even half the way ! And worse than that was to come. Even supposing that the said velocity was imparted, and that the said velocity was sufficient for the purpose, why, the shell could never resist the terrific pressure caused by the combustion of 1600 thousand pounds of powder ; and even supposing it did resist this pressure, it could never bear the enormous heat sure to be developed, and therefore it would melt like wax the moment it left the Columbiad, and fall in showers of burning rain on the heads of the spectators that were foolish enough to expose themselves to such evident danger !

But not even a frown from Barbican, who calmly continued at his labors.

Then McNicholl took up the question in its other aspects. Not to speak of the utterly unmitigated inutility of the project viewed from every possible point, he considered the experiment to be one of a highly dangerous nature, both for the lookers on who would be silly enough to encourage such proceedings by their presence, and for all the cities comprised within a radius of a hundred miles from this obnoxious cannon. He went on to prove that if the projectile did not attain its object—an irredeemable impossibility—it should evidently fall back on the earth, and then what terrible consequences would be the result !

Multiplying the weight of the enormous mass by the square of the distance through which it should fall, he produced an array of figures it would give you a headache to look at. The least possible harm it could do was to make a hole in the earth big enough to swallow up a city fully as large as Baltimore. *Absit Omen !* As for his own personal safety, he, McNicholl, was not in the least concerned. He could and would take care of himself. But as a citizen concerned in the welfare of his country, he

lifted up his voice against the whole nefarious proceeding. It was a clear case for government
interference; in no other country on earth would
such a thing be allowed; but when would the
United States learn that the safety of all should
never be hazarded for the sake of humoring
the folly, or gratifying the selfishness, of some
insignificant individual ?

Evidently the Captain ran riot in his spirit
of exaggeration. But, one comfort, nobody
shared his opinions. Nobody ever read his
letters, except the proof-corrector and he had
forgotten all about them in five minutes. They
did not shake the faith of a single one among
Barbican's millions of worshippers. The President of the Gun Club never deigned to reply
even by a gesture, but sat aloft enshrined in the
majesty of his calculations, to all appearance as
serene, calm and composed as the great Olympian
Jove himself. Nevertheless the mighty thunderer's
ambrosial locks were to be shaken at last.

The greatest sporting paper of the United States
is the well known *New York Living Age*. It
is the recognized organ for theatres, billiards,
base ball matches, horse races, boat races, prize
fights and gambling of all kinds, except the
little gambling now and then done in stocks.

Its circulation is therefore immense, though its literary matter—apart from its authoritative decision of bets—does not attract much attention. In its issue of October 17th, the following challenge appeared in its editorial columns, printed in double leaded type :

" PHILADELPHIA, *October* 16, 186–.

" To the Editor of the *New York Living Age.*

" MY DEAR SIR :—To convince you and every right thinking man that I am quite in earnest when I denounce the Baltimore gun project as a ' phantom, a delusion and a snare, ' the shallowest humbug of the easily gulled nineteenth century, I take advantage of your widely circulated and influential journal to make the following propositions :

" 1. I assert that *the funds necessary for the enterprise will never be raised,* and I back my assertion with the sum of, ... $1,000 00

" 2. I assert that *the casting of a cannon nine hundred feet long is impossible,* and this I back with the sum of, ... $2,000 00

" 3. I assert that *it is impossible to load the Columbiad, as the gun cotton would take fire under the pressure of the bullet,* and this I back with the sum of, $3,000 00

" 4. I assert that *the Columbiad will burst at the first offer* and this I back with the sum of, . . $4,000 00

" 5. I assert that *the projectile will not rise even 6 miles*

and that it will fall back in a few moments afterwards ;
this assertion I back to the sum of, . . . $5,000 00

" These bets, Mr. Editor, are open, separately or
collectively, for the acceptance of any man whomsoever,
only with this well understood preliminary condition,
that the moment they are taken the corresponding
amount of money will be put up immediately, and at
once deposited in the *Wall Street Bank,* subject to your
check alone.

" This *bona fide* offer of mine must of course meet
your approval. If I am not very much mistaken, it
will at last succeed in tearing the mask off those shame-
less hypocrites who, with no risk to themselves, have
so far found it an easy task to abuse the credulity of
their simple countrymen.

" Your obedient servant,

" JOSHUA D. MCNICHOLL."

The New York morning papers cannot reach
Baltimore much sooner than three o'clock in
the afternoon, the hour at which the Captain,
punctual as clock-work, sat down to dinner every
day. Nevertheless, he had not quite got through
his soup when an envelope was handed to him,
containing the following laconic telegram :

" BALTIMORE, *October* 17,

" Taken !

" J. P. BARBICAN."

9

The same evening the editor of the *New York Living Age* received a note from the Cashier of the *Wall Street Bank,* stating that $15,000 had just been deposited there to be held subject to his order.

CHAPTER XI.

FLORIDA OR TEXAS?

An important question was still left undecided : that of choosing the ground where the great experiment was to be made. According to the directions received from Cambridge, the cannon was to be pointed in a line perpendicular to the plane of the horizon, that is, exactly in the direction of the zenith ; now as the Moon is never in the zenith, or directly overhead, in countries further than 28° from the equator, to decide on the exact spot for casting the Columbiad became a question that required some nice consultation.

At a general meeting of the Club held on the evening of October 9th, Barbican, having called the assembly to order, began unrolling one of Mitchell's beautiful maps of the United States, when Marston, who could never keep still five minutes, suddenly jumped up with the intention of offering a " few preliminary remarks."

" Mr. President and gentlemen," he exclaimed, " the question we are to treat of this evening is one likely to assume a national importance, and it is therefore bound to test every particle of patriotism that we can boast of."

He was altogether out of order, but everybody knew the eccentric Marston and his " great gift of gab," as his acquaintances termed it, an expression softened off by his friends into " fatal facility." Besides they all wanted to know what in the world he was coming to.

" High above, far high above all earthly considerations," the orator went on, " we set the glory of our noble country, and if anything *can* redound to her glory in a very remarkable degree, it is to contain within her territories the historic spot that is evermore to be inseparably associated with the grandest idea that ever flashed from human soul ! Yes, gentlemen, down through the shadowy vistas of future years, as through a vast cathedral's myriad aisles—down through the long echoing corridors of all time, I see a name—"

" Order ! order !" here broke in some voices.

" Question ! Question !" shouted others.

" Mr. Secretary——" observed Barbican.

" Allow me to conclude !" cried Marston excitedly, in a voice easily heard above the rest. " I mean to say that as this spot is to be sought for in a country nearer to the equator than our own——''

'' Question ! Question !'' again shouted many voices in different parts of the hall.

'' Come, Marston, dry up !'' cried some of his friends, who knew that geography was not the Secretary's strong point.

'' Wade in, old man !'' cried some of the younger members, highly amused, and too fond of fun to mind their manners. '' Go for 'em ! Sail in, lemons !''

'' Really, Mr. Secretary, I regret exceedingly,'' cried the President, ready to tap the detonating bell, '' but——''

'' Really, Mr. President, I also regret it exceedingly,'' interrupted Marston, not a particle cowed by the disorder he had excited, '' *but 1 will not* be bottled up before I finish, and there is no use whatever in trying to choke me off. All I mean to say is this : Since our experiment must be made on our own soil, and since our own soil does not extend to the 28th parallel, I propose that we advance our boundaries as far as the 28th parallel, even if we have to fight Mexico for it !''

The roars of laughter that greeted these words were so loud, hearty, and universal that Marston, at once concluding he had " put his foot in it," took his seat, somewhat mortified and even disconcerted. Barbican flew to the relief of his friend, by touching off the fulminating bell, and in an instant everything became as still as death.

" Gentlemen," said the President, calmly, " our honored Secretary knows so many things that he may be well excused if he happens to forget one or two. (Hear !) And if anything is excusable it is some slip of memory regarding the wonderful progress of our glorious country. Let only the innocent one throw the first stone. Which of us can tell off hand the exact number of States at present constituting our Union ? (Hear ! Hear ! and renewed applause.) Besides geography is rather a ticklish subject. The greatest minds have sometimes been known to succumb to its intricacies. Did not a British lord of the Admiralty speak of Pittsburgh as a seaport town ? (General hilarity.) Have we not all heard of the eminent English historian who spent several hours looking for Bunker Hill among the Allegheny Mountains ? (Roars of laughter.) If my accomplished but somewhat impetuous friend had only given me time to open my map, as I do now, he would have seen with his own eyes that there is no need whatever of a fight with Mexico. A glance at Florida and Texas shows that our boundaries not only include the 28th parallel of latitude, but approach very nearly to the 25th.''

In spite, however, of the President's well meant efforts to soften off Marston's blunder, it had excited the hilarity of the Gun Club too much to render any serious work possible that evening The meeting, after a few ineffectual attempts at serious business, broke up in some disorder, without deciding whether the cannon was to be cast in Florida or Texas. The unfortunate consequence of it all was that an exceedingly warm contest immediately sprung up on the subject between these two rival States.

The 28th parallel of north latitude, as every school boy knows, strikes the American continent a little below Cape Cannaveral, crosses the peninsula of Florida, and divides it into two parts pretty nearly equal. Then passing through the Gulf of Mexico about one degree south of the mouth of the Mississippi, it enters Texas at Aransas Bay, crosses over the Rio Grande into Mexico, meets the Gulf of California at Guaymas, and is soon lost in the waters of the Pacific Ocean. It was therefore only in those portions of Florida and Texas that lay south of this parallel, that the conditions regarding latitude recommended by the Cambridge Observatory, could be complied with.

The southern part of Florida, the amphibious country of hummock land, savannahs, swamps, lakes, and the immense stretch of marsh called the Everglades, contains hardly a town deserving notice. The settlements, " few and far between," generally consist of some huts in the neighborhood of the numerous forts erected about thirty years ago, the time of the Osceola war. The few Seminoles now left, live quietly enough under their old Chief, Tiger Tail, though, if so disposed, they could still give the whites considerable trouble, as the nature of the country affords them complete protection against every possible civilized appliance of war, except the bloodhound. Key West, a flourishing town on a little island in the extreme south, had the disadvantages of being both too distant and accessible only by water. Tampa, a small village at the head of Tampa Bay, seemed to be the only place which united the conditions of position and easiness of approach, both by sea and land.

Texas, on the contrary, even in the comparatively small angle of territory lying south of parallel 28, contained several important and thriving towns. San Patricio on the Nueces, Corpus Christi on a bay of the same name, Brownsville on the Rio Grande, Rio Grande City further up, Laredo higher still, at the point where the San Antonio and the Saltillo road crossed the river—these towns alone, not to mention several others, formed a very imposing obstacle to the claims made by Florida.

As was to be expected, the moment it was known that the Gun Club had not quite made up its mind, but hung fire between the merits of Florida and Texas, deputies from the rival States, commissioned to urge their claims by every means in their power, began to arrive in great numbers in Baltimore. The Club House was soon besieged night and day, and neither Barbican nor any other influential member could appear in the public streets without running an imminent risk of being talked to death. Angry collisions between the hostile claimants became of frequent occurrence. Seven cities of Greece fought of old for the honor of Homer's birth; here were two great States ready to fly at each other's throat for the sake of a cannon; such is the nature of man; if he has not one thing to fight about he soon finds another.

Happily in the present case the well organized police force of Baltimore, under the efficient direction of Marshal O'Kane, prevented the hot Floridians and Texans from having rifle duels in the streets, or ripping each other up with bowie knives. By way of safety-valve, however, they let off their angry passions in the columns of the daily papers. The Baltimore press having no circulation in Florida or Texas, the war was carried on by the great New York journals, which find their way to all parts of the Union—I was going to say of the world. The *Herald* and the *Tribune,* agreeing for once in their lives, sustained the claims of Texas ; the *World* and the *Times,* a union unprecedented in the annals of journalism, fought side by side, their bitter old feuds suppressed or forgotten for the moment, in their keen desire to uphold the cause of Florida.

Texas advanced to the attack, boldly priding herself on her immense size, six times larger than the State of Pennsylvania, and her 162 counties. Florida replied that her 37 counties were more creditable in a State six times smaller. When Texas pointed to her population of 800,000 souls, Florida met her with a figure of 200,000, which was a higher proportion, considering the respective size of the States. Besides, she accused her rival of her unhealthy soil, which, giving rise to chills and fevers, consumption and pneumonia, carried off her in· habitants by the thousands. Texas replied that as far as regards chills and fevers, the less Florida had to say the better, her climate in the southern part of the peninsula being so deadly that no white man could live there; adding, that when the last Seminole died, the Everglades forever after would become the abode of no-thing but alligators, bears and monstrous serpents.

Apparently by mutual consent, both States soon changed this subject of the question, and went on to another tack.

" Is no account to be made of a State," indignantly cried the *New York Herald*, " that actually ranks fourth in the production of cotton, whose forests of magnificent live oak stand un-rivalled on the continent, whose silver mines of San Saba, worked in the old Spanish times, are among the richest in the world, whose coal beds on the Trinity, on the Brazos, on the Rio Grande, are at least equal to those of Pennsylvania, and whose supply of iron ore in almost every quarter of the State is simply in-exhaustible ?"

"Why," sneered the *World* in reply, "why did not Texas brag, since the fit was on her, of her ' Llano Estacado,' and her other grassless deserts in which she likewise ' stood unrivalled ' ? Why not plume herself on her terrific ' Northers,' the scourge of the Gulf of Mexico, in her winter supply of which she is ' simply inexhaustible ' ? But all this had nothing at all to do with the question, which, cleared of all turgid bombast, stood as follows : Which State offered the most favorable conditions for the moulding and casting of the great Columbiad ? Clearly Florida, her soil being generally sandy or argillaceous, and therefore easily excavated."

"Granted for argument's sake," spoke the placid *Tribune.* " But surely before casting a cannon anywhere, you must first succeed in getting there. Now, as the *Gulf Railroad* is not finished yet, nor likely to be for some years, how is central Florida to be approached ? The Spaniards, the great road builders, had never built roads in Florida, as the settlers would never venture into the interior. But look at Texas ! Besides Corpus Christi Bay and Laguna del Madre, was there not the Rio Grande, navigable 450 miles from the sea, and affording perfect communications with the interior by the

Presidio road, the Laredo road, and the Camargo road, that had been found so useful in the Mexican war? Not to mention Galveston Bay, one of the finest harbors in the world, and in regular communication with New Orleans by the Morgan steamers."

"Ha! Ha! I like that!" laughed the pert *Times*, "the old lady of the *Tribune* has forgotten her geography. Galveston! Why, it is more than 29 degrees north! She might as well tell us that Texas could be entered by a sail up the Red River to Shreveport. Corpus Christi Bay, and Laguna del Madre! What were they? Quicksands covered with water at high tides! The Rio Grande navigable for 450 miles! What did the old lady mean? Navigable! Yes, perhaps for *mudscows*. But surely, the old dame with her usual ponderous awkward wit could hardly mean to imply that the members of the honorable Baltimore Gun Club were no better than *mudsills!* But suppose they had paddled themselves up the Rio Grande for some distance, to what place would these roads, paraded with such display, take them? To the most miserable corner in Texas, unproductive prairie land, mere thickets of chaparal, 'with gigantic cactuses here, sharp pointed Yuccas there, cat-claw briars everywhere, and a good drop of water no-where !'

" Now let the old lady put on her spectacles and look at the map of Florida, crossed by the 28th parallel itself. On the western coast could be seen the beautiful Bay of Tampa, 40 miles long, and navigable for the largest vessels. If the *Tribune* had no atlas of her own, the *Times* would send her one with the greatest pleasure ; the *Times* being particularly fond of geography, and desirous to encourage people in such a highly interesting study."

" The *Times* is undoubtedly the highest au-thority in the country on geography !" roared the *Herald,* " its masterly monogram on the ' Elbows of the Mincio,' put that point beyond dispute long ago." (This was giving a rap on the knuckles to the *Times* for an egregious blunder in geography, which it had once made in describing some military operations in the Italian war, and which it had innocently believed to be long since completely forgotten. But the *Herald* never forgot anything, and, as usual, he now sought to cover his retreat from weak ground by trying to turn the laugh on his op-ponent.) " Was it not a well known fact," he demanded, " that the *Times'* profound ob-

servations on the ' Quadrilateral,' compelled
Humboldt to suspend for a time his work on
the *Cosmos*, and even to re-write his three best
chapters ? Did not Guyot regard the *Times* with
such veneration as never to venture on the
slightest geographical generalization without its
previous endorsement ? When such luminaries
bowed in submission to the geographical oracle,
what could humble journalists do but gracefully
imitate their example ? The *Herald*, therefore,
would not waste printer's ink by repeating that
the whole State of Florida, almost from end to
end, was primeval forest, alternating with pine
barrens, wilderness and unreclaimed swamp-land,
hideous with alligators, howling with panthers,
and sprinkled with a miserable human population,
one half negro, the other half partly Indian,
partly Spanish, partly ' poor white trash.' Dr.
Livingstone, suddenly dropped into it, would
still think himself in the worst parts of Africa.
From its history Florida could hardly be otherwise. The *Times*' cranium, too swollen with
geography to have room for history, had to be
reminded that Florida, discovered by Ponce de
Leon in 1512, had remained in possession of
the sleepy Spaniards for 300 years, with the exception of the short time that the English were

in possession. What could be expected from a country held by do-nothing Dons and blood-sucking mercenary English ? Did not both parties, jealous of the neighboring United States, instigate the Indian marauders to commence depredations against the Georgia settlements, until General Jackson made peace by invading the country, taking some forts, and hanging some Englishmen ? Was not Spain glad to settle the matter by selling the peninsula for 5 millions of dollars ? But though this happened in 1821, was not the real trouble of the United States government then only at its commencement ? Who could describe the horrors of the Seminole war ? or enumerate the millions of dollars expended, and the thousands of valuable lives sacrificed ? Not until 1845, 24 years after her purchase, was Florida admitted into the Union, the costliest State that ever became a member of our glorious confederation. These things considered, and remembering that her population was even yet half negro, $\frac{1}{6}$ Indian, $\frac{1}{6}$ Spanish, and the other $\frac{1}{6}$ " Crackers," was not it rather cheeky in Florida to call herself American at all ?"

" Cheeky !" repeated the *World*, shocked at the term. " But according to the eternal fit-

ness of things, were not the *Herald's* columns
just the place to expect such slang ? Poor Texas
might well exclaim ' Save me from my friends !'
Had she never heard of the proverb about
glasshouses ? Why call up memories that had
better be buried in eternal oblivion ? Before
sneering at the population of Florida, should she
not have remembered that she was first peopled
herself by runaway slaves ? Were Georgia " Crackers" worse than the despised " Greasers ?" Was
not a Spaniard at least as good as a Mexican ?
As for the Indians, the brave Seminoles certainly ranked as high in the scale of humanity
as the plundering Kiowas, the murdering Apaches,
or the treacherous Comanches. American ! What
was American if Florida was not ? What city of
the United States had a better right to the name
than Saint Augustine, the oldest town in the
Union ? Her streets were lively and flourishing
300 years ago, that is, many years before the
Cavaliers saw the James ; the Puritans, Plymouth
Rock ; the Dutch, the Hudson ; the Swedes, the
Brandywine ; or the French, the Mississippi. It
was an old city ere the Catholics saw the Potomac ; the Huguenots, the Ashley, or the
Quakers, the Delaware. In other words, for pri-
ority of claim to the name *American,* Florida

10

could enter the list with even any of the old glorious THIRTEEN !"

" Facts before fancy !" hotly objected the *Tribune.* " Dates proved nothing. Florida may have been settled 300 years ago, but what had she ever done for the country ? What had she ever done for herself ? The man that spoke of Florida and the glorious THIRTEEN in the same breath, was a premium idiot ! Now if any State could claim the glory of being inscribed among those deathless names, it was Texas, and Texas alone ! The THIRTEEN had fought and bled, and at last achieved independence under General George Washington, who by the great victory of Yorktown, October 19th, 1781, expelled the foe forever from our soil. Texas, single-handed, had fought and bled, and at last achieved independence under General Sam Houston, who by his great victory of San Jacinto, March 2d, 1836, delivered the country forever from the Mexican invader. What other State could say as much ? To conclude, did not the State of the *Lone Star,* full of admiration for our institutions, and desirous to participate in their advantages, voluntarily relinquish her independence, and, unbribed and uncorrupted, annex herself to our glorious Union in 1845 ? Could any

State show a cleaner, sounder, or more creditable record ?"

"*Achieved her independence !*" yelled the
Times. " That *was* 'cheek,' to borrow the phrase
of a cotemporary, more remarkable for force
than elegance ! A crowd of Northern rowdies
and Southern slave-drivers, calling themselves
Texans, happened one day to frighten the wits
out of a miserable set of Mexican Greasers, led
by Santa Anna, one of the half dozen Presidents at that time pretending to rule the
wretched Republic ! Would not Sam Houston
and his whole band of hungry adventurers have
been easily gobbled up, as Walker was afterwards, by the Mexicans, the very first moment
they had freed themselves from the French
complications, and their own intestine squabbles ?
Voluntarily annexed herself to our Union ! There
was richness ! We should soon have men chal-
lenging our gratitude, because they showed sense
enough to run under an arch when they saw a
storm coming. Why not call on us to admire
the English fugitive from justice for his mag-
nanimity in landing at New York ?"

And so the war ran on for many a day, but
we must spare our readers the rest. In fact,
in order not to weary their patience too much,

we have given only a very feeble and meagre
summary of what appeared every day in these
great organs of public opinion. Every morning
they let fly at each other an editorial, at least
three columns long, written in a style worthy
of Macaulay, not to mention the squibs, jokes,
puns and conundrums that flashed all over the
paper. For several weeks the sub-editors had
a very hard time of it indeed, working night
and day, one set in the Cooper Institute, another
in the Astor Library, ransacking the shelves in
diligent search of such facts in American history
as were most easily manipulated into telling
points.

Of course this war of the newspapers did no
good whatever towards settling the main question.
Not that what they stated was not true or not to
the purpose, or not even highly instructive to
those million readers who rely on their paper for
history as well as for news, poetry, and general
information. Not that every member of the
Gun Club did not religiously wade through his
half-dozen papers every morning at breakfast
time. The trouble was that the more they read
the more they were puzzled, and the more undecided they became. The advantages and disadvantages presented by both States were balanced

to a hair, and the Gun Club was too strictly philosophical, too severely logical to come to any decision whatever, without being compelled to it by a cogent preponderance of argument. Recent political events, of course, counted neither way. The club, "Union men" to the core, were too generous, too high toned to make the slightest allusion to the part taken by either Florida or Texas during the great civil war.

The case was fast becoming another instance of the ass starving between the two bundles of hay, because he could not make up his mind which one he should begin at; overvitality, in fact, was threatening the enterprise with sudden dissolution, when all at once, a luminous idea struck Barbican. He instantly called the Club together and spoke as follows:

"Gentlemen, you are aware of what a difficult matter it is to decide between the conflicting claims of Florida and Texas. Has it ever occurred to you that when we have settled on the *State*, the difficulty will still be far from ended? The respective merits of the *towns* in the favored State will then have to be discussed, and who can tell when we should come to an end? Now Texas possesses at least *six* towns ready to fly at each other's throats for the honor of being the scene of our great enterprise, and therefore certain to cause us more delay and more vexation. Whereas Florida has but *one*. You see the idea ? It solves all difficulties at once if we decide on Florida for the State, and Tampa for the town !"

It is needless to say that this proposition was instantly and unanimously carried. The preponderance of argument in its favor was too overwhelming to be resisted. But the decision when reported in the evening papers, struck the unfortunate Texan commissioners actually speechless. In their paroxysms of rage they challenged every member of the Club to a duel, to be fought next morning with rifles at 20 paces distant. The police authorities had but one course to take, and they took it. They made a *coup d'état* that very night on the Texans in their hotel, the *Eutaw House*. They captured every man of them, put them into a special train well provided with food and drink for a week, and started them at once out of the city at the rate of thirty miles an hour.

The commissioners, as they recovered from the stunning effects of the surprise, by degrees came to a true sense of the situation. Feeling that violence would not mend matters, they spent tbe rest of their journey in concocting some plan to console their people at home for their failure. Putting on faces expressive of the greatest joy, they warmly congratulated the disappointed Texans on their extraordinary good fortune in having escaped the presence of the " consarned thing," which would be sure to " bust" at the first chance and blow up little " Florry," Crackers, Spaniards, Niggers, alligators and all, into " one grand, almighty, and everlasting smash !"

This evil omen had no effect on the jubilant Floridians. " Let her rip ! Who's afeard ?" they unanimously exclaimed, with a spirit worthy of Curtius when he jumped into the yawning chasm.

CHAPTER XII.

THE FINANCIAL QUESTION.

The astronomical, mechanical and topographical difficulties of the enterprise once squarely met and satisfactorily settled, next came the financial question. Without the dollars, "the sinews of war," nothing could be done. The immense sum required would evidently reach too high a figure for any private individual, any club, any State, or even any government.

But though the enterprise was of American origin, Barbican had determined to enlist the sympathies of the whole world in its success, and to demand the financial co-operation of every civilized people. It was clearly the right as well as the duty of every nation of the earth to be interested in the matter so closely concerning our common satellite. The subscription therefore opened at Baltimore was not to be confined to that city alone; it was to extend from that city to the world at large—like the Pope's blessing at St. Peter's on Easter Sunday —" *Urbi et Orbi.*"

(152)

This subscription was to be no stockbroker operation or government loan; it was not started for the redemption of territory; it did not propose building a railroad to Hudson's Bay, certain to pay every shareholder 150 per cent. on his investment; it did not propose to pay any interest at all; it did not even propose to return one cent of the principal; not a single human being was ever to make a penny by it; yet it was destined to have a success unparalleled in the annals of subscription. Why so? Because in the United States, as in the world at large, the nature of man has been so improved by the teachings of this 19th century, so elevated above mere consideration of self, that hard, vulgar utility has become unprized—an obsolete barbarism. Consequently, the moment an enterprise is announced which touches our fancy, appeals to our ideality, or plays upon our abstract love of the sublime, our purse strings fly open as with a spring, and the fortunate originator of the envied idea is soon almost smothered beneath the piles of our contributions. It was thus with the proposition of the Gun Club.

For the effect of Barbican's communication had not been circumscribed by the frontiers of the United States. It had bounded over the Atlantic and the Pacific, invading at once Europe, Asia, Africa and Oceanica. All the great observatories of the Union immediately put themselves in telegraphic communication with the observatories of foreign countries. Most of the latter flashed complimentary offers to the Gun Club. The warmest and most enthusiastic were the observatories of Paris, St. Petersburg, Berlin, Altona, the Cape of Good Hope, Stockholm, Hamburgh, Bologna, Dorpat, Milan, Rome, Warsaw, Buda, Lisbon, Benares, Madras and Pekin. Others kept a prudent silence, waiting results. As for the great English Observatory of Greenwich, with the full approval of the twenty-two other observatories of Great Britain, it came out "flat-footed" on the question. It boldly denied the possibility of success, and sided altogether with Captain McNichol. Instead of sending deputations to Tampa, as the other learned societies had promised to do, the Greenwich staff, in full assembly, the Astronomer Royal presiding, unanimously tabled Barbican's communication, and passed on to the order of the day. All pure English jealousy and envy, nothing else. But as everybody had expected it, nobody minded it, and it had not the slightest effect in counteracting the popularity of the enterprise.

As a general rule it was the scientific men who showed the most enthusiastic interest in its success, but, what does not always happen, their hearty fervor, spreading among the masses, soon produced a general response from all ranks fully as ardent as their own. This was a most fortunate result, as the zealous co-operation of the masses could easily meet an expense that otherwise would have soon swamped all the resources of the scientific men.

On the 9th of October, Barbican had issued a manifesto, glowing with enthusiasm, intended for all the nations of the earth, and having for its motto the beautiful words of the angelic hymn, " *Et in Terra Pax hominibus bonæ voluntatis !* " It was translated into all languages, and in a few months its accents resounded in every quarter of the globe.

Subscription books were immediately opened in all the chief cities of the Union, the head office being the Patapsco Bank, 13 St. Paul Street, Baltimore. The chief subscription offices in the two Continents, outside the United States, are given in the following list :

Vienna :—Solomon Rothschild.

St. Petersburg :—Thomson, Bonar & Co.

Paris :—Drexel, Harjes & Co.

Stockholm :—Arfwedson, Sutthoff & Co.

London :—J. S. Morgan & Co.

Turin :—Ardouin & Co.

Berlin :—Mendelssohn.

Geneva :—Lombard, Odier & Co.

Constantinople :—The Imperial Ottoman Bank.

Brussels :—Brugmann Fils.

Madrid :—O'Shea, Goldsmith & Co.

Seville :—Cahill, White & Beck.

Amsterdam :—Hope & Co.

Rome :—Torlonia & Co.

Lisbon :—Fortunato Chanico, Junior.

Copenhagen :—Frolich & Co.

Mexico :—Martin, Drana & Co.

Rio Janeiro :—The Mauà Bank.

Buenos Ayres :—The O'Donoju Bank.

Lima :—La Chambre & Co.

Valparaiso :—Alsop & Co.

The success of the subscription all through the United States was immediate and immense. Even in Philadelphia, the sedate " Quaker City," so eager was every one to contribute his share, that at an early hour of the evening previous to the day for opening the subscription books, the people began taking places along Chestnut street, in the neighborhood of the Bank of Pennsylvania. Some who could not conveni-

ently stay up all night in the streets, hired boys
to do it for them; others even paid a handsome
premium next morning for a good place in the
line. *Ex uno disce omnes.* In less than a week
after the appearance of Barbican's circular, the
subscriptions of the principal cities of the Union
had amounted to the enormous sum of a little
more than four millions of dollars. With such
a snug balance in their favor, the Club need
have no hesitation in commencing at once. But
even from foreign countries the telegraphic dispatches were equally encouraging. Some nations
especially distinguished themselves by their lib-
erality; others, of course, " forked over" with
much less readiness—all a pure matter of temperament.

Figures being more eloquent than words, we
shall here give a short statement of the principal
sums paid in by each country, and, at the close
of the subscription, openly announced to be
lying in the vaults of the Patapsco Bank, subject
to the orders of the Baltimore Gun Club.

Russia's contingency reached the very large
sum of 368,733 rubles, nearly a quarter of a million dollars. Should any one be astonished at
this generosity, he must remember that the
scientific taste of the Russians is very highly

developed, particularly in the direction of astronomy. They possess at least ten famous observatories, of which two, one at Dorpat and the other at Pulkova, are at least equal to any in Europe.

France, as usual, began by making fun of what she considered the irresistible (*impayables*) eccentricities of the Americans. The Moon became a target for every *homme d'esprit,* nine out of ten is the average in France, and no one could count the jokes, puns, epigrams and even *vaudevilles* made on the new " American notion.'' Patti's marriage was nothing to it. But a Frenchman often after his laugh, like an Englishman sometimes after his growl, is the most generous, if not the most sensible of men. It was so at least in the present instance. France laughed so heartily over the American absurdity that she ended by falling in love with it. Instantly the question arose : Who would do the most for its advancement ? It was just before the German war, when France was in a fine condition to gratify her scientific fancies to almost any extent. This accounts for her princely contribution of 1,253,930 francs, more than a quarter of a million of dollars. The Americans took the money and never said a word about the jokes.

Austria showed herself, considering her serious financial embarrassment, very kind and generous indeed. Her contribution amounted to the sum of 216,000 florins, about 108,000 dollars, which were very thankfully received by the Club.

52,000 riksdalers, or about 15,000 dollars, were contributed by the United Kingdoms of Sweden and Norway, a subsidy in tolerable proportion with the resources of these countries, but it would have probably been much more considerable had the subscription been opened in Christiania as well as in Stockholm. For some reason or other, the Norwegians have never liked sending their money to Sweden.

Prussia showed her high appreciation of the American enterprise by a remittance of 250,000 thalers, about 175,000 dollars. Her different observatories alone raised a large sum, and in other respects showed themselves extremely desirous to encourage the enterprise.

Turkey also—in spite of the fact that her expenditures are far in excess of her revenue, and that the government publication of a budget exhibiting a surplus, is invariably followed by a new loan—showed herself remarkably liberal, though it cannot be denied that her interest in the enterprise partook of the selfish as well as the purely scientific. Her years are altogether regulated by the Moon, particularly her celebrated ninth month, called *Ramadan,* the month of the great fast, when from dawn to sunset, from the moment a white thread can be distinguished from a black one, complete and entire abstinence from all kinds of food and drink, even medicine, is strictly enjoined on every good Mussulman. As this holy month depends entirely on the Moon for its beginning and end, and is therefore impartially distributed through every season—sometimes occurring in the freezing depths of winter, sometimes in the roasting blaze of summer—it is easily seen that the Mahometans have very special reasons for regarding the beauteous Queen of Night with an interest far surpassing our own. Still I must say, that both the amount of the sum itself, 1,372,640 piastres, about 60,000 dollars, and the readiness with which it was contributed, were somewhat extraordinary for Turkey, and smacked decidedly of some gentle but very effectual "hint" on the part of the Ottoman government.

Among the States of the second class, Belgium distinguished herself by a donation of 513,000 francs, about 102,500 dollars. This handsome sum—an average of 2½ cents for every inhabitant, three times greater than the French average —spoke no less for the public spirit of the flourishing little kingdom than for her industry, and the prudence and honesty that kept her free from oppressive debt.

Holland and her colonies interested themselves in the enterprise to the extent of 110,000 florins, about 44,000 dollars. Only as the Netherlanders are all good business men, they insisted on getting back a discount of five per cent. for cash.

Denmark, though rather cramped both in territory and population, still gave 42,264 rigsdalers, about 24,000 dollars, a sum showing that Tycho Brahé's countrymen are still interested in scientific inquiries.

The North German Confederation pledged itself to the amount of 34,285 florins, about 14,000 dollars. You could not ask her for more, and if you did she would not give it.

Italy, though staggering under such a fearful public debt that the interest alone eats into half her revenue, contrived to scrape together 200,000 liras, about 40,000 dollars, but it was only by turning her pockets inside out. In spite of the annexation of Venetia, and the confiscation of the Church property, she was still " hard up."

Rome—this was before the invasion of Victor

Emanuel—sent as her share 7040 scudos, almost exactly the same number of dollars; and Portugal, though with a yearly increasing deficit, by a remittance of 20,376 milreis, about 23,000 dollars, showed her good will towards the advancement of science.

Poor Mexico, in the middle of the troubles that ended so disastrously for Maximilian, could only give the widow's mite, 345 silver dollars. Maximilian is now dead and gone, but I have not heard that Mexico's condition is much improved.

257 francs, or 51 dollars and 40 cents—such was the modest contribution of Switzerland towards the great American enterprise. I must speak plainly on the subject; Switzerland looked on the idea altogether from a *practical* point of view: What was the good of sending a bullet to the Moon? Was it not a pure waste of capital? How could it possibly "pay"? Therefore, she politely begged to be excused taking stock in any such risky proceeding. After all, perhaps Switzerland was right.

Spain could give no more than 220 reals, about 11 dollars. She said she had her railroads to build. The truth is that this was the time when Spain was engaged in her fight with

Queen Isabella, or rather when everybody was in a fight with everybody else, and nobody seemed to know what anybody wanted. Prim would be prime minister to-day; an insurrection would put O'Donnell in his place to-morrow; on the next day Narvaez would be master of both. Then all would unite in a conspiracy against the Queen. No wonder if the subscription languished. Besides, Spain, once the head of the nations of Europe, is now, for want of a good government, one of the lowest. She has been fighting so much and so ineffectually that she seems to be relapsing into barbarism. Wherever love of science is dying out, unreasoning terror takes its place. Too much occupied in getting up insurrections to read books, a pretty good number of Spaniards all over the kingdom, not calculating the relative proportions of the projectile and the Moon, were afraid that our satellite might be so much disturbed in her orbit by the shock, as to be unable to keep her course. Therefore, she might either be compelled to wander off into space, or to fall to the surface of the earth. Neither contingency being pleasant to contemplate, they resolved to abstain from the subscription, which they did, with the exception of the 11 dollars mentioned above.

England yet remained to be heard from; but the manner in which the Greenwich Observatory authorities had acted, left little room for conjecture regarding the nature of her answer. The fact is, that England, never very friendly, entertained at this time particularly bitter feelings against the United States for several reasons. The chief one was the Alabama claims, still unsettled, still difficult to settle, and, like Damocles' sword, hanging over her head, silent, glittering, terrible; and her guilty conscience saw the thin thread growing thinner and thinner every day. Another was the Fenian troubles. The sudden ending of the Civil War had set free from both armies a few hundred of soldiers who, hardly knowing what to do with their spare time, and considering themselves injured by England, for her double dealing on the one side, and her blockade running on the other, thought they could bother her a little by kicking up a "shindy" in Ireland. Here again England's guilty conscience terribly frightened her, but, Heaven bless you! she never thought of attributing her terror to its real cause—her long continued evil treatment of Ireland—but altogether to the inveterate animosity with which she considered herself to be always regarded by the

United States. Besides, the mortification of her old defeat still rankled in her breast. The crime of catching two of her fine armies, like a rat in a trap, was too great for ordinary human, not to talk of English, nature to forgive. When John Bull is in good humor, he may not be insensible to the cry of some great distress—a terrible conflagration for instance—but when his pride is hurt, his envy or jealousy aroused, or his money-making opportunities interfered with—that is, on an average nine times out of every ten—he buttons up his breeches-pocket as tight as a salamander safe, and would see you in Halifax before he gave you a single farthing. Of course he would try to conceal this absurd meanness by some high sounding title, the more inappropriate the better. In the present case the English refused the Baltimorians point blank, on the dignified principle of strict " non-intervention." " It was so well known that England never interfered on any account in the affairs of other countries—witness India, Italy, Spain, Ashantee, etc.—that however willing she might feel under other circumstances to show her friendship for her trans-Atlantic Anglo-Saxon cousins, the brothers of her Shakspeare, etc., she could not now compromise her honor by departing in the slighest degree from the grand principle which it had been always her glory unswervingly to pursue." So England did not send the United States as much money as would jingle in a tombstone.

But the Baltimorians were soon consoled for this sulky refusal by a remittance from a quarter as welcome as it was unexpected.

The very causes that had rendered England unfriendly towards the United States, had intensified the contrary feeling in another part of the British Kingdom. Ireland had always hated England, and had always loved America. With very good reason : She had always been treated badly by the one, and always kindly by the other. Her people had risen to high places of honor and influence in the one country, without compromising either their faith or their patriotism; this they had never done in the other country, without smothering, or at least suppressing both. In the years of her terrible famine, her cry of anguish had been heard at the other side of the Atlantic, and war ships laden with corn had sailed immediately for her relief. Since that time a stream of money had been constantly flowing from the West, like the Gulf Stream, towards the suffering island : every dollar

a new link in the great chain that attaches for
ever the heart of Ireland to the people of the
United States.   Recent events had only strengthened this feeling.   In the great civil war her
sons had fought bravely, on both sides it is
true, but anyway was it not for America ?   The
question of the Alabama claims possessed an intense interest for them, because they knew it to
be so embarrassing to their hereditary foe ; and
the generally accepted report that American
officers secretly directed the operations of the
Fenian movement, made every Irish eye, for the
time being, look on every American as something
very little short of a regular angel.

This being the case, it is not surprising that
Ireland pursued a course on the present question most distinctly contrary to that of England.
As soon as Barbican's circular appeared in the
papers, a self-appointed committee—not a scientific man among them except two : one a distinguished chemist of Trinity College, the other a
young professor of the Irish University—held its
first meeting in a little room back of the *Nation*
office, Dublin, and that very evening sent a
rousing appeal to the chief cities and towns of
Ireland, calling their attention to the great Balti·
more project, and soliciting their immediate and

warm support. The idea was everywhere embraced with enthusiasm, and, to make a long story short, in less than two weeks the committee were able to send to America the creditable sum of 11,625 pounds sterling, about 60,000 dollars. This was accompanied by a letter stating that the remittance was exactly one-half penny a head for every man, woman, and child in Ireland, but that if it was ten pounds a head it would still fall far short of showing the gratitude and kindly feelings entertained by Ireland for America. In a postscript it was added that poor old Baltimore (the little fishing village in the south of Ireland, which had given Lord Baltimore his title), had sent all she could to her big, full grown, beautiful daughter across the ocean, the small sum of one pound ten, but her best blessings had gone along with it !

The reading of this letter caused a very pleasant excitement in the Club Room, and J. T. Marston, who being a New Englander, had of course always been pretty hard on the Irish, wrote a recantation on the spot. It was composed in his best style, and he was so well pleased with it himself that he had it published a few days afterwards in the *New York Herald*, but nobody ever read it.

The chief States of South America, namely, Brazil, Colombia, Peru, Chili, Bolivia, and Argentina, together with a few of the smaller republics, having contributed for their share a little more than 300,000 dollars, the Club now found itself master of the very considerable capital represented as follows:

Total subcriptions from the United States,	$4,000,000
Total subscriptions from foreign States,	1,446,675
Total, ...	$5,446,675

But large as this sum undoubtedly was, every cent of it would be required. After paying all the expenses attendant on the casting, the boring, the masonry, the transport of the workmen, and their support in an almost uninhabited country, the construction of furnaces and machine shops, the supply of tools, the powder, the projectile, not to mention the thousand and one incidental expenses impossible to foresee—after paying all these, very little of the 5½ millions would be left. But what matter? During the Federal war every ball shot by certain cannons was said to cost the government a thousand dollars. Barbican's ball, unique and unprecedented in the annals of gunnery, could be readily excused for costing five hundred times as much.

On the twentieth of October, a contract was concluded with the Cold Spring Iron Company, at whose great works on Harlem Creek, not far from New York, the largest and most reliable Parrott guns had been cast during the war. By this contract, in consideration of a certain sum, the company pledged itself to transport to Tampa, a town in Florida, on the Gulf of Mexico, all material, whatever, necessary for the casting of the Columbiad. There the whole operation was to be performed, and the cannon delivered in good condition, at a period of time no later than the 15th of the following October, under pain of forfeiting a hundred dollars a day until such time as the Moon should present herself again in the same conditions; that is to say, in 18 years and 11 days. The company was furthermore to hire, pay, support and take general care of the workmen.

This contract, carefully written out and duplicated, was duly signed, sealed, and delivered on the part of the Gun Club by J. P. Barbican, President, and on the part of the company by John Murphy, Director and Chief Engineer, as well as the Superintendent of the Iron Works, Cold Spring, Harlem, near New York.

CHAPTER XIII.

STONY HILL.

As soon as the decided preference of Florida for Texas by the Gun Club was officially announced, every American that knew how to read—which is equivalent to saying all without exception—considered it his sacred duty to study up the geography and history of the fortunate State.

Luckily, works treating on the subject were abundant enough. Those most sought after by the general reader were :

The Conquest of Florida, by Don Fernando de Soto and his 600 *followers* (a translation from the Spanish) ; *The Spanish Main, the Floridas, with some account of the Seminole Cannibals* (of which more anon) ; *A Journey up the St. John's, by John Bartram of Philadelphia, Botanist ; W. Darby's Memoir on the Geography and History of Florida ;* Theodore Irving's *Conquest of Florida.* The last three Philadelphia publications, being rather antiquated, aroused in the public mind a keener desire for more modern works. Of these the chief favorites were :

J. T. Sprague's *Florida War ;* Parkman's
Huguenots in Florida, and Professor Bailey's
Microscopical Researches in Florida. At school,
instead of the ordinary French Reader, the
children read *Vue de la Floride Occidentale,* and
Volney's *Eclaircissements sur la Floride ;* and
the young ladies and gentlemen taking Spanish
lessons, threw aside *Don Quixote* for *La verdadera
Historia de la Florida del Inca,* by *Garcilasso
de la Vega.* The works were numerous enough,
as already mentioned, but the books in print
could not supply the thousandth part of the demand. In less than a day all the old stock
on the shelves was thoroughly cleared out, and
the public had to groan impatiently for the
next few days, while new editions were being
hurried through the press with all the dispatch
the quickest printers in the world were capable
of. It was during this interval that a little
episode occurred which, as it is by no means
unusual in the book business, and as it furnished
food for a good deal of public comment at the
time, may as well be here related.

A great Philadelphia publishing house had
been very much pleased with the appearance of
the second book given on our list. The title
was catching, the style was neat and crisp, the

information was sensible and interesting, but, above all, the work was English, no copyright was to be paid, and therefore it was a goose chockful of golden eggs, the legitimate and well established prey of whoever made the first grab ! It was at once stereotyped, an edition of 5,000 copies prepared for immediate sale, and 5,000 more announced to be ready in a few days. Unfortunately, a great Boston publishing house, having been equally captivated by the same seductive points of the work, announced an edition of 10,000 copies to be ready the very same day. The two great houses were telegraphing to each other some possible means of effecting a compromise, when, most unfortunately of all, a great New York publishing house, decoyed by the very same identical appetizing charms of the book, announced in the evening papers as ready for immediate sale an edition of 15,000 copies ! Then it was war to the knife. As a newspaper wit of great originality remarked, it was the terrible encounter of pirates over the prostrate body of their victim. The published price of the book had been about two dollars ; this the Philadelphian immediately cut down to one dollar. The Bostonian replied by reducing the price to fifty

cents. The great New York house demoralized
them both by offering the work for nothing at
all ! The plucky Philadelphian, recovering from
the blow, and determined to do something for
the honor of his city, offered *his* book also for
nothing, but accompanying it with the beautiful
chromo of " *The Babes in the Wood.*" The
proud Bostonian's premium to every one
accepting a copy of his book, immediately rose
to a neat *Boydell's Shakspeare* by the Heliotype
process. But the gigantic New Yorker com-
pletly knocked the wind out of both his opponents, by offering the enormous premium of a 5
years' subscription to his magazine together with
one share in the great *Centennial Stock*, the par
value of which was ten dollars !

The best part of the joke, however, was to
come. The book was not English at all, but
the work of an old gentleman of Delaware,
who had written the book about 30 years before,
published it at his own expense and carefully
taken out a regular copyright. The work, though
really a good one, not appearing at the right
time, naturally mouldered on the shelves, and
at last found its way to the trunkmakers—all
but one copy. This had somehow caught the
eye of a London publisher, who found it to

his advantage to give the public an edition or two, being very careful, however, to suppress the name of the author, and in fact everything in the work that might betray its American origin.

No one was more surprised at the resuscitation of the book than the author himself; but acting under the advice of one of those Philadelphia lawyers, who are famous all over the Union for their superior shrewdness, he kept perfectly quiet at first, and for a little while enjoyed the sublime sight of a publisher pounding his rivals to jelly, and then standing over them in majestic attitude, eye flashing scorn, and terrible arm lifted on high to "crush" the next one who would be mad enough to provoke his ire. Then, by the advice of his lawyer, the old gentleman wrote the great New Yorker a polite note, explaining the whole case and enclosing a bill for $3,000, the author's usual royalty at 10 per cent. on the published price. The Bostonian and the Philadelphian received equally polite notes, enclosing equally peremptory demands. All remonstrances were in vain. How resist the author's claims on a work of such unprecedented popularity, 30,000 copies having been disposed of in three days? The six thousand dollars had to be paid, and were paid, to the great joy of the public at large. Perhaps in no country in the world is there a greater love of even handed justice than in America ; therefore nobody pitied the poor great publishing houses ; on the contrary, the unanimous verdict from all quarters was, " served them right !"

These inanities, you may be sure, never troubled Barbican, who had something better to do than bother his head with books. One of his maxims was, " *Read to know ; then stop.*" He sometimes quoted another : " *A great reader is a poor thinker, and a poor thinker is a poor creature.*" He would trust nobody with the selection of a site for the Columbiad, and he wished to see everything with his own eyes. Accordingly, without losing an instant, in the name of the Gun Club, he placed in the hands of the Director of the Cambridge Observatory, money enough to pay for a large telescope, the construction of which Professor Belfast had promised to superintend. Then having made a contract with the house of Meneely & Co., Albany, for casting the aluminium projectile, he started from Baltimore, accompanied by Marston, Elphinstone, and also Murphy, the Director of the Cold Spring Iron Works. The bad condition of the Southern railroads, which had not yet recovered from the damaging effects of the war, put their patience to the test, but in less than a week the travellers had arrived in New Orleans, embarked in the *Wissahickon*, a United States revenue cutter which the government had placed at their disposal, and found themselves in the midst of the dreary region called the Delta of the Mississippi, sailing down one of the mouths through which that mighty river discharges its waters into the Gulf of Mexico.

The low coast of Louisiana soon disappeared, their eyes ceased to trace the line that for hundreds of miles separated the fresh water of the river from the salt water of the gulf, the warm breezes of the tropics played around them, the *Wissahickon* steamed on at the rate of ten miles an hour, and on the second morning after leaving New Orleans, the flat, barren shores of Florida came into view. Skirting, for some time, several low lying keys and many little creeks, rich in oysters, lobsters and turtles, the steamer at last entered the fine harbor formerly called Espiritu Santo, but now generally known as Tampa Bay. It is about twenty miles long, and at its northern end, a projecting tongue of land divides it into two smaller bays or havens,

12

that of Old Tampa on the northwest, that of
Hillsborough on the northeast. It was into the
latter that the *Wissahickon* headed, full steam ;
the batteries of Fort Brooke were not long in
revealing themselves ; the chimneys of the little
town of Tampa were soon perceived ; and early
in the evening of October 29th, the steamer
cast anchor in a small natural port formed at
the point where the Hillsborough river entered
the bay.

Barbican felt his heart beating with unusual
violence the moment he touched the soil of
Florida. His feet seemed to test its capacity,
as a doctor feels his patient, an architect sounds
a doubtful wall, or as a smith taps the wheels
of a train before it is allowed to start on a
new trip.

" Gentlemen," he cried earnestly to his companions, " there's not one moment to be lost.
To-morrow morning at day-break we shall examine the country on horseback———"

He would probably have said more if he had
not been cut short by a sight that actually froze
the marrow in his bones. This was a procession formed by the 796 inhabitants of Tampa,
men, women, and children, white and black,
headed by Squire Jones, the longest winded

TAMPA TOWN PREVIOUS TO THE UNDERTAKING.

orator that ever spoke in Tallahassee, carrying
all kinds of flags, banners and streamers, and
shouting fearfully. It was in fact a grand parade
got up for the occasion, and intended as a high
mark of honor for the illustrious President of
the famous Gun Club, whose choice had conferred such an eternal distinction on their city.
They had been all up since day-break ready to
receive him, but the poor people, becoming tired
with the delay, had tried to amuse themselves
by firing off the cannon until they ran out of
powder. Then a part had gone home to get
something to eat ; another part had adjourned
to the taverns to get something to drink ; indeed they had almost completely forgotten their
expected visitors, when the sudden cry startled
them that the vessel was in sight. It took so
much time to form the demoralized masses into
line, that Barbican and his friends had been permitted to land in peace—a most fortunate circumstance, for the loud shouts and energetic gestures
of the advancing multitude reminded the President of the Gun Club more painfully than pleas-
antly of a similar ovation which had nearly cost
him his life in Baltimore. Being a man of
quick decision, his resolution was formed in an
instant. Instead of waiting for the crowd, he

plunged headlong into it, where, as nobody knew him, nobody could shake hands with him, or, still worse, harangue him ; so that he soon reached the *De Soto Hotel*, where he immediately locked himself up in his room, positively refusing admission to all strangers. A great crowd remained up all night under his window, shouting, playing music, and roaring " speech ! speech !" A volley of stones even would every now and then rattle against his shutters, but they never disturbed his slumbers for a moment ; all night long he slept the sleep of the just. Decidedly Barbican would have made a splendid President of the United States. He had precisely the temperament that would never permit him to take pleasure in acting " the great man."

He was up next morning before sunrise, brisk as a bee, and after a hasty breakfast, the four artillerists started on their tour of observation, mounted on those well known small sized horses of Spanish blood that are so full of fire and vigor. Though late in October, the thermometer marked 84° in the shade, but this excessive temperature was much modified by the cool morning sea breezes.

Quitting Tampa, the little troop took a

southerly direction, skirting the eastern shore of
the bay till they came to a small stream called
Bullfrog Creek, emptying into it eight or ten
miles below Tampa. Turning their horses'
heads eastwardly, they followed the right bank
of this creek for some time with much difficulty,
the horses sinking almost to the knees in
mud and sand, though Barbican was repeatedly
assured by one of the guides that they were on
the great military road leading to Fort Meade.
Soon they lost sight of the waters of the bay
altogether, and veritable Floridian landscapes
alone presented themselves to their eyes.

Florida, one of the United States, may be considered as divided into two parts : the northern,
healthier, more advantangeous every way, and
therefore more thickly settled, contains, besides
Tallahassee, the capital, St. Augustine, the oldest
town in the United States, and the flourishing
modern cities of Jacksonville and Pensacola ;
the other part, a projecting tongue of land, is
the well known peninsula, about 300 miles long
by 50 wide, washed on one side by the Atlantic
Ocean, on the other by the Gulf of Mexico, with
its southern extremity gnawed into thousands of
keys or reefs by the tropical waters of the famous
Gulf Stream, which here seems to take its rise.

The whole State, almost exactly the size of England and Wales united, is larger in area than either Illinois or Iowa. It was in a region considerably south of the centre that Barbican had to find a suitable locality for his great enterprise ; this was no easy task, considering the profile of the country and the alluvial nature of the soil.

In 1512, twenty years after the discovery of America, the adventurous old *hidalgo* Ponce de Leon sailed northwest from San Domingo in search of the fabled *Waters of Eternal Youth.* On Easter Sunday, called by the Spaniards *Pascua Florida*, the festival of flowers, he struck the coast of the main land and named it *Florida*, the land of flowers, which is therefore the proper name of the North American Continent. But however appropriate the name might be for the country at large, the barren and burning coasts of the peninsula could lay little claim to the charming appellation. Such at least was the first idea that occurred to our Gun Club men. However, a few miles from the seaboard the nature of the soil began to change by degrees, and the country looked as if it really had some right to its name. The sand began to disappear under the masses of verdure, and the explorers soon found themselves in the midst of a net work of creeks, tarns, pools, ponds and little lakes. You could have easily imagined yourself in Holland or in Guiana. As they advanced they gradually reached higher ground, and soon came to vast plains, capable of producing every vegetable of the North and South in the greatest abundance. Little need for cultivating soil like that ; the tropical sun and the moisture retained in the rich clay, did all the hard work. " Tickle it with a harrow," as Marston said, quoting somebody, " and it will smile with eternal harvests !" Finally they came to those vast fields where pine apples, sweet potatoes, tobacco, rice, cotton, sugar cane, extending further than the eye could reach, displayed their treasures in the most prodigal and luxuriant profusion.

But it was the gradually increasing elevation of the land that gave Barbican the most pleasure. To a remark of Marston's on the beauty of the scenery, he replied somewhat absentmindedly :

" Yes, my dear friend, it is a necessity of the first order that our Columbiad be cast in ground of commanding elevation."

" To be nearer to the Moon ?" asked the Secretary.

" Oh, no," replied the President with a quiet smile. " What signifies the difference of a few rods, more or less ? On elevated ground, you know, our labor will be both diminished and simplified. We shall not have to contend with the water by means of hard pumping and expensive tubing—a very important consideration when you remember that we have to sink a pit nine hundred feet deep."

" You are quite right, Mr. Barbican," observed Murphy, who was to superintend the works personally. " We must, of course, do everything possible to avoid water, but if, in spite of all our efforts, water *will* come, we shall soon get rid of it by pumping it off or turning it aside. This is not like sinking an Artesian well, narrow, dark, deep, where the bits, the reamers, the sinkers, the augers, all the boring tools in fact, are compelled to work where no eye can see to direct their operations. I know all the difficulties presented by the boring of rocks, having sunk wells in the oil regions of Pennsylvania for a year and a half. I even helped Major Welton to bore the Artesian well at Charleston—the hardest job I ever had in all my life. And we got only salt water after all. Digging out our well here will be mere

child's play. We shall work under the open
sky, with plenty of room ; the pick, the spade
and the shovel will be quite enough ; except the
help we get from a blast now and then. Oh,
we shall get along famously, I promise you."

" However," replied Barbican, " if by the
elevation of our ground above the surrounding
level, or by its favorable nature, we can avoid
difficulties resulting from water or quicksands,
our labor will be so much rapider and more
satisfactory. Let us, therefore, try to sink our
shaft in the summit of some hill, if possible a
few hundred feet above the level of the sea."

" Quite correct, Mr. Barbican, and I have
no doubt that in a short time we shall come
across what suits you exactly."

" I should like to see the first stroke of the
pick," said the President.

" And I the last !" exclaimed Marston.

" The last will come as sure as the first,"
observed the engineer. " Our company knows
better than to make itself liable to the forfeit."

" By the great United States ! I should think
it did," cried Marston. " Do you know how
much a hundred dollars a day for 18 years and
11 days amounts to ? Do you know that it
comes to the snug little sum of 658,100 dollars ?"

" No, sir," answered Murphy, " I don't know anything about it ; we never took the trouble of calculating what we shall never have to pay."

After a short halt, at the point where the Fort Meade trail broke off, the little band resumed their march. Quitting the fertile flats, they soon entered the forest region, where they found themselves surrounded by almost every species of tropical trees, growing in truly tropical profusion. They could hardly follow the trail through the labyrinth of pomegranate-, orange-, citron-, olive-, apricot-, and banana-trees, hung with exuberant vines, rich in color and fragrant in perfume. In the balmy shade of these magnificent developments, countless thousands of birds flashed and glittered in plumage of the most brilliant dye. The most conspicuous among them was a beautiful little heron, the *gold winged fire-bird*, as it is called by the natives. The sight of it threw the excitable Marston almost into an ecstacy. " It is not a nest," he cried, " but a precious jewel case that should enshrine a gem of such oriental effulgency !" Elphinstone and Murphy, though in a quieter way, expressed their great delight at all they saw.

But the splendor of this wonder-land was all lost on Barbican. Nay, the prodigal fertility, so indicative of the presence of water, positively annoyed him. Dry, solid ground was what he looked for, and that he knew he could not find where vegetation flourished in such unstinted measure.

Onward, therefore, was still the cry. They had to ford several creeks and even rivers—a feat not always quite free from danger, as alligators twelve or fifteen feet long would sometimes approach to a proximity too close for comfort. Marston's fierce shouts and occasional pop with a pistol seemed to have hardly the effect of frightening even the pelicans, strawtail ducks, green herons, and the other wild denizens of these untravelled regions, where the orange-red flamingo quietly regarded the travellers with the innocent stare of unsuspecting stupidity.

Finally, the waders, the web-footers, the spoonbills, and the other birds that favor marshy bottom lands, disappeared in their turn ; the trees gradually decreased in diameter, the forest became less dense, the trail less encumbered, the ascent steeper and more decided, and the rich sunlight streaming through the branches rendered the labor of the guides superfluous. The little party soon left the tropical forest altogether, and, approaching the pine region, for the first time they had an unobstructed view over the great park-like plains before them, where several herds of frightened deer could be seen scampering in all directions.

All at once Barbican's eye flashed with excitement and his pale cheek flushed red, as at a sudden turn he caught sight of a rocky mound about half a mile further on, a few hundred feet in height, of easy ascent, and its flat summit comprising an area of probably twenty or thirty acres.

" Halt !" he cried in thrilling tones. " We have exactly what we want. Guides, have you a name for that eminence yonder ?"

" The Tampa people call it Stony Hill," replied the younger and more intelligent of the guides, " but the Seminoles call it *Pilakleena*, meaning, as I have heard, *the mound of the white bones.*"

Barbican wrote down " Stony Hill" in his tablet and pushed on without another word, but Elphinstone's curiosity being somewhat excited, he asked :

" Why do they give it such a strange name ?"

" Because for hundreds of years it was white all over with the bones of the Spaniards slain in the great massacre."

" What Spaniards ?" asked the Major.

"What massacre?" asked Marston, also somewhat interested.

"The massacre of those Spaniards who, shortly after the country was discovered, tried to reach the interior, in search of gold, silver and diamonds. They landed in Tampa Bay."

"Well?" asked the Major and Marston in one breath.

"Well, gentlemen, luck, you see, was dead against them. In the first place, there was no gold, nor silver, nor diamonds in Florida. Then their fleet got destroyed by a tornado, and at last themselves were all massacred by the united Creeks, Euchees, and Chickasaws."

"And Seminoles," suggested Marston.

"No, gentlemen, excuse me; there were no Seminoles, you see, in those days, being as Seminole is the name given to the runaway Indians of all the other tribes."

"Did the massacre take place on that hill?" asked the Major.

"So they say," answered the guide. "There they made their last stand, and all perished to a man, except a few who were taken prisoners and escaped at last, after many years' captivity."

"Are the bones to be seen there now?" asked the Major.

"Oh, no; in the Seminole war General Gaines, considering the hill as a good point for a fort, had them all cleared off and burned or buried, I don't know which."

"Did you ever see the bones yourself?" asked the Major.

"I was too young myself, at the time, but my father often said he saw them."

"Or said he saw the man that saw the man that said he saw the man that saw them!" laughed Marston incredulously.

"Marston," said the Major quietly, "it is an established fact in early Floridian history that Narvaez, so well known in connection with Cortez———"

"Who knocked his eye out—*vide* Prescott," interrupted Marston.

"Exactly; Narvaez, jealous of the great conqueror of Mexico, landed somewhere in Florida, about 1528, and perished there with all his companions except four, one of whom, Vaca, afterwards wrote a history of the disastrous expedition. But I always thought that it was the northwest part of the country that had been the theatre of their sufferings. Surely, Vaca, the first historian of North America, could not have been guilty of a false statement."

" Of course not !" laughed Marston, " considering the infallibility of historians generally."

By this time they reached the summit, where they found Barbican, on foot, coat off, hard at work, trying to take the bearings of the locality by means of an improved portable theodolite of the latest pattern, which he had taken the trouble of carrying in his own hands all the way from Tampa. His companions formed a little group near him, keeping perfect silence and watching his proceedings with the utmost interest.

They had made such good time on the road as to reach the hill a little before high noon. Consequently, the sun at this moment was crossing the meridian, which shortened Barbican's calculations so considerably that in a few minutes he was able to give his friends the following result of his observations :

" This hill, nearly a thousand feet above the level of the sea, lies in 27° 7' north latitude by 5° 7' west longitude, counting from the meridian of Washington. It is probably the highest point in southern Florida, its base being washed by the head waters of the chief rivers : the St. John's on the east, the Withlacoochee on the north, the Pea Creek on the southwest, and on the south the countless streams that flow into Lake Okeechobee. By its position, its dryness, its rocky soil mixed with sandy alluvium, it appears to me to possess every condition desirable for the success of our experiment. Here then on this plateau shall rise our store houses, our workshops, our foundries, and the habitations of our workmen. And it is from this very spot," he added emphatically, stamping strongly as he spoke, " from this very spot, the highest point of Stony Hill, that our projectile——"

" Shall wing her triumphant way through the boundless fields of ether towards our peerless Satellite's resplendent orb !" struck in Marston, who could never resist the temptation of giving vent to the fiery inspirations of his grand Byronic soul.

CHAPTER XIV.

SPADE, SHOVEL, PICK AND TROWEL.

Though it was late that evening when the exploring party returned to Tampa, Mr. Murphy, unwilling to lose any time, started at once in the *Wissahickon* for New Orleans. Thence he was to telegraph to the great cities of the North for the army of workmen already collected there by his foresight, and who were now impatiently awaiting his signal. The Gun Club men remained at Tampa, where they had no difficulty in obtaining all the help they needed for starting the preliminary operations.

In less than two weeks, Murphy was back again in the *Wissahickon*, accompanied by several other smaller steamers, containing in all about fifteen hundred first-rate hands. He had experienced no difficulty in obtaining them. The famous climate of Florida, the renown and popularity of the enterprise, and, above all, the offer of very liberal wages, had secured to him the very pick and choice of the best workmen in every department. Machinists and firemen from New England, foundrymen and brick-makers from Philadelphia, lime-burners from New York, miners from Pennsylvania, Irish railway laborers, Negro hod carriers, together with masons, bricklayers, carpenters and smiths —all had been personally selected in the most favorable localities, and it is not too much to say that for intelligence, industry, cheerfulness, and general good conduct it would be hard to match such a body of men in any other country. Many of them had even brought their families along—the very want most felt in the South, where Nature, lavishing her gifts in most bounti-ful measure, requires the genial fingers of labor to prune their rank luxuriance.

On the 11th of November, at 10 o'clock in the morning, the little fleet landed at Tampa, and you may guess what bustle, activity and confusion consequently prevailed immediately in a small town whose population was tripled in the course of a few hours. In fact, from this day forward the worldly prosperity of the place advanced with gigantic strides, not merely on account of the im-mense number of workmen and their families, for many of whom food and shelter were to be found, but also from the great crowds of strangers impelled by curiosity to converge from all quarters of the world to this one point of the peninsula. As it was expressed by the clever correspondent of the *Boston Globe*, who always hits on grand historical contrasts, " Tampa and the Gun are the precursors of Philadelphia and the Centennial."

The first days were spent in discharging the vessels of the machinery, the tools, the provisions, and likewise of a great number of cast iron frame buildings, with the pieces marked and numbered, so as to be put together and taken apart at pleasure. In the meantime Barbican had set with his own hand the first sleeper of a railroad about twenty miles in length, that was to connect Stony Hill with Tampa. He also projected another railroad to connect Tampa with Waldo, on the *Gulf Railroad*. This would have placed him in immediate and direct communication by rail with Baltimore and the North, and for awhile he was very earnest about it. But he abandoned the idea at once, as soon as he learned that in all probability he would have to finish the main road as well as the branch road, work on the *Gulf Railroad* having been suspended for some time, and its resumption being anything but probable. Though a scientist and a patriot, he was also an honorable man, and therefore he never dreamed of spending other people's money in any other way than in strictly forwarding the views for which it had been subscribed. Not only that, but by his extraordinary intelligence, his untiring energy, his wonderful ubiquity, his inspiriting enthusiasm, his decided conviction of ultimate success, his friendly thoughtfulness for the comforts of the workmen, but above all, by his unscrupulous *honesty* which never tolerated imposition from any quarter—he actualty wrought wonders ; the railroad was finished in a short time ; it had neither deep cuttings nor high bridges, nor did it attempt to follow a straight line ; yet it was safe and tolerably smooth ; its expense was comparatively small, and it had cost no human life whatever—a decided contrast with the *Aspinwall and Panama Railroad*, whose sleepers are said to rest on the bones of the perished laborers !

In fact Barbican was the life and soul of the whole enterprise. No difficulty, no obstacle, no embarrassment could conquer him. His practical genius always contrived some plan to overcome them all. He was by turns miner, mason, machinist, draughtsman, with a ready answer for every question, and a ready solution for every problem. He corresponded daily with the Gun Club or the works at Cold Spring, and the *Wissahickon* kept up steam day and night, waiting his orders in Hillsboro Bay.

About the middle of November he left Tampa, accompanied by a detachment of workmen, and the very next day a little city of frame houses was erected around the foot of Stony Hill. It was soon surrounded by a neat fence, and from its bustle, stir and life, you might for a moment take it for one of the great cities of the Union. Strict discipline prevailed in everything, and the works were immediately commenced with perfect order and system.

Having ascertained the geological nature of the hill by some careful boring and drilling, Barbican called his foremen together on the morning of November 19th, and addressed them as follows :

" You know already, my friends, why we are all assembled here on this wild spot in Florida. We have to cast a cannon measuring nine feet in the interior diameter, six feet in thickness, and nineteen feet and a half from its external surface to the outside of the stone wall that is to surround it. We have, therefore, to excavate a pit sixty feet in diameter and nine hundred feet in depth. This serious piece of work must be completed in eight months; therefore you have 2,543,400 cubic feet of earth to remove in 223 days, omitting Sundays, or, say in round numbers, 11,500 cubic feet per day. This amount of work would not present any serious difficulty to a thousand workmen who had plenty of elbow-room, but it will prove rather embarrassing by being confined within such comparatively narrow limits. Nevertheless, as the work has got to be done, done it must be, and I rely on your energy as firmly as I do on your intelligence.''

That very morning at eight o'clock precisely, Barbican led off the operations by breaking ground himself with the spade. From this day forward until the work was completed, that valiant weapon, the queen of implements, never rested one moment idle in the hands of the workmen, except for twenty-four hours every week, from 12 o'clock Saturday night until 12 o'clock on the following Sunday. Even in the wilds of Florida, Barbican insisted on the Christian Sabbath being observed as a day of holy rest. On that blessed day even the horses were not disturbed, and were allowed a double allowance of food. Moreover,

on that day, as clergymen of different denomi-
nations held divine service on the hill, Metho-
dists, Presbyterians, Baptists, and Catholics could
be seen worshipping within sight of each other in
perfect harmony. What country but America
could show such a sight? The men were told
off in squads and relieved each other every six
hours.

The job, though a colossal one, by no means
exceeded the limits of human resources. Far
from it. Many works of a similar nature, but
of far greater real difficulty, have been brought to
a successful termination. To give one or two instances out of many, it will be enough to mention
the famous *Joseph's Well*, constructed at Cairo,
Egypt, by the Sultan Saladin, 700 years ago, a
period when machinery multiplying the strength
of man was unknown. This well, a parallelo-
gram in shape, 20 feet by 12, is nearly three
hundred feet in depth. Still more remarkable
is the well in Orvieto, Italy, called *St. Patrick's
Well*, in honor of the patron saint of Ireland.
It is 180 feet in depth, 46 feet in diameter, and
encloses two spiral staircases, so that you can descend by the one and ascend by the other. It
was excavated through the solid rock on which
the city is built, by San Gallo for Pope Clement

VII., in 1527. What then was to be done at Stony Hill? Nothing more difficult than to make the depth five times greater, with 14 feet increase of diameter, which would render the work much more convenient. That was all! Not a single man, whether boss or laborer, had the least doubt of the ultimate success of the work.

A happy thought of Mr. Murphy's considerably accelerated the progress of the operation. An article of the contract has spoken of binding the Columbiad with red hot hoops of wrought iron. Such a precaution being useless, as the engine could easily dispense with all such compressing bands, this clause was cancelled, and much time saved in consequence, as there was nothing to prevent them now from employing the new plan adopted in sinking wells. This is, simply to begin building the wall as soon as the pick reaches the solid foundation, and to continue the mason work as fast as the excavation advances. The descent of the wall, by its own weight, renders it altogether unnecessary to use stays or props to prevent the earth from caving in. The circular wall does that part of the work completely; on the principle of the arch, the more it is compressed the more firmly it resists the pressure ; besides, as it continually descends by its own weight, an immensity of time and trouble is saved to the masons, who remain constantly at work on the top of the wall, which is kept on a level, or nearly so, with the surrounding surface.

The first object encountered by the pick and the spade, was a layer of black earth, about six inches in thickness, which the shovels soon got rid of. Then came a stratum of fine sand two feet thick; this was carefully piled away as it was to form the core or interior mould of the cannon. Then appeared a bed of white clay, pretty stiff and somewhat resembling English marl; this bed was fully four feet thick. Then the clashing point of the pick struck fire against the solid stony formation of the hill, a kind of dry, hard flinty rock, formed of petrified shells. Here, the pit being now six feet and a half deep, the masonry commenced, and Murphy's happy thought was put into execution.

At the bottom of the well, they constructed a kind of disc, shaped somewhat like a quoit, sixty feet in diameter, more than a foot in thickness, formed of strong oaken planks, riveted, bolted, and screwed together, so as to be rendered as solid a mass as human skill could make it. In its centre it had a hole 21 feet wide, corresponding to the external diameter of the Columbiad. This disc supported the first layers of stone wall, the stones of which were to be held together by hydraulic cement, with inflexible solidity. The masons then built up the wall till it was flush with the summit of the hill, and the miners found themselves working in a pit twenty-one feet in diameter.

As soon as the wall was considered perfectly solid and " all of a piece," as it were, through the hydraulic cement, the miners went to work at the rock under the disc itself, taking great care to support it here and there by solid iron studs of extreme solidity. Whenever they had sunk the pit a clear foot in depth, they removed these studs, which were so constructed that they could be readily knocked away. The disc sank by degrees, and with it the circular pile of masonry, at the upper portion of which the men were kept continually at work—not too closely, however, to forget leaving occasional vents for the future escape of the gases during the operation of casting.

This kind of work, of course, required from the men extreme skill and the most wakeful attention. The most dangerous part was knocking away the studs, and for the first month

THE WORK PROGRESSED WITH GREAT REGULARITY.

the loss of legs or arms was most unpleasantly
frequent. But being very intelligent men, and
perfectly submissive to Barbican's and. Murphy's
orders, by degrees they learned to avoid accidents. Like coal miners, they left very thick
pillars standing, on the top of which an immense number of the studs supported the disc ;
another immense number of studs rested on
other pillars a few inches lower ; the first set
being removed, the disc sank to the second set,
which easily supported it, whilst the first set
were being prepared to do the same duty in
their turn. The ardor of the men never relaxed a moment, night or day. Though they
were so far south, the mean average of the
thermometer stood no higher than 56° Fahrenheit, a temperature very favorable for work.
During the night, the white sheets of electric
light that blazed all over the hill, the ringing
of the picks against the flinty rock, the puffing
and whirring of the engines, the volumes of
smoke continually rising from the summit, turned
Stony Hill into a diminutive Vesuvius, and
would have frightened the Indians more than
all the De Leons, Narvaezes, Jacksons, or Gaineses,
that ever invaded Florida.

The work in the mean time progressed with

great regularity. Immense derrick cranes, worked by steam, did all the hard labor. Some of them supplied the masons with the smaller stones, some laid the great blocks, whilst others removed from the mouth of the well all the *débris* as fast as it was sent up by the miners. Unexpected obstacles gave very little trouble; all difficulties had been foreseen, and were therefore readily met and conquered.

At the end of the first month, the averaged amount of work was accomplished, the pit having reached a depth of a little more than 112 feet. By the middle of January this depth was doubled, and it was tripled on the 19th of February.

But about this time the miners began to have trouble with some subterranean springs of water which had managed to trickle through from the surface. They were obliged to employ pumps of great power and machines worked by compressed air, in order to get at the orifices and stop them up with concrete, as the seams of a ship are caulked with oakum when she springs a leak. At last, those vexatious currents were mastered, but not before they had done serious damage. They had washed away some of the sandy veins of the rocks, so that the disc sunk unevenly, and in fact partially caved in. Just imagine the tremendous force and weight of this pile of solid masonry 300 feet in height. Three weeks fully were consumed in staying and propping the sides of the opening and in underpinning the disc in order to restore it to its former state of solidity. By that time, thanks to Barbican's fertility of invention, fully seconded by an extraordinary skill in managing his powerful machinery, the enormous pile, for a while compromised, recovered its perfect perpendicularity, and the work could go on as regularly as before.

Henceforward, no new incident arrested the progress of the work—in fact, it marched on now at such an accelerated pace as to be finished on the 10th of June, considerably more than a month before the term appointed by Barbican, who always left sufficient margin in his calculations for delays that *might* turn up though they could not possibly be seen at the time. At six o'clock on the evening of that day, the pit, completely faced with its revetment of masonry, had reached the depth of nine hundred feet. At the bottom, the pile rested on solid block stone work thirty feet in thickness ; at the top, its surface was exactly flush with the summit of the hill. Barbican and the other members of the Gun Club warmly congratulated Murphy on the unexampled rapidity with which he had so successfully accomplished his cyclopean task.

During the whole time, Barbican had never left Stony Hill for a moment—not that he imagined that the work could not advance without him—but because he wished to witness every portion of its progress with his own eyes. He particularly made it his especial care to see after the health and comfort of the numerous workmen, who had cut themselves away, as it were, from the world at his instigation, and for whose safety he therefore considered himself in a great measure responsible. His sanitary precautions were simply perfect. His quick eye in an instant perceived a drooping man, who was immediately sent to the hospital, where he soon recovered, because the treatment was kind and intelligent, and because the disorder had been arrested before it had made much headway.

Barbican's countrymen in general, unfortunately, have not the reputation of being over attentive to such details. In their regard for the rights of humanity, they sometimes forget the rights of man. In the roaring onward march of the triumphant majority, who, they ask, can find time to pick up the individual unfortunate enough to faint on the way?

But Barbican did not believe in these unholy principles, and he showed it in all his actions. At war, he had tried to put an end to war by destroying the greatest number of his enemies in the shortest possible time. Even then, his experimental researches in gunnery had been continually inspired by the idea of rendering guns at last so terrific in their discharges that even the most bellicose of nations would shudder at the idea of engaging in a war. His scientific enthusiasm, combined with his extraordinary practical skill, had often led him into visionary undertakings, but his profound science had taught him that in this world there is really nothing more valuable than human life. Therefore, thanks to his care, his intelligence, his promptness in difficult cases, his extraordinary sagacity, and particularly to his true humanity by which he secured a wonderful influence over his men, the average of accidents attendant on the sinking of the shaft, fell short of even the average of France, where only one accident occurs for every 200,000 francs spent in hazardous operations.

CHAPTER XV.

THE CASTING.

Sinking the pit had not been the only work done at Stony Hill during these eight months ; the preparations preliminary to the casting had been carried on simultaneously with extreme rapidity. A stranger arriving at the place, would have been very much surprised at the scene presented to his view.

At a distance of six hundred yards from the pit, and forming a regular circle around it, twelve hundred fire brick furnaces or *cupolas* had been erected; each six feet wide, and separated from each other by an interval of three feet. The circumference of the circle was therefore more than two miles in length. All the furnaces were constructed on the same plan ; and the immense four cornered chimneys, all precisely the same height, and all precisely the same distance apart, produced an effect which, according to Marston, who admired exceedingly the whole arrangement, " if not strangely beautiful was at least beautifully strange."

The reader may perhaps remember that the committee had decided, at the third session, to employ cast iron for the Columbiad. In fact this metal, when of the kind called the *grey pig*, is remarkable for its tenacity, ductility and softness ; it is easily cast and readily bored ; and when fused in a coal furnace, it is a very superior material for cannons, steam cylinders, hydraulic presses, and for all kinds of machinery where great powers of resistance are indispensable.

But metal melted only once, is seldom homogeneous ; it requires a second fusion to purify and refine it, by ridding it entirely of slag and its other earthly impurities. Accordingly, the ore roasted in the great iron regions of central and southeastern Pennsylvania, before being sent to Tampa, had been carefully smelted in the blast furnaces of the Cold Spring Iron Works, where combining with charcoal and silicium, raised to a very high temperature, it had formed the variety called cast iron No. 1, or *grey pig*.

To transport 136 million pounds of cast iron to Tampa was no slight undertaking, but the Cold Spring Company were equal to the task. On the third of April, a fleet of no less than 68 full rigged ships, each at least 1000 tons burden, laden with the metal, started from New

14

York, passed Sandy Hook, turned south, doubled stormy Hatteras safely, entered Florida Strait, passed within sight of Key West city, where they were hailed with the cheers of at least 5000 throats, and then skirting the west coast of Florida, soon came in sight of the entrance to Tampa Bay. On the tenth of May they began unloading at the Stony Hill Railroad wharf, and by the middle of the following month the enormous mass of metal had safely reached its destination.

It is easy to understand that the 1200 furnaces were none too many to melt simultaneously these 68,000 tons of metal. Each of them could hold about 114,000 pounds of melted iron ; they had been constructed on the very same plan as the cupolas which Rodman had employed when casting his columbiads. That is to say, they were trapezoidal in shape, with the roof coming down very low ; the fire and the chimneys being at different ends, the heat was equally distributed throughout the whole extent. Built of the best Philadelphia fire bricks, these furnaces consisted principally of a grate to burn the coal and a "hearth" on which the iron to be melted was deposited in bars. The hearth, not horizontal but sloping at an angle of 25 degrees, allowed the fused metal to flow into troughs conveniently placed for its reception ; from these it was conveyed by twelve hundred converging trenches directly towards the central pit.

The morning after all the work attending the sinking of the well and its solid stone lining had been completed, Barbican proceeded to the formation of what was to be the " core" of the Columbiad. His idea was to erect in the middle of the pit, and in a direct line with its axis, a solid cylinder nine hundred feet high, and nine feet wide, the dimensions of the gun's interior. This cylinder consisted of a stiff yellow clay mixed with sand and held firmly together by hay and straw. The interval between it and the masonry was to be filled by the melted metal, which would thus form the walls or sides of the Columbiad, six feet in thickness. To be kept perfectly vertical, it had to be strengthened by iron braces, and propped by cross pieces firmly imbedded in the masonry. After the casting, these cross pieces, forming as they did a portion of the solid metal, would, of course, do no harm to the gun.

On the eighth of July the core was pronounced " all right," and the casting was to take place on the tenth.

" What a grand and impressive sight this casting must afford to all present !" said Secretary
Marston to President Barbican, on the morning
of the ninth.   " The Tampa people are delighted that it did not take place on the fourth
of July, last week, as they will now have two
holidays instead of one."

" What are you talking about, Marston ?" replied Barbican.   " We shall have no holiday
here !"

" How ?   Are not the gates to be thrown
open to every one that wants to see the magnificent sight ?" asked the Secretary.

" I should never think of such a thing, Marston," replied the President.   " Casting our
Columbiad will be a very delicate, not to say
a very dangerous, operation, and I should prefer
to have it done in private.   When the projectile is shot off, holiday as much as you chose,
but till then, no."

Barbican was perfectly right.   The operation
might easily present unforeseen dangers and difficulties towards the successful grappling with
which a great crowd of strangers should certainly prove an obstacle.   He himself also should
have perfect liberty to move about from point
to point.   Nobody, therefore, was admitted

within the enclosure except a delegation of the Gun Club, which had come over the railroad early on the morning of the tenth, from Tampa, by the 4.30 train.

It consisted of Elphinstone, Morgan, our old friends Billsby the brave, Tom Hunter and Colonel Bloomsbury, and of several others who had played a very active and successful part in the financial operations of the great undertaking. Marston was their guide, and as it was not yet six o'clock, he made the most of the occasion. He allowed them to pass no detail unnoticed or misunderstood. He took them everywhere ; to the store houses, the workshops, the machines ; he had them let down by " man-engines" to the bottom of the pit ; he even compelled them to make the " grand tour" of the 1200 furnaces, assuring them that they could do it in half an hour at a brisk pace. Before they were half through, some of them felt like giving up the ghost, but most of them persevered manfully. They were protected from the burning rays of a July sun by the dense volumes of black smoke issuing from the immense circle of 1200 chimneys, and overspreading the inclosed area like a huge awning.

At noon precisely, the casting was to take

place. The previous evening, each furnace had been supplied with 114,000 pounds of pig iron in bars, which were piled in layers alternately crossing each other, so as to be more readily reached by the heat. Since early in the morning, the 1200 chimneys had been vomiting forth thick smoke in torrents, and the earth sensibly quivered from the roaring of the flames. As many pounds of metal as were to be melted, so many pounds of coal were to be burned. Judge, therefore, if the smoke must have been dense, which was produced by 68,000 tons of coal, all burning together and at a comparatively short distance apart.

Towards 11 o'clock, the roaring of the flames resembled the rumbling of an earthquake near at hand. But it was not able to drown the shrill whir of the powerful fans forcing the hot air with its oxygen in continuous streams on to the masses of incandescent metal. The heat became intolerable, but the success of the casting depended altogether on the rapidity of the operation. The signal was to be given by a cannon, and, at the appointed instant, every furnace was to open and give discharge to its fiery contents immediately and completely.

Every arrangement being now perfected, over-

seers and workmen awaited the appointed
moment with an impatience mingled with emotion. Nobody had been allowed to remain in
the central enclosure, and every foreman stood
at his post, beside his trough and at the head
of his trench. Barbican and his colleagues,
outside on a little eminence, stood behind the
cannon that was to be discharged at the engineer's signal.

A few minutes before 12, the first drops of
the metal began to trickle down the inclined
hearths ; by degrees the troughs began to fill ;
when they were quite full, the white hot, hissing liquid was allowed to stand a few instants,
so as to permit any impurities still remaining
in it to come to the surface as scum.

A great bell struck noon ; at the last stroke
the report of the cannon roared out the signal.
Instantly the 1200 trough doors flew open, and
1200 blazing torrents, billowing, hissing, and
sparkling like serpents of living fire, shot down
the trenches towards the central pit. There,
forming a mighty cataract, they plunged, with
deafening uproar, into an abyss nine hundred
feet deep. It was an exciting and magnificent
spectacle. The earth shook with the concussion,
as these pillars of molten iron, dashing through

whirlwinds of smoke and dust, broke against the core and fell in great fragments around its base, rapidly volatilising its moisture as they rose, and sending it out in floods of steam, shrieking, glowing, reeking through the vents that had been left in the masonry. Immense clouds, formed of smoke, steam, dust and gases, streamed up vertically from the pit, whirling their spiral volumes as they rapidly ascended, and forming themselves into a shape somewhat resembling that of an enormous tree half a mile in height. A traveller, 20 or 30 miles away, seeing this gigantic pillar, and reminded of Vesuvius, would probably suppose that a new Jorullo had sprung up in Florida. Yet it was neither an eruption, nor an earthquake, nor a waterspout, nor a whirlwind, nor any of those terrible commotions that nature, ordinarily so quiet, is sometimes capable of producing. No ! It was man alone that had sent up those blood-red clouds worthy of a burning forest, that tower of blazing fire seldom seen on the summit of Etna ; it was he that had unchained those hollow rumblings terrific as those presaging the earthquake shock, and that ear-splitting, unearthly roar loud as a shrieking tempest ; it was his feeble hand that had pre-

cipitated into a yawning chasm, which he himself had previously dug out, a whole Niagara of
tearing, raging, scintillating, blazing, liquid
metal !

CHAPTER XVI.

THE BIG GUN.

Had the casting succeeded ? This question for the present could be answered only by conjectures, though there was every reason to hope for the best, as the entire mass of melted metal had been completely absorbed in the mould. There was no certainty however on the subject, and a good many days should still elapse before a decided answer either way could be obtained.

If Rodman's gun of 160,000 pounds took no less than fifteen days to cool, how long might the monstrous Columbiad, wreathed in whirlwinds of vapor and defended by her intense heat, succeed in keeping herself hidden from the gaze of her ardent admirers ? That was a question of difficult calculation.

It was a severe test to the Gun Club men's patience. But there was absolutely no help for it. On July 26th, 15 days after the casting, the clouds of black smoke still rose apparently as dense as ever, and the soil within a circle

(218)

of two hundred feet from the pit was as hot as cooling lava. Marston, the rashest of men, as well as the most curious, lost several pairs of shoes and boots by approaching too near. Indeed, his devotion to science almost cost him his life one day, a sudden change in the wind enveloping him in a cloud of sulphurous smoke that nearly smothered him.

The days slipped slowly away one by one. The time could be counted even by weeks, still the monstrous cylinder gave no sign, whatever, of cooling, and was as difficult as ever of approach. The Gun Club men, completely powerless to mend matters, fidgeted and fumed, chafed and raved, in a state of impatience altogether impossible to describe. Marston almost exploded under the pressure.

" Here we are at the tenth of August !" he exclaimed one day to, a crowd of grumbling and disgusted Club men. " Less than four months from the first of December ! And what a lot of work is yet to be done ! Clear out the core, adjust the calibre, lodge the powder, introduce the projectile ! We shall never be ready ! You can't even go near the darned thing ! I burned another pair of boots off this morning !"

Nobody attempted to calm the impetuous Secretary. In the present state of general irritation he was regarded as a public benefactor, on the principle of the safety valve. Barbican alone never said a word ; yet even his silence betrayed a secret impatience. To find himself so persistently encountered by an obstacle that time alone could overcome, and not a particle of that precious time to be spared—this was indeed hard to be borne by a man whose resources were limited only by the impossible.

In another day or two, however, careful observations noted a decided change in the temperature of the soil. Towards the middle of the month the ascending vapors had visibly diminished both in rapidity of motion and in density of column. A few days more, and they exhaled only a little whitish moisture, the last breath of the dying monster shut up in his stone coffin. By degrees the succussions of the soil became less sensible, and the circle of heat contracted its radius. The impatient spectators, standing around in a circle, approached each other little by little. One day they gained as much as twelve feet, the next day twenty-four, and on the 22d of August, Barbican, his colleagues, and the engineer Murphy, were able

to keep their place on the warm sheet of cast
iron that had overflowed the summit of Stony
Hill. Marston had hardly a sole left to his
boots, but he easily consoled himself for his
loss by saying that in such a spot you could
not get cold in the feet if you tried. Barbican said nothing, but he heaved a deep sigh
of profound satisfaction.

That very day the works were at once resumed. The first thing to do being to clear
out the core, pick, shovel, spade, and boring
tools were put into instant and incessant application. The clay and sand, under the action
of the heat, had acquired an extreme hardness,
but, by means of their powerful machines, the
workmen soon pierced it, cracked it, and broke
it into pieces small enough to be hoisted up
in enormous iron buckets, and rapidly carried
off on trucks running night and day on a tram-
way that started from the very mouth of the
pit. The work now progressed with wonderful
rapidity, deriving new energy from its previous
forced inaction, like a mighty river temporarily
restrained by some obstacle—not to mention
the inspiring effect of Barbican's incessant and
ubiquitous activity, which the promise of doubling
the men's wages had now rendered absolutely

irresistible. No wonder then if by September 3d, every trace of the core had disappeared from the interior of the Columbiad.

Then commenced the work of smoothing its internal sides and giving them the proper calibre. The machines proper for the purpose, being made beforehand, were installed without delay; circular cutting tools of immense power attacked the roughnesses and inequalities of the cast, and in a few weeks the interior surface, made perfectly smooth and cylindrical, shone with the brightness of a silver reflector.

At last, on the 22d of September, less than a year since Barbican's famous communication, the enormous engine, accurately calibred, and perfectly vertical, as proved by the rigidest tests, was pronounced ready to do its work. Now if the Moon would only prove as punctual —but about *her* ability to be up to time, nobody, of course, entertained the least doubt.

Marston's joy at the result was actually beyond expression. That day, just as his friends, having come up from one of their last visits to the bottom of the cannon, were standing around its edge, he insisted on " boring them," as he said, " with a little extempore speech in honor of the occasion." There was surely no great harm in this, but as he had the ugly and not uncommon trick of springing backwards and forwards whilst under the impulse of his oratorical furor, a most deplorable accident was very near being the result. As long as he kept still, all was well ; the edge of the pit was a lovely spot whence to address an audience, the occasion was exciting, and every word told. But the fit soon came on him ; he could not begin his sentences without running backwards, and to finish them he had to run forwards. The audience was spell-bound under the stream of his burning eloquence, and not one saw the danger—not one but Barbican, who was fire proof against poetry, and no more minded the gilded phrases of oratory than so many puffs of a locomotive. Just as his friend, having run back a few yards while delivering the first half of a particularly long and thrilling sentence, was racing forward to finish it, with a momentum towards the edge of the pit that would certainly have sent him over, Barbican grasped him like a vice, and by his immense physical strength, easily saved this modern Curtius from a frightful death in the profound depths of the mighty Columbiad.

The cannon being finished, the news was immediately telegraphed all over the Union, and, of course, Captain McNicholl was the first to hear of it. Having satisfied himself that he had lost his wager, he immediately sent Barbican, in payment, a bill of exchange drawn by Drexel & Co., and on the 1st of October the President of the Gun Club had the gratification of writing on the receipt column of his cash book the sum of two thousand dollars. The Captain's fury was so great that it actually made him sick—at least that was the way his friends accounted for a few days' confinement to his room. However, as there were still three other wagers to be decided, of 3, 4, and 5 thousand dollars respectively, and as he was pretty certain of winning two of them, the affair, looked at financially, was not unpromising. But the financial aspect of the question gave the Captain the least trouble. It was the wonderful success of his rival, in casting a cannon which a plate armor of sixty feet thick would be incapable of resisting, that now galled him to the quick, and rendered him a perfectly miserable man. (We forgot to mention that long before this, the Captain had ordered his first wager to be paid, as soon as he saw that from the state of public feeling the success of the subscription was assured. The Captain was a strictly honorable man ; like all great geniuses, he was, of course, rather cranky and stubborn, but there was not a particle of trickery in his composition.)

On the 23d of September, the gates of the enclosure at Stony Hill were thrown open to the public, and you can hardly imagine what crowds of visitors immediately availed themselves of the opportunity to visit the great curiosity.

In fact visitors from all parts of the Union, and even from Europe, Japan, China, and other civilized quarters of the world, had been flocking into Tampa ever since the beginning of the travelling season. Instead of passing the summer on the Continent, or at Newport, or at Cape May, or at Saratoga, or the Yosemite Valley, or amid the grand scenery of the heart of the Rocky Mountains, the fashionable American world had determined to devote it to a sight of the wonders going on at Stony Hill. The working classes strictly followed suit as far as they could, which was eminently right and proper in a country where " one man is as good as another." The great Pennsylvania Railroad organized " excursion trains" from all the principal cities of the North, which took you to " Tampa and back," with the privilege of remaining over at any place of interest on the route, tickets good for a month—all for 5 dollars, a sum any good man in the United States can earn in two days. As a matter of course, this great influx of strangers had greatly increased the size of Tampa. From less than 800, the population had risen in less than a year to nearly 50,000 souls. The city no longer knew itself. Having surrounded Fort Brooke in a network of streets, it began extending itself along the tongue of land that separates the two divisions of Tampa Bay. Block after block, square after square, of good substantial dwellings, now covered what only a few months before had been a mere sandy waste, or a marsh croaking with bullfrogs. Churches and schools had sprung up like magic, and you may be sure that such indispensable elements of the success of every new American settlement as newspaper offices and drinking " saloons," were to be found in gratifying abundance. In less than a year, the extent of the city was decupled. This progress was wonderful even in America, and beat out Chicago, who only quadruples herself every ten years.

Everybody knows that the American, or Yankee as he is called in Europe, is a natural born

TAMPA AFTER THE UNDERTAKING.

trader. Wherever fortune throws him, on the
ice of the Arctic regions, or under the burning
sun of the torrid zone, his instinctive talent for
business is at once called into play. To the
grand and beautiful in nature he is as impres-
sionable as any one else, but if there is " any
money in it" his nose of unerring keenness is
the first to smell it out. Somebody said with
more truth than poetry that if a Yankee was
shipwrecked on a South Sea island, the very
next morning you would find him selling cotton
suspenders to the natives. It is in fact to this
irrepressible instinct of looking at everything
with the practical eye of utility, that his great
country, the envy of the world, is indebted for
her wide spread activity, the abundance of her
resources, and her unexampled prosperity.

It was just the same at Tampa. Many a man
of means from Baltimore or Boston, visiting
Florida with the sole desire of witnessing the
curious operations of the Gun Club, finding
himself in the midst of those luxuriant savannahs,
so suitable for rice and the sugar cane, of those
flourishing cotton fields and orange groves, of
those avenues of live oaks and olive trees draped
in Spanish moss, of those Florentine gardens
where the fig, the date, the palm, the banana,

the citron, and the pomegranate flourish in the open air, of those woods and streams so stocked with game as to make Florida the sportsman's paradise, of those virgin forests untouched by axe, so suggestive of millions to be made by the saw-mill and lumber trade, but, above all, charmed by the balmy incense-breathing climate not surpassed by that of the lovely Riviera—I say, many a Northern man of means, who had come so far South out of mere motives of curiosity, saw such unexpected advantages presented by a residence there that he never went back, except to return with his family. Many a mechanic too from New York or Philadelphia, where food is dear, fuel scarce and rent high, the winter icy and the summer roasting, finding food to be so plentiful in Tampa as almost to be had for the asking, coal to be absolutely useless, wood in superabundance, no winters, mild summers, plenty of work to be had the whole year round and no working days spoiled by the weather—many a mechanic, I repeat, concluding at once to stay where he was, forfeited his " excursion" ticket privilege of returning, and sent for his wife and children as soon as he had earned money enough to pay their passage. The great fleet laden with pig iron was only the precursor of others, not so numerous, it is true, but more frequent, and every day increasing in importance. Very soon you could see vessels of all shapes, sizes, and descriptions, loading and unloading along wharves miles in length. Great shipping houses lined the water's edge ; behind them stood immense store houses belonging to the agents of the chief Northern firms ; not far off, brokers of every staple article of merchandise displayed their abundant wares ; in short, Tampa, where a few months ago an oyster smack had been an object of the curiosity, and the monthly arrival of the government cutter with dispatches for Fort Brooke had been an event of absorbing interest, was now declared a port of entry, and an appropriation was made in Congress for the erection of a Tampa Custom House and a Tampa Bonded Warehouse, one in the Greek style of architecture, the other in the ornate modern style, with a French roof, each to cost one million of dollars.

The facilities for reaching the now famous city, by water and by land, had increased in a similar ratio. You could not turn your eyes in any direction along the busy wharves without being encountered by immense posters displaying the respective merits of *Murray's Line*, and *Black Star Line*, from New York ; *Clyde Line*, and *Southern Steamship Line*, from Philadelphia ; *Boyce's Line*, from Baltimore ; besides other lines of steamers from New Orleans and Havana. The *New York Journal of Commerce*, the great business man's paper, added Tampa to the list of the other important seaports of which the arrivals and departures were to be chronicled every day.

The *New York Tribune*, generally pretty good authority on matters of fact, was all wrong when it asserted so positively that the *Gulf Railroad* would not be finished for many years to come. Starting from Fernandina, an interesting old town with one of the finest harbors on the east coast, this railroad had been intended to cross the peninsula in a southwesterly direction and to terminate at Cedar Keys on the Gulf of Mexico. But after struggling through the swamps for forty or fifty miles until it reached Baldwin, there it had stuck fast, and so continued for several years. Then it slowly crawled along as far as Waldo, which was the point, as may be recollected, that Barbican had struggled so earnestly but so ineffectually to unite with Tampa.

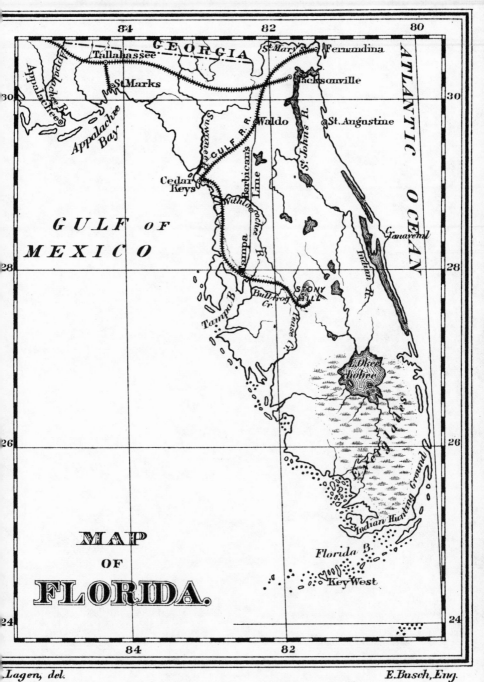

MAP
OF
FLORIDA.

Scene of the Operations.

But the influx of Northern capital consequent on the Stony Hill enterprise, soon changed this state of things. Not only was the railroad completed as far as Cedar Keys, but also the latter town was connected with Tampa by a branch constructed along the low marshy Gulf coast at great trouble and expense. Barbican had made the company a present of the drawings of *his* route, strongly recommending it as being higher and healthier, more picturesque and fertile, besides being shorter and less expensive. But Barbican, though a great artillerist, was unfortunately only a Baltimore man, and no mere Baltimore man could by any possibility teach a Boston man, as the President of the *Gulf Railroad* Company prided himself upon being.

For, outside of Boston, as you must know, everything in the United States is provincial; literature, fashion, society, at best only second rate; all the boys and girls in the Union learn their lessons out of Boston newspapers, Boston magazines, and Boston books; the Revolutionary War began and ended within sight of Bunker Hill; the Boston people single handed had licked the British in 1812; aided a little by some other New Englanders, they had put down the great rebellion of '61; Faneuil

Hall, " the cradle of American Liberty," was
the only place where the " Centennial" should
be celebrated ; her municipal system was un-
equalled ; her fire department was simply perfect ; no act of cruel bigotry had ever disgraced
her lofty minded and enlightened people ; her
men were all corresponding members of learned
societies, and her women read so much that
they all wore eye glasses ; her public schools
produced the profoundest of scholars and the
most virtuous of citizens. Such, at least, was
the Nicene Creed repeated every Sunday by
every good Bostonian. The President of the
Gulf Railroad happened to be an extra good
Bostonian. A Baltimorian to dictate to *him ?*
Never ! Of course he had his way ; the branch
followed the worst possible route, because a
Baltimorian had pointed out the best possible
one. What matter if it cost the company an
additional million of dollars and five thousand
poor Irish laborers their lives ? A grand moral
principle had been successfully vindicated. If
Boston is not to have her way, the world is
not worth living in !

By the completion of the branch railroad to
Cedar Keys, and of another, much smaller, con-
necting Fernandina with Brunswick, passing near

the famous Okeefinokee Swamp, the home of millions of alligators, frogs, lizards and cranes, Tampa was put in direct and constant communication with all the great Northern cities.

As may be readily supposed, this flourishing state of things in Florida was looked on with no friendly eye by the inhabitants of southern Texas. Every gain accruing to the peninsula in consequence of the grand experiment, they considered as so much lost by themselves. Those ships, those railroads, those emigrants, those capitalists, all the developments of prosperity attending in their train, by right belonged to southern Texas, and would have been hers too, only for the absurd preference of the crazy fool Barbican for that miserable one-horse, slink of a place called Tampa. In the meantime, they fell back for consolation on the awful prophecy still confidently uttered by their disappointed commissioners ; and every morning the Texans opened their newspapers with the pious hope of feasting their eyes on something like the following, printed in the largest and most startling type :

ASTOUNDING INTELLIGENCE !

THE GREAT COLUMBIAD BURST ! !

3000 PEOPLE KILLED ! ! !

WE STOP THE PRESS TO ANNOUNCE THAT
BARBICAN AND THE OTHER CLUB MEN HAVE BEEN
BLOWN OFF THE FACE OF THE EARTH !

THEIR BODIES CANNOT BE FOUND ! !

INTENSE EXCITEMENT, ETC., ETC., ETC. ! ! !

N. B.—We shall issue extras every ten minutes, giving our readers the latest and most interesting details regarding this

TRULY TERRIFIC BUT NOT UNEXPECTED
CATASTROPHE ! ! ! !

Tampa troubled herself very little about either
the ill will or the good will of the Texans.
But though her commercial activity and her in-
dustrial prosperity were now in full blast, she
was not so wholly engrossed in them as to forget what had given birth to them both. Quite
the contrary. The slightest detail of the Gun
Club's operations interested her keenly. Not
a delve with a spade, a stroke with a hammer,
or a chop with an axe, escaped her notice.
The coming and going between Tampa and
Stony Hill was incessant night and day; the
trains could not accommodate half the visitors;

even the vehicles were far from meeting the general demand ; and the roads were black with people, all facing in one direction, like pilgrims bound for some holy shrine.

It was easy to foresee that on the day when the grand experiment was to be finally made, the spectators could be counted by millions. So many strangers now began to arrive that for several months the Floridian peninsula must have been the great centre towards which the prow of every vessel in every sea was turned.

Up to this time, it must be acknowledged, the strangers who had expected to see much had in reality seen very little. Many had come early, expecting to witness the magnificent spectacle of the casting. The sight of nothing but smoke was a sad disappointment to their hungry eyes, for Barbican, as we already know, had turned a deaf ear on their remonstrances and would allow nobody's presence at such a dangerous operation. The consequence of course was grumbling, dissatisfaction, irritation ; such epithets as " too darned stuck up," " big dog of the tanyard," " bumptious," were circulated from mouth to mouth, though in under tones ; in fact, there came very near being a serious riot around the fence on the day of the casting. Still, as previously mentioned, Barbican even on that day had shown himself inexorable as fate.

But the labors in the interior of the Columbiad once completed, the face of things was immediately changed ; the gates were thrown open ; every one was allowed full opportunity to gratify his curiosity ; only, Barbican, like the eminently practical business man that he was, had determined to make the public enthusiasm contribute considerably towards the success of the enterprise.

To get a glimpse at all of the immense Columbiad was something to be proud of, but to descend down into its yawning caverns nine hundred feet deep—that *was* a sight worth all the trouble of going there to see. Everybody wanted to be the first to go below. Neat carriages with cushioned seats, and bars all round high enough to prevent all danger, were suspended by great ropes made of many strands of iron wire, and let down and drawn up by great revolving drums working day and night at the mouth of the pit. Even the timidest travellers, not excluding the women and children, could not resist the desire of seeing the mysterious wonders of the colossal cannon. The sensation many allowed to be far and away ahead of that produced by a ride down the famous *Switch Back*. The "excursion" tickets from the Northern cities always included a coupon, giving you the right to a descent in the "Big Gun," as the people commonly called it. No wonder, therefore, if the sight considerably swelled the cash receipts of the Club. The tariff fixed by Barbican of five dollars for a season ticket and one dollar for a single admission was readily paid, and, for the two months that the gun kept open, the public curiosity was so great and incessant that, after paying all the extra hands employed for selling tickets and attending to the comfort and safety of the visitors, a net profit of 500,000 dollars was made by the operation, and, what was still better, not a single life was lost, though the registers showed an average of more than 10,000 visitors a day.

It is almost needless to mention that the first regular guests let down into the Columbiad by the apparatus of the revolving drum and the cars, were the chief members of the Gun Club, an honor to which that illustrious body had every right. The solemn opening of the gun took place on September 25th. A car of honor, of double size, and made especially for the occasion, waving with the flags of all the known countries of the world except England, descended with President Barbican, Secretary Marston, General Morgan, Colonel Bloomsbury, Major Elphinstone, Chief Engineer Murphy, and several other distinguished members of the celebrated Club, about ten altogether, that number being about all there was room for. They took five minutes to go down, at the rate of three feet to a second ; this was rather slow, but Barbican had observed that a quicker descent than this made many people sick. They came up, however, in two minutes, and hardly felt the motion. They found it pretty hot at the bottom of this long metal tube, but they were in too good spirits to mind it. A table, with covers for ten, had been laid on the solid rock that served as a foundation for the Columbiad, and a brilliant electric light made everything as bright as day. Dishes of exquisite cookery and of every variety, seeming to descend from heaven, arranged themselves before each guest, and the best wines of Burgundy and Champagne crowned a splendid dinner, that was enjoyed heartily by the joyous party nine hundred feet below the surface of the earth.

As the wines circulated, the laughter became merrier and the voices louder ; speeches began to be made and toasts to be offered by several gentlemen at the same time. They drank to the health of everybody and everything appropriate to the occasion, beginning of course with the President of the United States, and ending with the " Ladies." They drank to the health of the Gun Club, to which Barbican replied in a neat speech two minutes long, and Marston by a flowery oration which he was finally compelled to stop only on the assurance that his own turn would come by and by. They drank the health of the terrestrial globe, our old dear mother Earth. But the favorite toast of the evening was the Moon ! Every member gave her a name of his own : *Our Satellite ! Queen of the Night ! Isis ! Astarte ! Phœbe ! Artemis ! Diana ! Luna ! Noctiluca !* and said something *apropos* to the name, and whatever he said was sure to be soon drowned in a tumult of applause. The cheers, the laughter, the cries, the acclamations, the rappings on the table and the other noises, though nothing extraordinary down there, had become by the time they arrived at the mouth of the Columbiad, so reverberated, reflected and re-echoed by this gigantic speaking trumpet that they sounded like peals of terrific thunder in the ears of the vast multitudes assembled on the summit of Stony Hill. The unearthly uproar, however, no way frightened them, for they continued till late in the night, answering cheer with cheer, acclamation with acclamation, yell with yell, whilst the depths of the mighty forests around them rang back responsive echoes, like the screams of a gigantic organ.

This reminds us of Marston, who, his health by this time having been drunk with all the honors, made a speech in which he actually surpassed himself. " It was the proudest moment of his life ; he was in a condition that emperors might envy ; and he would not change places that moment with the mighty emperor of all the Russias. No ! Not even though, in the very next instant, the mighty Columbiad, loaded, primed and discharged, were to sweep him, J. T. Marston, dismemembered, comminuted, disintegrated into a million fragments, through the vast, the illimitable regions of starry space !"

CHAPTER XVII.

BY THE ATLANTIC CABLE.

The most exciting and interesting portion of the great preparatory labors undertaken by the Club were now, so to speak, almost terminated, and the grand and final catastrophe was little more than two months off. "How near and yet how far!" In one sense, to the busy men whose hearts and souls were wrapped up in the experiment, the days would fly past with the rapidity of the "swift winged arrows of light;" in another sense, to the public at large, thus suddenly deprived of its daily allowance of absorbing excitement, without which existence was scarcely endurable, how miserably slow should those crawling sixty-four days be in dragging their dull length along! Sixty-four cycles in Cathay, or even on the eastern shore of Maryland, could hardly be more humdrum. Everybody determined that when making up his age for the approaching census of 1870, he would drop the next two months altogether, as they would not be worth counting in.

Everybody was wrong. In less than one

week after the events recorded in our last chapter, an incident the most unexpected, the most extraordinary, the most incredible, the most improbable, fell like a clap of thunder on the public ear, and once more aroused the astounded people to the highest pitch of excitement and surprise, Barbican himself not excepted.

On the 30th of September, at forty-seven minutes past three o'clock in the afternoon, a messenger handed Barbican an envelope containing a telegram transmitted by the Atlantic cable from Valentia, Ireland, to Trinity Bay, Newfoundland, and thence overland to Tampa, Florida. Barbican broke the envelope, read the dispatch, and, in spite of his great self-control his lips quivered, his cheeks lost their color, and his brow winced a little at the sight of its contents.

They were only about thirty words in all. Here they are, copied literally from the original, still to be seen among the archives of the Gun Club :

" PARIS, FRANCE, *September* 30, 4 P. M.

" BARBICAN.

" Tampa, Florida, United States.

" For shell spherical, substitute projectile cylindroconical, and I shall take a place inside. Shall arrive per *Atl.nta.*" " MICHEL ARDAN."

CHAPTER XVIII.

WHO WAS HE?

If this startling communication, instead of flying over the wires, had come simply by post in an ordinary letter; if the telegraph operators, French, Irish, Newfoundland, and American, had not already known and fully understood its meaning, Barbican would not have hesitated a single instant. He would have simply given it the deaf ear, and quietly proceeded with his work. Was not it most likely a silly hoax, particularly as it came from a Frenchman? Could any man living ever dream of attempting such a fearful trip? If he was in earnest, a bullet *inside* him was what he wanted, not one *outside;* at all events, a place in a cylindro-conical projectile would not suit him half as well as one in the strongest cell of a lunatic asylum.

But the dispatch, from its nature, could not be kept secret, and by this time, no doubt, it was flying about through every State of the Union. Silence on the subject being evidently absurd, Barbican called all his colleagues together and, without uttering a word for or against the credibility of the dispatch, read it aloud several times for his amazed, but not easily gulled, auditors.

"Impossible!" "Stuff and nonsense!" "Catch a weasel asleep?" "Good joke!" "Not so verdant!" "Wakes up the wrong passenger!" "Bogus!" "Can't come it!" "Played out!" —in short, the whole vocabulary of phrases serving to express doubt, incredulity, suspicion, and contempt, formed the chorus that, with appropriate gesticulation, greeted the reading of this most singular telegram. They laughed at it, they pooh-poohed it, even the least suspicious shook their heads over it. Marston, however, differed decidedly with his colleagues. His first exclamation on hearing the dispatch was:

"What a grand idea!"

"Very grand," replied the Major, "but such ideas as that should not be left lying about loose."

"Why not?" asked Marston, ready for a discussion, but the Major did not feel like arguing such a question. Barbican said nothing, but he thought to himself that if the dispatch really was a hoax, its sender must not only be very fond of a laugh but also very well able to pay for it.

Thirty words at five dollars each, the Atlantic cable tariff, made a very pretty sum in gold.

In a few minutes, the name of Michael Ardan was as well known as Barbican's all over Tampa, where his proposition encountered pretty keen criticism. Everybody, stranger as well as native, considered it to be his duty to crack his little joke on the Quixotic proposition, and as Ardan himself—a myth, a phantom, the baseless fabric of a dream—was not there to hear their views on the matter, they spoke pretty freely to the best substitute they could find, namely, J. T. Marston, who was crazy enough to believe in his existence. The warmth of their expressions was certainly quite reasonable. Barbican's proposition to send a ball to the Moon—what was it ? A perfectly natural, feasible, legitimate enterprise, a simple question of ballistics ! But that a being endowed with reason should volunteer to take a passage in this projectile, to tempt Providence by such an absurd piece of desperate recklessness—it was preposterous, monstrous, silly, outrageous—in fact, it was unpleasant to talk about, and the fellow that started such an idea, should be treated at once to a straight jacket ! Marston was within an inch of being tarred and feathered.

This way of viewing the question lasted nearly four hours—which is rather strange in a country where the word impossible has been omitted in the school dictionaries, and where the greater the difficulties an enterprise has to encounter the greater the favor by which it is regarded.

Towards evening Ardan's idea began somehow to lose a little of its absurdity. To their surprise people began to find themselves thinking over the proposition without flying into a passion about it. They could not get it out of their heads. Its very novelty had a certain fascination that was irresistible. Absurd! What was absurd? Had not Doctor Lardner proved the utter absurdity of ever attempting to cross the Atlantic in a steamer? Had the world kept so still since that time that the new Doctor Lardners were more likely to be infallible than the old? Besides, if a man is crazy enough to venture his life in such a mad undertaking, the world can easily bear his loss. Why spoil our tempers about him?

Was he or was he not a myth? The name, it is true, was as well known in America as in Europe. Its owner had already figured in some enterprises of extraordinary daring. Disguised as a dervish, he had travelled further and seen more than Vambery in Central Asia, where to be discovered was certain death. He had slain more lions in Africa than Gerard and Cummings put together. Balancing himself without a pole, he had carried two dogs in his arms on a tight rope stretched across the Grand Canal, Venice—a feat in which Blondin, after several unsuccessful attempts, acknowledged his utter inability to imitate him. But the name in itself proved nothing—it was the very one that, in case of a hoax, was most likely to be employed. Still, this expensive telegram, the name of the vessel in which he was said to have taken passage, the very short period beyond which it was impossible that the hoax could be prolonged—all these considerations began to strike the people as having something genuine about them. *Was* it a hoax after all? Doubt, uncertainty, suspense set in, and every one knows how painful it is to be in a state of suspense during a great excitement. Isolated individuals could not keep apart; they formed groups; the groups under the pressure of curiosity, like atoms acted upon by molecular attraction, condensed into crowds, and finally the throng became so compact that, unable to bear their condition any longer, they made a " bee

line" for the hotel where Barbican had his
rooms.

Ever since the arrival of the dispatch, the
President of the Gun Club had maintained a
profound silence on the subject ; he listened to
Marston's decided assertions, without opening
his lips either in censure or encouragement.
He was maintaining a masterly inactivity, quietly
awaiting the march of events, fully determined
not to compromise himself by any overt act,
when all at once, to his utter disgust, he looked
out and saw the whole population of Tampa
assembled in dense masses under his windows.
His old manœuvres were now of no avail. The
yells, outcries, and vociferations of the excited
multitude soon brought him out on the balcony
before them. Greatness has its inconveniences
as well as its enjoyments.

His appearance produced immediate and profound silence, which, after a few seconds, was
broken by a voice in the crowd saying :

" Mr. Barbican, we want to know if the man,
Michael Ardan, the writer of the dispatch, is
on his way here or not ?"

" Gentlemen," replied Barbican, " that is a
question that I am no more able to answer than
you are yourselves."

"Too thin! Too thin!" roared several impatient voices.

"We must have an answer!" roared others.

"Time will give you an answer," replied Barbican coldly.

"Live horse till you get grass!" cried some wit in the crowd, but all were too excited to laugh.

"Answer! A plain answer!" resounded from all quarters.

"Gentlemen," replied Barbican in a clear voice, emphasizing his words by earnest gesticulation, "really I have no answer to give you."

"Mr. Barbican, we believe you," cried the man in the crowd who had first spoken, "but there is another question that you *can* answer. Have you made the change in the plan of the shell that is suggested by the dispatch?"

"Not yet, gentlemen; but now that you remind me of the dispatch, I think I shall be able to give answers satisfactory to your questions in the course of a few hours. I am going directly to the telegraph office."

"Let us all go to the telegraph office!" cried the crowd, following Barbican to the *North American Buildings*, corner of *Marion* and *Magnolia* streets.

A few minutes afterwards a dispatch was sent to the office of the *Inman Line* of steamers, Liverpool, asking an immediate reply to the following questions :

" When was the *Atlanta* to set sail ? For what port was she bound ? Had she on board a Frenchman named Michael Ardan ?"

In about two hours an answer came back, too formal and precise in its assertions to leave any further doubt possible.

" The steamer *Atlanta*, of Liverpool, was to leave port on the 2d of October, bound for Tampa direct, having on board a Frenchman named, as recorded on the registry book. Michael Ardan."

This confirmation of the first dispatch made Barbican's eyes glitter with a sudden flash ; his fingers clenched themselves violently, and a few quick-eared bystanders heard him muttering hoarsely :

" It is true then ! He's in earnest ! And he'll be here in little more than two weeks ! He must be crazy ! No matter ! Crazy or not, I shall never consent ———— " But in spite of his resolution, he wrote that very night to Meneely & Co., Albany, telling them to suspend operations on the projectile till further orders.

But as for undertaking to describe the state
of feeling produced throughout all America by
the startling dispatch ; how it completely eclipsed
even Barbican's famous communication ; how
the papers went into ecstacies about the idea
and its originator, the trans-Atlantic hero whose
arrival on the American Continent they were
so soon to have the delight of recording ; how
everybody counted the hours, the minutes, even
the seconds, in their feverish agitation ; how the
minds of all, rich and poor, old and young,
without exception, succumbed completely to the
dominant idea ; how the laboring people of
Tampa could not work, the dealers could not
sell, the ships ready to sail remained moored in
port, waiting the arrival of the *Atlanta ;* how
the trains arrived choking with passengers, and
went away empty ; how Tampa Bay was alive
with steamboats, sailing ships, yachts, schooners
sloops, and coasters of all dimensions ; how
the endless crowds of visitors kept flocking into
Tampa from all quarters in such numbers as to
be obliged to camp out in tents like a vast
army—I say, to describe these things adequately,
or even to give the reader more than a faint
idea of what an excited state of feeling prevailed everywhere, is a task so much above the

powers of the ordinary writer that even Dickens'
magic pen would recoil before it in despair.

On the 20th of October, early in the morning,
the watchman at Cary's Fort Light House, in
southeast Florida, signalled a thick smoke in
the offing. Two hours later he telegraphed to
Tampa that a large steamer named the *Atlanta*
was passing before him. Though her arrival before the next day was impossible, nobody slept
in Tampa that night. At four o'clock next
morning she was seen entering the Hillsboro Nar-
rows with full steam on, and a little after five,
she cast anchor at pier No. 6 South Wharves.

Long before this, however, while she was
treading the mazes of the channel at less than
quarter speed, the *Atlanta* had been surrounded
by innumerable boats, and boarded by excited
crowds, who could *not* be kept off. Barbican
was the first man that cleared the nettings and
jumped on deck.

" Michael Ardan !'' he shouted, in accents full
of an emotion which he in vain tried to suppress.

" Present !'' was answered by a somewhat singular looking individual standing on the poop-
deck.

Barbican said no more, but with arms

folded, he leaned against the bulwarks and took a long, steady, and searching survey of the wonderful passenger by the *Atlanta.*

He was a man of some forty-two years, tall but stooped a little already, like Atlas when carrying the world on his shoulders. His head, large and shaggy as a lion's, showed a flowing mass of reddish hair that reminded you of a mane. A face short, round, and wide at the temples, a moustache bristling like a cat's, little tufts of yellow hair almost covering his cheeks, eyes large but a little unsteady in their glance and evidently nearsighted, completed a physiognomy essentially feline. But the nose was bold, the mouth particularly sweet and human, and the forehead high, intelligent, and furrowed like a field never allowed to lie fallow. Finally, a body stout, shapely and well set on long legs, arms light and easy of movement but powerful as sledge-hammers, with a general air of decision and self-reliance, gave Barbican the idea that this man was a right good fellow, well built in body and mind, or, as he expressed it himself in a foundryman's phraseology, that he was " forged not cast."

A phrenologist would have no difficulty in detecting his bump of " combativeness," that is, courage in danger and readiness to face obstacles ; a strong development of " benevolence and wonder," that is, a love of the marvellous carried to a total forgetfulness of self ; but, on the other hand, for the bump of " acquisitiveness," or a desire to get and keep, Gall himself might search long, but search in vain.

His clothes were well cut, but remarkably ample and easy fitting, the ends of his cravat fluttered in the breeze, a low turn down collar revealed the proportions of his robust neck, and his ungloved, restless hands never gave themselves the time to button his wristbands. Looking at him, you readily felt, somehow, that no danger was so appalling, no winter so piercing as ever to give such a man as that a chill, either in heart or limb, body or soul.

Never keeping still a moment on deck, he hurried continually here and there, " dragging his anchor," as the sailors said, gesticulating, talking to everybody, and gnawing his nails with feverish inquietude. He was, in short, one of those originals spoken of by somebody as being occasionally framed in one of her whimsical moods by Dame Nature, who then immediately breaks the mould. He was well worth analyzing if we had only the time to do it. A perpetual prey to hyperbole, he could never get over his love of superlatives ; the retina of his eyes giving gigantic proportions to whatever he looked at, he passionately loved the extravagant, and naturally magnified everything—except difficulties.

Of a nature luxuriating in vitality, he was an artist by instinct, and a humorist in spite of himself ; only he never said epigrammatic things, which always betray an effort, but, feeling intensely whatever he expressed, his manner rather than his words invested even his most fleeting thoughts with a light, a color, a variety, a spontaneity that rendered them far more charming, and certainly far less oppressive, than the vividest scintillations of the professional wit.

In discussion, regardless of logic, deaf to syllogism, he fought his battles his own way ; little caring for cunning of fence or superiority of vantage ground, the more desperate the case the more he delighted to defend it, and he plied his blows so rapidly, striking his opponent right and left, assailing him tooth and nail, never giving him an instant's breathing time, that not unfrequently with all the odds against him, he ended by flooring his man, no one could tell how.

One of his favorite manias was to proclaim himself "a sublime ignoramus," as Voltaire called Shakspeare, and he actually prided himself on his profound contempt for scientific men. "What are they good for?" he would often ask. "Like billiard markers, they use their figures just to score the points, while you and I play the game." Adventurous, but no adventurer; a Bohemian, but not of the ordinary type; a Don Quixote, but not a Tom Sayres; a Phæton, but no timid youth driving his father's horses at half speed; an Icarus, but not trusting to one pair of wings; he rushed recklessly, "bald-headed" as the Americans say, into every new enterprise of the hour, burned his ships behind him more defiantly than Cortez, and though thousands of times exposed to the most imminent dangers, he ended invariably by falling on his feet, like a cat flung out of a fifth-story window.

If Barbican's motto,—*Nil desperandum !* Never give up the ship !—showed the undying game of the Saxon, Ardan's favorite expression—*Quand même !* What of it !—proved the dauntless and irrepressible pluck of the Celt.

Such qualities carried to excess seldom benefit any man. "Who risks nothing, nothing has,"

is a proverb of very doubtful utility. Ardan
risked every thing and still had nothing !
Giving him money, was throwing it into a bot-
tomless pit. Not that it had all gone in mad
adventures ; on the contrary, his heart being
just as good as his head was flighty, he was
quite as ready any day to relieve a family in
distress as to start on an expedition to the
North Pole ; chivalrous, disinterested, incapable
of selfish calculations, he would tear up the
death warrant of his bitterest enemy, and cheer-
fully forfeit his own liberty to set a poor slave
free.

Well known in France—what country of
Europe indeed had not witnessed his escapades ?—
his name figuring every day in the public papers,
every action of his known, every word of his
quoted, he had been fair game for every wit,
and he had pointed the moral of every magazine writer. For you may be sure, he had
made for himself a noble army of enemies by the
way he had of jostling, pushing, treading on
corns, and even upsetting people as he fearlessly
elbowed his way through the crowded sidewalks
of social life.

Still, though looked on somewhat as a spoiled
child, he was generally liked ; yes, take him all

17

in all, he was rather admired than censured by the world at large. When people got wind of some new foolhardy enterprise of his, they would even put on airs of concern, and remonstrate against the folly of running himself into inevitable danger. But he easily got rid of such friends by a quiet smile and one or two favorite expressions that he was very fond of quoting. "Danger! Threaten a duck with water!" "Danger! Not a particle, if you only keep your top eye open; it is only its own trees that burn a forest!"

Such was the restless, daring, emotional, impulsive, passionate, incomprehensible being that Barbican had been now gazing at for nearly a quarter of an hour with the most absorbing interest. No wonder if he had found him an attractive subject, for, independent of Ardan's object in coming to America, surely nature had never formed two creatures presenting a stronger contrast to each other, mentally and physically, than the European and the American that were now standing so close to each other on the deck of the *Atlanta*.

Barbican's perspicacity was gradually beginning to convince him that a man as brave, enterprising, and full of resources as himself, though in a different way, stood before him, when he found his study of character suddenly cut short by the hurrahs and the cheers of the crowd, become by this time perfectly frantic in its enthusiasm. Their shouts were now so loud, their demonstrations of friendship so bois- terous, their hand shaking in particular of such a violent nature, that Ardan not relishing the idea of having his fingers crushed into a jelly, found himself compelled to make a precipitate retreat below into his state-room.

After a little while, Barbican followed him, knocked quietly at the door, and presented his card without saying a word.

" Hello ! Barbican, is it you ?" cried Ardan, as heartily and familiarly as if he were talking to an old friend of twenty years' standing.

" Yes," replied the President of the Gun Club, quietly.

" Glad to see you, old boy ! How are you ? Quite well ? Glad to hear it, Barbican. De- lighted to hear it !"

" You are still determined on that idea ?" replied Barbican, paying no attention to outside matter.

" What idea ? Oh ! Going to the Moon. Certainly, quite decided."

" Nothing can change your mind ?"

" Nothing whatever. Have you made the modifications in the projectile alluded to in my dispatch ?"

" Not yet. I was waiting to see you. But," continued Barbican, again asking the question, " have you reflected on all the——"

" Reflected ? Never did such a thing. Mere waste of time. I find I have a chance of getting to the Moon, and I avail myself of the opportunity. That's *my* way of putting it."

Barbican's gaze expressed a new instalment of surprise when he heard the man talking as coolly and unconcernedly as if the trip meant no more than a day's shooting on Lake Okeechobee, or a flying visit to Havana.

" But, of course," he resumed, " you have considered the difficulties—devised some means of overcoming them—adopted some plan——"

" You're right, my dear Barbican," interrupted Ardan, " I *have* considered, devised, adopted, as you express it in your admirable concise English. Excuse mine—I picked it up here and there—never took a lesson—never read an English book—talked a good deal with Kossuth for practice—it is like myself—jerking, outlandish, nondescript. But it serves my pur-

pose—allow me, I know exactly what you're
going to say. The very thing I'm coming to.
I have no objection whatever to tell you all
about myself and my plans. But it would be
pure waste of time—should have to tell it all
over again to the next man. Know something
better than that. You put a little notice in the
papers, calling your friends, the whole city, all
Florida, all America, if you like, to a meeting
in some handy place to-morrow or day after.
There I shall develop my plans, and answer in
public every possible objection. Don't be uneasy—I know what I'm about—used to this sort
of thing. That suit, eh?"

" That suits exactly," replied Barbican, returning immediately to the deck. There he
took advantage of the momentary silence produced by his reappearance, to announce to the
impatient multitude Ardan's intention of addressing them all next day at a public meeting,
and answering every objection that could be
made to his extraordinary project. It is needless to say that this intelligence was hailed with
the most joyful acclamations. It gave instant
satisfaction ; all uneasy impatience was at once
allayed ; to-morrow everybody would have an
opportunity of hearing and seeing at his ease

the wonderful European. By degrees the immense crowds began to disperse, but all the morning and even all the afternoon excited groups of spectators filled the deck of the *Atlanta*, and hung around the neighboring wharves in such numbers that the passengers could hardly get their trunks out, and the custom house men gave up all idea of unloading the freight before the following day.

Many, indeed, in their excitement, remained on deck all night in spite of the remonstrances made by the captain, who, however, like a wise man, had no notion of resorting to extreme measures ; for the enthusiasm was confined to no class, color, or section. The Southern people of the Union are said to be much less notorious than their brothers of the North for their proneness towards hero worship, or their avidity to see sights. But on this occasion the most impartial observer could find no especial sectional preponderance in the crowds remaining on deck. North, South, East, and West were very near equally represented. The particular idioms, the preferences for certain pronunciations, the singularities of accent which a practised ear can proclaim to be characteristic of certain sections of the country, were mingled together with wonderful regularity. The *hyar's*, the *tote's*, the *shenanigan's*, the *allow's*, the *Howdy's?* the *at's*, the *reck'n's*, the *enthuse's*, the *thar's*, the *jáb's*, the *mout's*, the *scaly's*, the *you-uns*, the *we-uns*, the *Yanks*, and other peculiarities of the South and West were fully counterbalanced if not neutralized by the *swan's!* the *calc'late's*, the *flunk's*, the *guess's*, the *keow's*, the *hendy's*, the *hull's*, the *hum's*, the *kiver's*, the *shet's*, the *stoop's*, the *haint's*, and other solecisms of the North and East.

The most enthusiastic of the enthusiastic was Secretary Marston. Securing the camp chair, which he had noticed to be occupied for a moment during the day by Ardan, he had established himself comfortably in it, and there he remained all night, sitting on the poop deck, and haranguing an audience that never grew tired of hearing him. The subject of his text of course was Ardan, and the refrain which occurred every ten minutes or so, tickled his hearers so much, that they took it up at once and repeated it most enthusiastically and with very great effect. It was as follows:

"He is even as one among ten thousand: the best of us beside him are nothing but small potatoes!"

Barbican had slipped away early in the afternoon and rejoined Ardan in a private parlor, where they had taken dinner together, and where they remained talking together as earnestly and as familiarly as two old friends, until eight bells rang out the midnight watch, ordered all the lights to be extinguished, and told the Club man that it was time to retire.

He made his way as well as he could over the decks, which he found still thronged with people mostly all awake, drinking in Marston's endless discourse with delight—and even occasionally joining in it, for Barbican had not quite reached his hotel, which stood a few squares off, when he heard a mighty chorus like the sound of many waters, rising high and clear and strong in the sweet autumn night, and bearing on the sea breeze of the fragrant Southern clime words that his ear could plainly distinguish:

" *For he is one among ten thousand : the best of us beside him are nothing but small potatoes !*"

CHAPTER XIX.

ARDAN DEFINES EVERY PLANK AND SPLINTER OF
HIS PLATFORM.

Never did a more lovely sky display its
sapphires, amethysts and rubies in the glowing
East than that of October 22d, and never were
its glories more completely wasted on unap-
preciative spectators than they were that morning on the people of Tampa. The sun rose
punctually at his appointed time, eight minutes
after six, but in their impatience they would
have considered him a laggard had he even
wrought a special miracle in their behalf by
rising two hours earlier. Many saw him rise
for the first time in all their lives, and most
probably also for the last. Long before seven
every man in the town had breakfasted, shaved
and dressed, and by eight the streets were
alive with people hurrying to the meeting,
though it was not to take place before three in
the afternoon.

Barbican, apprehensive of the effect of indis-
creet questions addressed to Ardan, would have,

perhaps, preferred confining his audience to a few learned friends ; but he might as well attempt to dam Niagara with a Virginia fence, or keep out the Atlantic with a sweeping brush. It was no doubt exceedingly risky, but nothing else could now be done than to let his new friend run the chances of a public meeting.

The new City Hall, though a very spacious building, being altogether too small to accommodate the immense numbers desirous of seeing the orator, a large level plain about half a mile east of Tampa, not far from the camping ground, had been fixed on as the place of meeting. From the previous evening a large force of workmen had been employed in preparing it ; their labors continued all the night and next morning, with such unremitting industry, that, a little before twelve o'clock, the ropes surrounding the enclosure could be taken away, and free admission given to the public. The principal object of their labors had been to defend the audience from the fierce rays of a Florida sun, which even at the end of October often sends the thermometer up to 90. By means of spare masts and sails, readily furnished by the ships in the harbor, telegraph poles, of which a large supply had just arrived, and old condemned canvas obtained in almost unlimited quantities at Fort Brooke, where it had been mouldering away since the Osceola war, they succeeded in erecting a monstrous tent nearly a thousand feet long, eight hundred wide and fifty high. Ample as was the space it afforded, it was not an inch too large for the 300,000 spectators, who had taken possession of every available spot in less than half an hour after the circumscribing ropes had been withdrawn. Here, in a sweltering heat, for three long hours, they waited for the arrival of the Frenchman, with tolerable tranquillity and even with something like good humor. With good reason an American crowd is considered the most patient in the world. Of the immense number here assembled no more than the first third could both see and hear, the second third might possibly see but could not possibly hear, and as for the others, they could not possibly either see or hear. Still this last third was quite as orderly as the rest, except at the applauding time when, once commenced, they could never tell at what time to stop, and kept on shouting until they had become a nuisance.

At three o'clock, Ardan made his appearance, accompanied by the principal members of the

Gun Club. He had on his right hand Barbican, and on his left Marston, radiant as the
midday sun and strutting like a drum-major of
the Home Guards.

A small platform, four or five feet high, had
been erected in front of the middle of the
stage. This he immediately ascended, and
calmly surveyed the ocean of black hats that
lay at his feet. He did not manifest the least
embarrassment ; he struck no oratorical atti·
tude ; he appeared as he really was, quite at
his ease and in excellent spirits. The cheers
that welcomed him he acknowledged by a
graceful bow, then, raising his hand as a signal for silence, he commenced his speech, his
foreign accent only very slightly marring his
English pronunciation.

" Gentlemen," he began, " though it is exceedingly warm, I must trespass on your attention for a short time, while I try to present
some explanations regarding certain projects
which appear to interest you. I am no orator ;
I am no scientific man. I try to hold my
own at an argument, but I could never make
a speech. I have the honor of appearing before you in public, simply because, in the first
place, by doing so I save you and myself

much valuable time, and in the second, because·
my honorable friend, President Barbican, has
assured me that such an arrangement was most
in accordance with your wishes. Listen then
for a little while with your six hundred thousand ears and don't be too hard on the slips
of the speaker."

This free and easy exordium seemed to please
the fancy of the audience, who testified their
satisfaction by loud murmurs of applause.

"Gentlemen," he continued, "I want it to
be distinctly understood that I require no further
favor. Hiss or applaud, as you feel like it. I
absolve you from all constraint. For I must
warn you that I am an extremely ignorant fellow, and, moreover, that my ignorance is of
the very worst possible kind. I read somewhere that you had once in your armies a general so exceedingly stupid that, though he often
and often lost the battle, he never had the
sense to know it. Often and often he was
thrashed so badly that any other general in his
place would at once have displayed surpassing
ability in running away to save the rest of the
army; but this ignorant general, being too shal-
low-brained to see that he was thrashed, of
course never thought of running away, and, as

some one *had* to run away, the enemy was always accommodating enough to do it. (Applause.) Now that's the kind of a man I am. I am so exceedingly ignorant that I am ignorant even of difficulties ! (Loud applause.)

" Instead of difficult, I think it the most simple, the most natural, and the most easy thing in the world to take passage in a projectile and start for the Moon. Such a journey must be made sooner or later, and the mode of effecting it is only a simple consequence of the great law of progress. Man begins locomotion on all fours, then he finds that two of his limbs are quite sufficient to propel himself with quite comfortably. Does he then stop? Not at all. He takes in quick succession to velocipedes, sleds, market wagons, omnibuses, sulkies, buggies, carriages, canoes, boats, yachts, ships ! Does he stop there ? So far from it that by this time he has got to steamers, railroad cars and balloons ! Is this to be the final impassable end ? Who says so ? What King Canute has drawn his mark on the shore powerful enough to resist for ever the great billows of progress so uncompromising in their onward sweep ? No, gentlemen. Man can no more come to a stand-still now than ever. A new era is dawn-

ing in the annals of locomotion. The projectile is the vehicle of the future. The simplest, the most natural, the most obvious of
all vehicles ! What is our old mother Earth,
the original vehicle, the easiest going and most
perfect of all vehicles, what is she but a projectile launched on her way by the omnipotent
hand of our Creator ? Are the planets and the
stars anything else than projectiles moving with
inconceivable velocity ? Does this velocity en-
danger their safety ? Not in the most remote
degree. But if not injurious in their case, even
when carried to an extreme, how can it be an
objection to our contemplated projectile ? Let
me give you a few examples in living figures,
which of course everybody already knows, but
which I must remind you of in order to
guide you to my .conclusions."

The audience listened with breathless attention. "I shall give only round numbers," he
went on, "which are near enough for our
present purposes. Neptune moves at the rate
of 12,000 miles an hour ; Uranus, 17,000 ;
Saturn, 22,000 ; Jupiter, 29,000 ; Mars, 55,000 ;
the Earth, 68,000 ; Venus, 80,000 ; Mercury,
130,000 ; certain comets as much as 3,500,000
miles an hour when at their perihelion ! Com-

pared with these velocities what is our projectile? A mere crawler, hardly better than a snail, as its initial velocity, at best only 25,000 miles an hour, is soon rapidly retarded. I appeal to your own good sense, if that is anything to be seriously excited about, especially as it is sure to be surpassed, some of these days, by velocities still greater, of which light and electricity will be the probable agents."

No one appeared disposed to dispute assertions made so positively and sustained so plausibly.

"Gentlemen," he went on, "if we are to believe certain narrow-minded partisans—just the word for them—humanity, enclosed forever in a vicious circle out of which there is no escape, must resign itself to perpetual imprisonment in this little earth of ours and to no closer acquaintance with yonder starry hosts than can be obtained by a look at them through a telescope. But we don't believe that those one-sided self-deluders know anything at all about it! For my part, I believe their notions to be all wrong, because they are founded on ignorance and are regardless of analogy. I believe that the day is coming when the great etherial ocean enveloping the universe can be crossed, when we can take passage for the Moon, for the planets, for the stars, as we now take passage from New York to Liverpool, as easily, as rapidly, as safely ! Distance ! Distance is only a relative term, and, within certain limits, will end by being reduced to zero !"

However favorably his hearers seemed to regard the orator, this astounding assertion was certainly too much for them. Ardan appeared to comprehend this as he resumed calmly :

" As I seem to be getting somewhat ahead of my story, gentlemen, let us argue the point a little. In what time, let me ask you, would an express train, running little more than thirty miles an hour, reach the Moon ? Three hundred days. No more. Not even nine times a trip round the world. Few travellers or sailors worthy of the name, have not gone much further in their day. Consider now that, once started, I shall be only 97 hours on the road ! Ah, you think the Moon is very far off, and that, before taking such a leap, I ought to see very well what I'm about. But what would you say if I thought of making an excursion to Neptune, wheeling as he does in an orbit nearly 3 billions of miles distant from the sun ! That is a promenade that few of us could take, even at the regular railroad charge of five cents a mile ! Rothschild himself, with all his 200 million dollars, would at last have to be shoved off the train for not paying his fare !''

The assembly seemed to relish this style of handling an argument, particularly as Ardan, full of his subject, went into it heart and soul. Feeling his audience and himself to be in perfect sympathy, he continued with an easy and graceful assurance :

" My friends, immense as is the distance separating us from Neptune, he is only our next door neighbor, when compared with some of the fixed stars. Here we are encountered with figures of such vast value, the least of them nine digits long, that we must take a billion for the unit. Excuse me for being so well posted on these points, and attribute it all to the absorbing nature of the subject. Listen and judge for yourselves ! Alpha Centauri, the nearest star to our system, is 20,000 billions of miles distant ; 61 Cygni is three times as far ; Sirius, seven times ; Polaris, sixteen times ; Capella, twenty-one times ; and the other stars, thousands and millions and even billions of times as far away ! Now talk about the distance of our planets from the sun ! Distance ! It is no distance at all ! Pure hallucination to

call such contiguity distance ! Do you know
what I think of our whole solar system, beginning with the orb of day and ending with
Neptune ? Do you really wish to hear my
notion of the matter ? (We do ! Yes, yes !
Let us have it !) Well, it is very simple ! To
me our whole solar system, in comparison with
the rest of the universe, is one solid compact,
homogeneous body. The planets composing it
touch, adhere, press together, and the space ex-
isting between them is only the space separating
the molecules of the densest metal, iron, silver,
platina ! Such being my conviction, I think
I have the right to affirm, and to repeat with
a confidence that must tell on every one that
hears me : Distance is but a relative term ;
and, taken in a certain sense, in fact, there is
no such thing at all as distance !"

" Hurrah !" cried the assembly, electrified by
the emphatic gestures and thrilling tones of the
orator.

" It stands to reason !" cried Marston louder
than the rest, jumping up from his seat ; " distance is an exploded idea !" he continued, forgetting in his excitement that he was on the edge
of a platform at least ten feet high. Barbican's
coolness, however, and strong arms once more

saved his friend from being convinced by painful experience that distance was anything but
an exploded idea. In the general excitement,
nobody seemed to notice this little incident,
and the orator continued in thrilling tones :

"Friends—for so I must now call you, as I
feel from your sympathy that my words have
not fallen in vain, and that this question has
been resolved to your satisfaction—if any one
still lingers among you unconvinced, it is either
because he has not heard me, or because I have
been too timid in my demonstrations, too feeble
in my arguments, or too little conversant with
illustrative details. (Loud cries of No ! No !)
However that may be, I repeat it again, that,
considering the infinite vastness of the universe,
in the eye of a thinking man, the distance between the earth and her satellite is something
altogether too insignificant to give him any
serious trouble in overcoming it. I don't think
I hazard too much when I say, the day is fast
approaching when we shall have projectile trains
to the Moon, mail, express and accommodation !
And in such trains what a luxury to travel !
The perfect realization of the poetry of motion !
What are your palace cars of the Pacific Railroad in comparison ? No collisions, ηo jarring,

PROJECTILE TRAINS FOR THE MOON.

no noise, no snapping of rails, no misplacement of switches, no telescoping, no burning passengers alive by the upsetting of stoves, no caving in of embankments, no crushing under falling tunnels, not a single one, in short, of the numberless accidents to which ordinary travelling is exposed, is possible on our great Lunar Railroad, the only one that really deserves the name of the Air Line!"

Loud applause greeted this sally, which was considered pretty good for a foreigner.

" In less than twenty years from now, half the Earth will have visited the Moon!"

" Hurrah! Hurrah!" cried the nearest part of the audience, taking every one of the orator's words for gospel truth.

" Hurrah! Hurrah!" cried those next, still louder, thinking he was going to start on his trip, then and there before their faces.

" Hurrah! Hurrah!" cried the third part, those farthest off, loudest of all, though they had not yet heard a word, nor even caught the first glimpse of the speaker.

" Hurrah for Ardan!" cried all together, with a cheer that made the great awning over head heave like the mighty billows of the Atlantic after an equinoctial storm.

"Nay, my friends," cried Ardan in reply, his clarion voice piercing the dense volumes of sound like a winged arrow, until it reached the outside edge, where it sounded like the faint far off cry of a bird at sea. "My dear friends, excuse me, surely you don't forget! Three cheers for Barbican! The worthy countryman of Franklin, who snared the lightning; and of Morse, who made it a postman; he has revolutionized travelling, by manufacturing a winged steed out of gun powder, and a triumphal chariot out of a cannon ball!"

The mighty yell that rushed out of the 300,-000 throats at this speech, lifted the central portion of the awning clean up off the timbers of the roof for ten or fifteen feet, and kept it there for a few seconds, extending over them without visible support like the dome of a vast St. Peter's. It would probably have burst with a terrific explosion, only for the fortunate ripping of several places which, on account of the hurry and confusion, had been sewed by inferior sewing machines.

Barbican bowed his thanks, but did not offer to speak.

When the hurricane of sound began to die away, and the violent excitement to be succeeded by a slight reaction, Ardan again addressed the meeting :

"Now, gentlemen, as we appear to have arrived at a good mutual understanding, I come to the second object of our meeting, and I have the honor to state that I shall be delighted to listen to any questions you may choose to make, and that I am willing to answer them as well as I can."

No one spoke, but all looked at Barbican.

The President of the Gun Club, so far, had every reason to be satisfied with the manner in which Ardan had acquitted himself. He had spoken on a subject of which he was complete master, and which his lively imagination had enabled him to handle brilliantly, if not logically. But if practical questions, where imagination went for nothing and actual experience was everything, should now come up for discussion, Barbican had very serious doubts regarding his new friend's ability to come off with flying colors. Before any one else, therefore, could give him some posing questions, he hastened to pull him off dangerous ground, by asking him if he thought the Moon or the planets were inhabited.

"That's rather a difficult question to answer

categorically," replied the unsuspicious Ardan,
readily falling into the trap. "Many men of
great intelligence, Plutarch, Bernardin de Saint
Pierre, Fontenelle, the elder Herschel, Sir
David Brewster, Doctor Lardner, have pronounced decidedly in the affirmative. Looking
at the question from a philosophical stand-point,
I am rather disposed to share their opinion. It
all turns on the answer to another question—
Are the planets habitable ? If they are, I should
say that, since nothing can be conceived to exist uselessly, they either are inhabited, have
been, or will be. Now, my opinion is that they
are habitable."

"Excuse me, Mr. Ardan, for differing with
such a distinguished gentleman," interrupted a
voice in the crowd, which Barbican recognized
at once as coming from the man who had been
the spokesman on the famous evening of Ardan's
dispatch, and whom he had since learned to be
a journeyman shoemaker of a literary turn, and
the president of the *Orion Debating Society*,
Catharine Street, Philadelphia. "Excuse my
boldness, Mr. Ardan," he went on, "but you
must be aware that there are very serious objections against your idea of the habitability of
other worlds than ours. To go no further than

the planets—some of them are so far from the sun, and others are so near, that creatures organized like us could not possibly live in either. We should be roasted alive or frozen to death."

" A very proper objection on your part, my dear sir," said Barbican, delighted to see the discussion taking such a harmless turn, " but one which, I feel confident, my friend can answer without the slightest difficulty."

" With none whatever," resumed Ardan, "and if only the time and the place permitted, nothing would give me greater pleasure than to answer the gentleman point by point and step by step. If I were a scientific man I should prove to him that the temperature of a planet depends on other causes than its relative distance from the sun. I should convince him that the condition of its atmosphere, the internal heat of its mass, the phosphorescence of its light, the electric effects of its chemical action, may so counterbalance relative proximity or remoteness that even a *Mercurian* may readily experience all the gloom and cold of our winter, and even a *Neptunian* enjoy all the light and warmth of our summer. If I were a naturalist, I could show the gentleman that even on our earth nature reveals to us many

examples of life flourishing under very different
conditions ; that fishes inhabit an element fatal
to other animals ; that frogs, lizards, alligators
and other *amphibia* enjoy a doublefold existence
very difficult to explain ; that certain sharks
and other inhabitants of the ocean sustain life
in depths where the pressure of the sea, though
as enormous as that of fifty or sixty atmospheres, does them no harm whatever ; that certain aquatic insects, perfectly insensible of temperature, are found alive equally in springs of
boiling hot water and in the frozen plains of
the Polar Ocean ; that even in strong acids
that would instantly kill any animal or even
insect they touched, myriads of living creatures
find their home ; that even in dark lakes in
the bowels of the earth below the craters of
active burning mountains, the volcano fishes
flourish so abundantly that an eruption often
shoots them out in thousands, mingled with
the cinders, the smoke and the burning lava ;
in short, that, as the omnipotence of the Deity
is not limited to one mode of action, life may
exist under such diversities of aspect as are
often perfectly incomprehensible, but still perfectly real. If I were a chemist, I should say
that the äerolites, evidently not belonging to our

world, still reveal to analysis undeniable traces
of carbon in such a state as to prove, according to Reichenbach, that it was once either the
food or the habitation of organized beings.
But I am neither a scientific man, nor a
naturalist, nor a chemist. Therefore, in my
profound ignorance of the great laws governing
the universe, I shall restrict myself to saying :
I don't know whether the other worlds are
inhabited or not, and as I don't know, I am
going to see !"

These words were hailed with such hearty acclamations and prolonged cheers that the literary gentleman in the crowd asked no further
questions—whether from a conviction of their
inutility or from the satisfaction he had de-
rived from the reply, it is now impossible to
state. The probability is that the uproarious
cheers and senseless applause of the outsiders
continued so long that he adjourned further
scientific inquiries to a more favorable moment.

Ardan soon resumed, the immense crowd coming to a dead hush as soon as he opened his
lips :

" Of course, my friends, you understand that
such a great question I only glance at, not
enter upon. I am no famous *Star Course* lec-

turer, exuding knowledge from every pore of his body at five hundred dollars a night, before a crowd of ladies and gentlemen seated at their ease and perfectly willing that somebody else should do their thinking. I am no learned professor surrounded with costly apparatus of the latest fashion, and attended by one or two dozen assistants doing all the hard work while he does all the easy talk. I am no orator, any more thàn one of yourselves, but a "plain, blunt man," according to the expression of your own Shakspeare, or, as we always enthusiastically call him in France, the "Divine Williams!"

The sudden fit of merriment that here shook the audience they did all they could to conceal by hemming, coughing, nose-blowing, etc., and even Barbican's grim features relaxed for an instant into a humorous smile. But the orator continued his discourse, evidently unconscious of the enormous success of his hit:

"Of all the many arguments that can be brought forward to sustain the habitability of the other worlds, I shall allude to one only, as that one, if not quite as conclusive as the others, is simple and within the comprehension of the humblest. To Doctor Whewell and the

other Star-smashers who deny the possibility of
the planets being inhabited, I would say :
Gentlemen, you may be right in your position, if you can only prove that the earth is
the best of all possible worlds. But she is
nothing of the kind. Far from it. In the
simple question of satellites alone she is far inferior to Jupiter, Saturn, Uranus and Neptune.
They have a great number at their service, she
has but one. But the strongest objection to
the optimism of our Earth is the great inclination of her axis to her orbit. This causes the
variation of our seasons, I admit, but that is precisely why I blame it. Variation of the seasons
is no advantage. Inequality in the length of our
days and nights is no advantage. Approaching
extremes in the heat of our summers and the
cold of our winters is no advantage. We are
alternately freezing or roasting. This planet of
ours is *par excellence* the planet of colds,
rheumatisms, coughs and catarrhs. But if you
want to see a planet really worthy of the name,
look at Jupiter ! His axis being inclined only
about 3°, his inhabitants can enjoy zones of
invariable temperature the whole year round.
They have their countries of perpetual spring,
perpetual summer, perpetual autumn, and perpet-

ual winter. Consequently, every *Jovian*, by choosing whatever climate or seasons he finds to suit him best, can protect himself completely against all possible variations of temperature. In this respect alone Jupiter enjoys such immense superiority over our planet that I need hardly allude to another one equally great—the length of his years, each one twelve times as long as ours. To me it seems that, living under such favorable auspices, under such advantageous conditions of existence, the inhabitants of Jupiter must be a very superior order of beings. Their scholars must be more learned, their artists more masterly, their good people more excellent, and their bad ones less depraved than with us. And what is it all owing to? What does our world want in order to become the pink of all possible worlds? Very little! Only a slighter inclination of her axis to the plane of her orbit!"

" That's so! All as true as gospel!" cried an impetuous voice. " But what is to prevent us from fixing it? Let us go to work at once and construct a machine to straighten up the earth's axis! What is it that Americans can't do if they only put their whole mind to it?"

Thunders of the most vociferous applause

hailed this bold proposition which, of course, could emanate only from the slap-dash, fidgety, excitable brain of our friend J. T. Marston, who was always ready " to fly off the handle."

The Secretary of the Gun Club was, in many respects, the type of a set of men who, though fortunately not very numerous in the Great Republic, are still to be found in every part of the country. Quick at catching an idea, but never improving on it ; ready at the tongue, but unable to control it ; abundant in mother wit, but apparently destitute of gumption ; acquainted with all the new books, but only skimmers of their froth ; rapid at figures, which they innocently believe can never lie ; full of the last idea, never masters of it ; lynxes at the strong points of an analogy, bats at its weak ones ; ready to pronounce at the moment a dogmatic opinion on the most puzzling question in politics or religion, though utterly deficient in the cool judicial mind—such men are often found occupying important positions in the land, where they evidently exercise great influence in the formation of public opinion. If wanting in the moral sense, they do more harm than all the rest of the politicians put together. If thoroughly honest, they are still more mischievous, by their proneness to " fly off the handle," as the popular phrase has it. Their reputation makes them respectable in the minds of the people, even when advocating extremely radical views regarding " Woman's Rights," " Maine Liquor Law," " Elastic Currency," " Credit Mobilier," " Educational Bureau," " Contraction," " Inflation," and other ticklish questions, not to mention their desire to introduce changes into the Constitution, of an extremely doubtful utility.

But Marston, so far, had done no harm whatever, except what resulted from his famous Baltimore experiment. His smartness had long before this been so fully appreciated that his friends had run him for Governor of Pennsylvania, in which State he possessed considerable property. But his unthinking, outspoken honesty made his election hopeless. He *would* speak his mind on every conceivable subject, and fill all the newspapers with his communications. His opponent, a man strongly similar in temperament, but less scrupulous and more cunning, or at least much more tractable in the hands of his backers, never uttered a word or touched a pen during the canvass. He was of course elected by a tremendous majority, but he has ever since been trying to indemnify himself for his period of forced silence, by giving full vent to his eloquence on every possible occasion.

Marston's new notion, " his latest kick," as a good natured friend called it, though quite on a par with all the others, was exactly the one to catch the popular fancy, excited as it was at the time by Ardan's novel audacities. To Barbican's delight, the whole meeting seemed to forget, for at least half an hour, every other question but that of "reconstructing" the earth's axis. They passed resolutions on the spot highly eulogistic of the idea, and appointed a committee of five, Marston chairman, to find out the best locality for the erection of suitable engines, and to report progress at the next public meeting, which they were likewise empowered to call.

That meeting has never since been called. Marston's engines have been as unfortunate in finding a $\Pi ov \ \Sigma \tau \tilde{\omega}$ as Archimedes' lever. Still I see by the New York papers that the question is by no means ·dropped. The committee hold their regular meetings, at which Marston's stream of eloquence, figures, speculations and poetry, gushes forth as hopefully, as abundantly, and apparently as inexhaustibly as ever.

CHAPTER XX.

A FENCING MATCH.

Marston's sudden proposition, as said in our last chapter, occupied the attention of the assembly for some time to the exclusion of every other consideration. In fact, the meeting had every appearance of being about to break up after the appointment of the Committee of Five and the reading of the eulogistic resolutions. But just as, the general agitation being somewhat calmed, somebody was on the point of proposing an adjournment, a loud clear voice with some asperity in its nasal twang, was heard to pronounce the following words :

" Now that the orator has given full swing to his fancy, perhaps he will have the kindness to return to the main question. We have had enough of the theoretic, will he not give us a little of the practical, side of his enterprise ?"

All eyes were immediately directed towards the speaker. He was a tall, thin, elderly man ; his face was clean shaven except where a stiff goatee hung from his chin ; his sourish features were full of energy ; and the gold spectacles could not hide the keen flash of his eyes. During the general confusion resulting from Marston's proposition, he had contrived to approach the smaller platform reserved exclusively for the speakers, and now he stood in front of the high stage before the eyes of the assembly, within a few feet of Ardan's left hand, calmly waiting an answer, with arms folded and eyes fixed steadily on the Frenchman.

Equally regardless of the thousands of angry glances shot at him, and of the thousands of angry murmurs excited by his unexpected appearance, he once more repeated his question, clearly, precisely, and in even sourer tones ; then he added :

" We are here, sir, to talk about the Moon, not about the Earth."

" You are perfectly right, my dear sir," replied Ardan, recovering a little from his surprise ; " we have wandered a little from the subject. Let us go back to the Moon."

" Sir," resumed the stranger, " you pretend that the Moon is inhabited. Now, those Selenite friends of yours must contrive to live without lungs, for, as you are aware, there is not a particle of air on the Moon's surface."

At this strong assertion, probing as it did the question in its vitalest point, Ardan suddenly straightened himself up and eyed his antagonist keenly while he answered :

" Indeed !   No air in the Moon ? Why not, pray ?"

" Scientific men say so."

" They do ?"

" Yes ; in such precise and positive language as to show that they know what they are talking about."

" My dear sir," replied Ardan quietly, " without meaning to be rude, I must say that for scientific men who really know something, I have the most profound esteem, but for those who only imagine they know something, I entertain nothing but the most profound contempt."

" Do you know any of those belonging to the latter class ?"

" Too many ; not a few of them seem to think that the profoundest knowledge consists in denying the simplest truth. I know a great scientist in France who proves by an incontrovertible mathematical demonstration that a bird can't fly. I know another who can show conclusively that a fish is not made for water."

" I don't speak of such simpletons, sir ; I can cite in support of my assertions the opinions of scientific men of world wide reputation for the depth and soundness of their knowledge."

" My dear sir, I shall be only too happy to hear what they have got to say. A poor ignorant fellow like me is always ready to take his lesson."

" Ignorant ! What business has an ignorant man to approach scientific questions ?" asked the stranger somewhat roughly. " Why should he do it ?"

" Why ? Why is he the bravest man who never suspects danger ? I am ignorant, it is true, but my honest ignorance often carries me further than another man's fancied knowledge."

" Your ignorance, I admit can carry you very far," growled the unknown, loud enough to be heard.

" I shall be quite satisfied if it carries me to the Moon !"

" The very place fit for you !" muttered the unknown, in a low but angry voice.

Since the beginning of the debate, the President and his colleagues of the Gun Club had been devouring with eager eyes this bold in-

truder, whose inopportune questioning might
seriously block the progress of their enterprise.
Nobody seemed to know who he was, but Barbican had his surmises, and he was therefore
doubly apprehensive regarding Ardan, who, so
far, certainly did not seem to be getting the
best of it. The assembly had been very attentive to the discussion, but it was now evidently
becoming somewhat restless at the idea of hearing something unpleasant regarding the dangers
or the actual impossibilities of the great enterprise.

"Sir," resumed Ardan's opponent, "arguments numerous and irrefutable prove the total
absence of all atmosphere on the Moon's surface. I might assert that, even if such an atmosphere ever existed, it must have been drawn
off long ago by the earth. But, instead of assertions, I prefer to adduce facts, sir; incontrovertible facts!"

"Adduce them, my dear sir, by all means,"
said Ardan, in his most polished style; "let
us have the facts."

"Of course you are aware," replied the
stranger, "that rays of light traversing a dense
medium, like the air, deviate a little from a
straight line, or, in other words, undergo refrac-

tion. Now, when the stars are occulted by the Moon, their rays, however closely they may graze her disc, never experience the least deviation, never show the slightest semblance of refraction. The evident conclusion from this is clearly that the Moon has no atmosphere.''

Every one looked nervously at the Frenchman ; the facts once admitted, the consequences were rigorous.

" Well," replied Ardan, " that is your best, probably your only argument, and a scientific man might have some difficulty in answering it. In my eyes, however, it has no value, as it takes for granted that the angular diameter of the Moon is perfectly determined, which is by no means the case. But let this pass for a moment, and answer me one question. Do you admit the existence of volcanoes in the Moon ?''

" Volcanoes extinct, yes ; volcanoes active, no.''

" They must have been active, however, at some period or other ?''

" Of course ; but as they might have furnished themselves with the oxygen necessary for combustion, the fact of their eruption by no means proves the existence of a lunar atmosphere."

"They might," replied Ardan, smiling, "and then again they mightn't. Conjecture proves nothing. Let us leave it altogether, and take to direct observation. I give you warning. I am going to lug in great names too."

"Lug them in !"

"In 1715, two astronomers, Louville in France and Halley in England, while observing a lunar eclipse, remarked on the surface certain glimmerings of a curious nature, resembling distant lightning flashes. They could account for them no other way than as signs of some terrible storms raging in the Moon."

"In 1715," replied the stranger, "Louville and Halley made a great blunder. They took mere terrestrial for lunar phenomena. The lightning flashes that they saw, were nothing but little meteors flying about in the upper regions of our own atmosphere."

"All right !" replied Ardan, no way disconcerted at this reply ; "let us again pass on. Did not Herschel, in 1787, observe more than a hundred and fifty luminous points on the Moon's surface ?"

"He thought so, at least ; but he offered no

explanation to account for them ; they never induced him to believe in a lunar atmosphere."

" Well answered," replied Ardan ; " I must
really compliment you, my dear sir, on being so
well up in selenography."

" Thank you ;" replied the stranger dryly,
" compliments are all very well, but I like arguments better ! Shall I quote you the opinions of Beer and Maedler, the great lunar map
constructors ? They are very decidedly opposed
to yours."

A thrill of anxiety ran through the assembly
at each reply made by the stranger. He was
evidently making some hits. But Ardan was far
from being a beaten man.

" Their opinions ?" he repeated with an arch
smile. " No, thank you ; opinions are all very
well, but I like arguments better ! (Laughter
and cries of good !) My dear sir, I don't care
a straw for any man's opinion as long as I have
facts to form one for myself. Once for all
then, let us drop opinions and come to one or
two very important facts. Laussedat, a French
astronomer, when observing the famous solar
eclipse of July 18th, 1860, saw that the horns
or cusps of the sun's crescent, instead of being
sharp, well defined, and coming to a point,

were truncated, jagged and blunt. Now, how is it possible to account for this very remarkable phenomenon any other way than by the refraction and even the absorption of the sun's rays as they passed through the lunar atmosphere?"

"But did Laussedat really make such an observation?" asked the stranger quickly and with some uneasiness.

"Really, truly and absolutely," replied Ardan; "I can refer you to the volume of the *Comptes Rendus* of the *Académie des Sciences* and probably to the very page on which it is recorded."

At this reply the stranger was evidently disconcerted, and for a few minutes could not utter a word. The audience withheld their hearty cheers at Ardan's triumph only because they saw that their favorite had not yet quite finished.

"I need not allude to *Bailey's Beads*," he continued, "which are so difficult to explain, without supposing the existence of an atmosphere, nor to Schroeter's *Lunar Twilights*, pointing almost irresistibly to the same conclusion, I cite these absolutely observed facts to show you that nobody should be in a hurry to decide that the

Moon has no atmosphere. Its atmosphere, it is true, may not be very dense, it may even be very rare, but its non-existence is far from proven, and therefore should not be positively asserted."

" It certainly does not exist on the mountains," said the stranger, unwilling to give in.

" On the summit of our Himalayas," replied Ardan readily, " the air no doubt is exceedingly subtile. But should we therefore conclude that there is no atmosphere on the earth ? Yet that is the strongest argument your scientific men adduce against the existence of one on the Moon ! As I said before, I respect highly the scientific men that know something, but I regard with very different feelings those who try to pass off their crude conjectures and flimsy fancies for profound knowledge. A negative proposition is the most difficult of all to prove, and your scientific men have a good deal yet to do before they can convince people that the Moon has no atmosphere."

A formidable shout of applause greeted Ardan's triumph, but his opponent, though disconcerted a little, was far from being dismayed, and still calmly surveyed the vast assembly. Ardan resumed, but quietly and without the air of desiring to press his advantage too much :

" Since we cannot deny the existence of a certain amount of atmosphere in the Moon, we are likewise obliged to admit the presence of a certain quantity of water. Besides, my dear sir, I must call your attention to another point. We know only one side of the Moon's surface. There may be but little air on the face presented to us, but how can we tell that there is not quite an abundance on the opposite side ?"

" Why should we think so ?"

" Well, as you are so fond of scientific men's opinions, I shall give you some. Professor Gussen, of Wilna, after a careful examination of the best Lunar photographs, has come to the conclusion that the Moon is egg-shaped, with its small end drawn towards us by the attraction of the earth. Professor Hansen, an astronomer of such celebrity that the British Government published his *Moon Tables* a few years ago, following up Gussen's idea, has calculated the Lunar centre of gravity to be in the external hemisphere. If this be so, the paucity of both atmosphere and water on the Moon's visible surface is easily accounted for. They have been all attracted to the other side, where they accu-

mulate in dense masses in accordance with well
known principles of gravitation.''

" All twaddle and fudge !'' cried the stranger
angrily.

" Twaddle and fudge, as you say, such opinions may very truly be," replied Ardan coolly,
" but, nevertheless, as they are founded on observation and calculation, they can be refuted
only by the same means.''

Loud applause greeted this ready reply. The
meeting, in fact, was becoming quite jubilant,
and, now seeing that the stranger was coming
off second best, it began to treat him with decided disrespect. He tried to speak, but they
would not listen to him. The more he per-
sisted, the louder they roared, and he soon
heard himself saluted with the refined wit so
common on such occasions :

" Dry up and bust, Old Spectacles !'' cried
some.

" Take a back seat, Old White Hat !'' cried
others.

" Go West, young man, go West !'' came
from the right.

" Change your base, General !'' came from
the left.

" Put him out ! Put him out !'' roared the

multitude at large, beginning to be tired of the scene.

But instead of being cowed by the storm raging around him, the stranger actually shook his stick at the yelling mob. Ardan, by some emphatic gesticulation, at last succeeded in somewhat calming the excited multitude, and, taking advantage of a lull in the storm, he addressed his unknown antagonist :

" Perhaps you desire to make a few more remarks ?"

" A few more ? A thousand more !" replied the stranger in a voice trembling with rage. " But no ! — further talk in such a pandemonium as this, would be mere waste of breath. I shall only say that if you persist in the idea of starting for the Moon in a conical cylinder, you must be the craziest simpleton living."

" A simpleton ! He calls me a simpleton for proposing to go to the Moon in a conical cylinder ! Would you have me start in a spherical shell, where I should never stop turning head over heels like a squirrel in a cage ? In a conical cylinder I shall always stand upright and go perfectly straight to the mark. Yet for this luminous idea I am called a simpleton !"

" But, you great baby, the tremendous concussion at the very start will be alone sufficient
to dash you into a thousand pieces !"

" My dear friend," replied Ardan, somewhat
seriously, " you have put your finger at last on
the real and only difficulty. That it is a
serious one I do not deny, but I have too
much confidence in the mechanical genius of
my American friends to entertain the least
doubt of their thorough ability to overcome it."

" Then, the enormous heat developed by the
projectile as it rushes through the various
layers of the atmosphere !"

" Oh ! The walls are thick and I shall be
only a few seconds getting through fifty miles.
There won't be time enough to get roasted
in !"

" But provisions ! Water ?"

" I shall take enough for a year, and my
trip will last but five days !"

" And the air to breathe in the meantime ?"

" I can make as much air as I like with
chemicals."

" But the shock of your fall on the Moon's
surface, if you ever get there !"

" It will be six times less violent than a fall

on the earth, the Moon's attraction being six
times weaker.''

"Still it will be violent enough to splinter
you like glass into a thousand fragments !''

"What shall prevent me from breaking the
fall by means of counteracting rockets suitably
disposed and let off at the proper time ?''

"But—well—in short, supposing all the difficulties gotten over, all the obstacles conquered,
and that you had arrived safe and sound at
your journey's end—how could you get back ?''

"I don't intend to come back !''

At the sublime simplicity of this reply, the
whole assembly was actually struck dumb. A
dead silence, infinitely more expressive than the
most enthusiastic exclamations, lasted for a few
seconds. The stranger took advantage of it to
make a last appeal.

"You will assuredly lose your life,'' he cried,
"and your death, though it leaves one mad-
man less in the world, will be of no other advantage to science.''

"Prognosticate, my dear boy, prognosticate !
Your cheerful predictions please you and do me
no harm !''

"Can't you be in earnest for a moment ?''
cried the stranger passionately. "But, in fact,

you're not so wrong in acting the jester regarding such a mad subject. I must be crazy myself to talk seriously even for a moment about it. Go to the Moon, or go to the—Halifax, if you want to ! I wash my hands out of the whole thing. I wish others could do the same ! You're not the one I blame most for it !"

" You're very kind !"

" Yes ; whatever may be the consequence of the silly piece of business no one will ever hold *you* responsible for it."

" Really ? I am not responsible for my own acts ! Who is, pray ?"

" The cowardly and shallow pretender that was the first to start a notion as absurd as it is ridiculous !" cried the stranger, in a voice loud enough to be heard by half the meeting.

The blow was direct and its animus unmistakable. Ever since the stranger's first appearance, Barbican had been making the most violent efforts to restrain himself, " to consume his own gas," as the stove makers say, but this public insult at once exploded him. Forgetting everything in the violence of his fury, he jumped from his seat, shook his fist at his antagonist and " went for him." The stranger, evidently expecting something of the kind,

20

stood on his guard. A violent collision seemed inevitable, fraught with heaven knows what consequences, when, all at once, Barbican found himself compelled, whether he liked it or not, to put off his deadly vengeance for a more favorable occasion.

We have already spoken of the small square stage—accessible by a few steps attaching it to the centre of the platform—which, enabling the speakers to come a little more forward, allowed them to be more easily seen and heard by the Gun Club men seated in rows behind. Before Barbican had time to descend the steps, this stage was forcibly detached from the platform by the vigorous arms of some admiring enthusiasts, who would be satisfied with nothing less than bearing Ardan and Barbican in grand ovation back to the city. The triumphal chariot was very heavy, difficult to balance, and exceedingly awkward to carry, but the broad shoulders made nothing of such trifles, and applicants for the honor were in such abundance that the right of precedence could not be settled in several instances without recourse to blows.

Marston jumped down and ran after his friends, but the stranger still maintained his post on the platform, gazing at the disappearing Barbican, who, for his part, in spite of the difficulties and inconveniences of his position, continued to shoot glances of the deadliest hatred at his adversary as long as he continued in sight. Could eyes kill, most assuredly these two men would have dropped dead then and there, shot through the brain by way of the optic nerve. This is only another illustration of the old Latin proverb regarding the savage hatred of scientific men :

Odium ignorantum
Est odium infantum ;
Sed odium Doctorum
Est odium ferorum.

Which may be thus rendered :

When ignorance ignorance offends,
The boyish quarrel quickly ends ;
But only let your *Savants* fight—
Not grizzly bears more fiercely bite !

The triumphal procession was a splendid success. The most rapturous acclamations greeted the conquering heroes as they advanced, and the cheers were so frequent and animated along the route as to seem one great continuous uninterrupted cry. The streets were gay with flags, and the ladies and children made the house-fronts alive with waving handkerchiefs.

Ardan enjoyed it intensely. His face radiated with smiles, and the air with which he bowed right and left to the vast multitude was grace itself. Not that he had not occasionally extreme difficulty to maintain the perpendicular, on account of the peculiar nature of the improvised triumphal chariot. Sometimes two short men would get hold of the front legs while two very tall men held the hind legs; sometimes the two short men were on the right and the two very tall men were on the left; the best of times the floor was far from level, and the triumphal car would .pitch and roll and toss and lurch like a ship in a chopping swell. But our heroes had splendid sea legs; if they did not always maintain an attitude rigidly vertical, they at least managed to escape being washed overboard, and their good ship at last safely came to anchor in the friendly port of Tampa.

It was so dark by the time they arrived in front of their hotel, that, by suddenly swinging themselves off the stage and mingling with the crowd, they easily managed to escape further inconvenient attention from their admirers. Ar-

dan stole up to his room, bolted his door, bar-
ricaded it with the furniture, and was soon fast
asleep, though the crowds kept shouting under
his windows till midnight, and were then succeeded by the German bands, who serenaded him
till half-past three in the morning.

In the meantime, a short, sharp and decisive
scene took place between the mysterious stranger and the President of the Gun Club.   Instead
of seeking his room, Barbican had immediately
retraced his steps back to the place of meeting,
expecting to find his adversary still standing on
the platform.   But he could see nobody there
but the workmen, who, lantern in hand, were
busily engaged in taking down the poles and
rolling up the canvas.   Greatly disappointed,
he returned to his hotel, but the very first man
he noticed there, talking to the clerk and probably inquiring about himself, bore the well remembered features of his adversary.   A light
tap on the shoulder, accompanied by a signifi-
cant glance, was understood in an instant.

Making their way as rapidly as they could
through the crowded streets, the two enemies
soon found themselves standing at the extreme
end of a lonely wharf, not far from where the
Atlanta lay at anchor.   They glanced at each

other for a few minutes without saying a word. The silence was first broken by Barbican.

" You are Captain McNicholl, of Philadelphia ?"

" Yes."

" We met to-day for the first time."

" Not my fault !"

" You have insulted me !"

" Deliberately !"

" You are ready to give satisfaction ?"

" Instant and complete !"

" Here we should be interrupted. We were watched at the hotel."

" Arrange it as you like."

" Do you insist on seconds ?"

" No."

" A few miles northwest of us is a wood surrounded by meadows bare of timber. Do you know it ?"

" I can find it."

" To-morrow morning at six o'clock will you enter its eastern end ?"

" As surely as you enter its western end."

" Bring your best rifle."

" Don't forget yours."

With these words, grim, cool, and determined as themselves, the foes separated.

Barbican returned to his hotel, but, instead of taking a few hours' rest after a most exciting day, he spent the remainder of the night in trying to find the means of counteracting the frightful concussion of the projectile at the instant of its departure—the serious problem alluded to by McNicholl, and on his successful solution of which Ardan had confidently counted.

CHAPTER XXI.

WAR TO THE KNIFE !

We left Ardan fast asleep in spite of the noise that surrounded him. Perhaps even the shouts of the impatient multitudes under his windows and the endless serenades of seven different bands had only excited his somnolency; for certain it is that, as soon as the reddening east told the last crowd of exhaustless Teutons that it was time to go home, his slumbers became less sound and his dreams more disturbed. He imagined that he had at last reached the Moon, but that, instead of alighting on the plains, the projectile had descended on the summit of a hill with such force as to bury itself two or three hundred feet below the surface. The shock had extinguished his light, broken his instruments, and thrown everything into the greatest confusion. He had already passed two days in profound darkness and dead silence, perfectly miserable and ravenously hungry (he had eaten nothing since noon). Completely helpless, he was at last quietly resigning himself to his fate, when, all at once, he heard a faint tapping at the upper end of the projectile. Some good Selenites perhaps coming to his rescue ! He shouted to let them know he was alive, and the tapping became louder. They were evidently approaching. Louder yet. He heard them talking ! Louder yet ! He could even distinguish their words : " Open, open, for the love of heaven !" At last, the tapping grew so loud that it awoke him.

But his dream was not all a dream, for, sure enough, somebody in the entry was knocking loudly at his door and crying with an anxious earnest voice :

" Open ! open, for the love of heaven !"

He jumped up at once and began pulling away the barricade from the door ; this was soon forced open, and Marston burst into the room like a bombshell, capering with excitement and consternation.

" Oh ! Ardan," he cried without further ceremony, " Barbican was insulted last evening at the meeting, as you know, but who it was you don't know. It was McNicholl of Philadelphia, his deadly enemy ! Of course he challenged him, and they are now fighting a Kentucky duel in the St. Helena Wood. I learned it all through a note of Barbican's, which by a lucky accident was handed to me two hours before its time. If the President is killed your Moon trip is all gone up!"

"Gone up where?" asked Ardan in some confusion, not understanding all the niceties of the American language.

"I mean the whole project is gone to smash, unless this duel is prevented. There is only one man in this world can stop Barbican once he has made up his mind, and, Ardan, that man is you!"

While Marston was speaking, Ardan was dressing, and in less than five minutes the two friends were tearing out of Tampa by the Fort Brooke road as fast as ever their legs could carry them.

The Secretary soon made the Frenchman complete master of the situation. He told him that though the real cause of the enmity between Barbican and McNicholl was of old date, chance and common friends had so arranged it that the foes had never before met face to face. As the real cause of the trouble was the rivalry between armor and ball, he had no doubt that the scene of the previous evening had been contrived by McNicholl, who was dying for an opportunity to vent his spleen. Then Marston told his friend something about the nature of the fight which they were hurrying to prevent.

This terrible species of duel, so common in the South and West thirty or forty years ago, is not yet, unhappily, quite extinct. Barbican and McNicholl understood it to perfection. Each was to go into the forest armed as he pleased, and was allowed to fight as he pleased, every trick, wile, or deceit employed to kill the enemy being considered perfectly lawful. Once engaged in such a duel, you could no more expect mercy or generosity from your enemy than from a tiger or a coppersnake or, worse still, from a savage Seminole tracked to death. Mere animal courage counted very little in your favor. The qualities of mind and body developed by a life long struggle for existence in a wild forest, where death lurks under a thousand forms—marvellous keenness of eye and ear and nose, rapid fertility in expedients and resources, ready ingenuity in throwing the enemy off the scent, unerring sagacity in following up his trail, skilful manœuvring so as to draw his fire on some " blind," the wonderful control of nerve which enables you to lie motionless for hours in an uncomfortable position when you think you have the advantage—these and other qualities of a similar nature were evidently of infinitely more account than mere animal courage. The slightest blunder, mistake or hesitation almost inevitably proved fatal.

"What perfect fiends you American fellows are!" cried Ardan, shuddering, as he listened to some details that would make your blood run cold.

"Well we ain't anything else!" replied Marston quite complacently. "I tell you what, when we're riled we can make the fur fly, and no mistake about it. But let us hurry up or we shall be too late."

"I'm afraid we are too late anyhow," observed Ardan, redoubling his speed after a short relaxation to take breath.

They had by this time left Tampa far behind them, and as they hurried over a flat plain covered with sea grass wet with dew, and crossed by several shallow creeks, they could easily catch sight of the "St. Helena Wood," skirting the edge of the plain at a distance of at least two miles. It was now half past six o'clock; if the duel had begun at six, by this time all was probably decided for ever. They saw a colored man at some distance before them, driving a loaded wagon drawn by four horses.

" Hello ?" cried Marston, a hundred yards off.

" Hello !" answered the man.

" Come from the woods ?"

" Yes, Boss ; from the saw mill."

" Did you see my friend Barbican there ?"

" How's that, Boss ?"

" I mean, did you see a sportsman—armed with a rifle, you know ?"

" Yes, two of them, Boss."

" Together ?"

" No ; in two different parts of the wood."

" How long ago ?"

" More than an hour."

" Did you hear any firing ?" asked Ardan, who had now come up.

" No, Boss ; nary fire."

" Sure ?"

" Sartain, Boss. Funny sports ! Yanks, I reckon. Ya ! ya ! Git along, Joe !" and on he went smacking his whip, and laughing heartily at the idea of a man being in St. Helena Wood for an hour without getting a shot.

Off they started again at full speed, but were obliged to stop a few hundred yards from the wood to take breath.

"What's to be done now?" asked Marston, when his companion had come near enough to talk to.

"Hard to say," replied Ardan. "If we enter the wood, it is at the risk of getting a bullet in the brain."

"I don't mind that," said the faithful Marston. "I would risk ten bullets in the brain to save Barbican."

"All right, then, dear boy!" cried Ardan, warmly shaking his hand. "Go ahead! You'll find no skulking about me, or ' backing out ' as you Americans call it."

In a few minutes they were making their way through the dense underwood that skirted the forest, and a half-hour's struggling brought them into the heart of St. Helena Wood. The vegetation was of the usual semi-tropical character. Gigantic cypresses, sycamores, palmettoes, limes, sweet and wild olive trees, tulip trees, tamarinds, pecans, live-oaks, and magnolias grew in such dense array and interwove their branches so closely that advancing was very hard work, and seeing ahead was actually impossible. Marston and his companion pushed on in Indian file, but on account of the obstacles presented by twining vines and luxuriant undergrowth, they had to change their course so often that they soon completely lost their way. For some time they wandered on at random, looking every now and then for some broken branch to tell of a human being having been there before them, and rather nervously expecting to hear every moment the crack of a rifle. Ardan, who, like most Europeans, had taken all his ideas of American forest life from Cooper's novels, was innocent enough to think that he might strike a trail by means of his reminiscences of "Leather Stocking," but Marston soon convinced him that the tactics of northern Indians would not work in a southern jungle, and, in fact, that a Kentucky duel was altogether out of place in a Florida forest.

After an hour or two's fruitless labor, the friends, tired, torn and dispirited, came to a halt under the shadow of an immense live-oak.

" It's all over, I'm sure," said Marston despondingly. " Barbican's gone up ! Bold as a lion, and smart !—smart is no name for him — he was as simple and straight-forward as a child. He would disdain to stoop to any of your Indian tricks. He went for his enemy fair and square, and that darkey was too far off to hear the shot that killed him."

" Not likely ;" said Ardan, " and certain it

is that no shot has been fired since we have been here."

"Oh! we've come too late!" exclaimed Marston, yielding to his despair. "Good bye, Barbican! Green be the sod above thee, friend of my early days!" he continued in doleful tones interrupted with sobs, whilst tears streamed down his cheeks.

Ardan's only reply was to call out as loud as he could :

"Barbican! McNicholl! Mac Nich — oll! Bar—bi—can—n—n !"

Flocks of birds, startled at the unusual sound, flew away through the branches, twittering and screaming in their fright; wild cats and ocelots rushed across the clearing with a scared glance and an angry growl; rattlesnakes, "coach-whips," and copperheads showed their glittering eyes for an instant amidst the surrounding foliage, and then rapidly wriggled away through the dried leaves; but no welcome human voice in reply saluted the listening ear. They shouted again and again; they heard nothing but the faint echo of their own voices feebly reverberated by the gloomy depths of the primeval forest.

They started once more, keeping the straightest line they could, and in considerably less than an hour they found themselves outside the wood on the north side. Having entered by the south side, they saw that the forest could not be very large, and this gave them new hope. Entering again, they tried to follow a southeast course, shouting, beating the bushes, and making just as much noise as ever they could. Once more they came to the edge of the wood without seeing anything. Over the plains to the south they could catch a glimpse of the United States flag waving in Fort Brooke, but that was the only sign suggestive of humanity that they could discover. Ardan, in his turn, tired and discouraged, began to fear the worst, but Marston, before giving up altogether, proposed a new exploration, this time in a northwesterly course, so that no portion of the woods should be left unsearched.

Resuming their course in perfect silence—too dispirited and tired to shout, they had not advanced more than a few hundred paces when Marston suddenly stopped.

"Hush!" he whispered, "I see something over there to the left."

"Something like a man?" asked Ardan.

"Yes it *is* a man! He is perfectly motionless. He has no rifle either."

21

" Who is he ?   Can't you tell ?'' asked Ardan, trying to fix his eye glasses.

" Hush !   He is turning this way !—Yes ! It's the man with the spectacles that catechised you yesterday !''

" McNicholl !'' cried Ardan with a sudden pang in the heart that almost stopped its beating.

McNicholl without his rifle !   No longer afraid of his enemy !   Then their worst suspicions were confirmed.

" Let us speak to him at once,'' whispered Marston.   " This suspense will kill me.''

They had not gone far before they stopped again to examine the Captain more attentively. Was that really the terrible duellist, implacable in his resentment, thirsting for the heart's-blood of his enemy, aud now gloating savagely over his fearful vengeance ?

He certainly did not look like it !

Amazement kept Marston and his companion riveted to the spot.

A net, with meshes close and strong, had been spread from one immense tulip tree to another, and it now hung between both like a beautiful screen of silver wire work.   In the middle of it, a poor little bird had got hopelessly entangled by the wings, and was now making its last efforts to escape, uttering the most pitiful cries. The hunter who had set this terrible trap from which there was no escape, was no human being, but a venemous spider of the *tarantula* species peculiar to the country, big as a pigeon's egg, hairy all over, and provided with enormous claws. The hideous animal had been just in the act of pouncing on his prey, when he was suddenly obliged to change front and seek safety in the higher branches of the tulip tree, being assailed in his turn by a formidable enemy.

The fact is, McNicholl, notwithstanding a temper compounded of vinegar and vitriol, was in reality such a kind hearted man that he had been made Vice President of the Philadelphia Society for the Prevention of Cruelty to Animals. He had entered the wood, breathing fire and fury, and if he had met Barbican any moment during the first half hour, the death of one or both would have been the inevitable result. But as he did not meet him, and as it was most unlikely that he ever would meet him in such a labyrinthine forest, he began to look around, and being an intense lover of nature, he soon found himself keenly interested in the various forms of animal life disclosed at every turn. It was not long until he had forgotten Barbican, armour, projectile, Moon, and all, so completely that he took the greatest amusement in throwing nuts at the squirrels, frightening off the wild cats from the rabbits, and killing the rattlesnakes that he saw climbing up the trees after birds' nests. While Marston and Ardan were watching him, he was completely absorbed in trying to extricate, with the gentlest of hands, the poor, timid, fluttering little creature, which, probably thrown into new ecstacies of terror by the efforts of her deliverer, was doing all she could to render his task more difficult. But he succeeded at last, and threw the little thing high up into the air; she fell back for an instant as if stunned, but soon finding herself at liberty, she shook her wings with joyful cries and in a moment vanished over the tree tops.

The Captain was still looking in the direction where she had disappeared, when he felt himself touched on the shoulder, and heard a voice full of emotion exclaim :

" McNicholl, you are a brave, noble man !"

Turning, he saw himself face to face with Ardan, who kept on repeating in every variety of tone :

" A brave man ! A noble man ! A gentle man !"

" Ardan !" cried the Captain, starting with surprise, " What are you doing here ?"

" Shaking your hand, Mac, my boy ; and going to keep you from killing Barbican and him from killing you !"

" Barbican !" cried the Captain. " Oh ! I had forgotten all about him ! Where can the coward be hiding himself ?"

" Coward ! Hiding !" exclaimed Marston, blazing with indignation. " Look out, Captain McNicholl ! My friend Barbican is as brave a man and as honorable a man as you are, and I will allow no one to traduce him in my presence !"

" Marston is right !" interposed Ardan, before the Captain could make an angry reply ; " Mac, you are unjust in imputing anything like cowardice or meanness to your opponent. He is incapable of either. No, no, no ! Your bad temper must give way to your good heart ! Let us hunt up Barbican. I want to talk over a little notion of mine in the presence of you both."

" Between Barbican and myself," replied the Captain with gloomy gravity, " there is a dispute which death alone————"

" Come, come, Captain !" interrupted Ardan, " none of that ! As much jaw as you like, as much ink as you like, but no blood, no powder and ball, no shooting !"

" I'll shoot him as dead as a door nail the first chance I get ! I'll shoot him like a mad dog !"

" You will do nothing of the kind !"

" I'll draw as fine a bead on him as I would on a rattlesnake !"

" Look here, Captain McNicholl," said Marston with much quiet dignity, " your expressions a few moments ago, referring to my illustrious friend, betrayed a forgetfulness of manners, and they now reveal a ferocity of heart, altogether inconsistent with the demeanor of a gentleman ! I repeat the insult deliberately ! If you want any satisfaction take it at once ! I am ready to die any day in behalf of my noble friend Barbican. Fire away !" and he struck a grand attitude, folding his artificial arms magnificently over his manly bosom.

" Sir, sir !" cried the Captain, convulsively grasping his loaded rifle, " I don't know you— you are not aware————"

" Again my friend Marston is perfectly right, Mac," interrupted Ardan, " and I honor him for his noble devotion to his calumniated friend. But the ball is not yet cast that Captain Mc-Nicholl is to fire either at Marston or Barbican. Mac, I have a little proposition to make, that will put all notions of fighting out of your head."

" Let us hear it," said the Captain, beginning to be rather ashamed of his violence and not knowing what else to say.

" Excuse me, Mac," replied Ardan, " I can't broach it until we are all in Barbican's presence."

" Let us go after him then right away !" cried the Captain, drawing the charge of his rifle, and starting off at a rapid but irregular pace, closely followed by his companions.

For a full half hour or more they had nothing whatever for their pains. Marston began to mistrust the Captain, and eyed him every now and then with a very suspicious glance. He even set himself to thinking what course he should follow if they came suddenly on poor Barbican's body weltering in his gore, his skull smashed with the Captain's bullet. Ardan too seemed to be troubled with the same idea, for he also began to survey the Captain with a decidedly uneasy glance.

All at once, Marston, who had the best eyes of the party, suddenly stopped, and pointing to the left, exclaimed :

" It is he !   Look !"

Peering through an opening in the foliage, they could see the motionless body of a man reclining at the silver gray foot of. a beautiful catalpa tree at least two feet in diameter and twenty or thirty paces off.   They could not see his face, the hat being over the eyes, and the body being half covered in the tall grass.   Again Ardan shot an eagle glance into the eyes of McNicholl, but the Captain never winced a moment.   Marston sprang forward, exclaiming :

" Barbican !   Barbican !"

No reply.   The three men, very much puzzled, advanced towards the prostrate form, but they suddenly stopped short, uttering exclamations of surprise at what they saw.

Barbican, stretched at his ease on the grass, his back resting against the tree, his rifle, uncocked, lying in the grass two or three paces distant, was drawing geometrical figures and calculating algebraic equations in his diary !

Before any one could say a word, he suddenly closed his book, jumped up, waved his hand over his head and cried out :

" Hurrah ! Hurrah ! *Eureka !* I have got it !"

" What ?" cried Marston, who was the nearest. " What have you got ?"

" My plan !"

" What plan ?" asked Ardan, taking him by the hand.

" My plan to counteract the projectile's concussion at the start !"

" No !" cried Ardan with a glance at the Captain. " You don't say so ?"

" Yes, I do ! It's all right ! Water will do the business !———Hello, Marston, you here ! You too, Ardan !—"

" My own four bones," interrupted Ardan, " and permit me to have the honor of introducing at the same time my good friend Captain McNicholl."

" McNicholl !" cried Barbican, making for his rifle. " Excuse me, Captain—I had forgotten—but I am ready—"

Marston had already secured the rifle, and Ardan now cut in before the enemies would have time to exchange words.

" By Jove," he exclaimed ; " how lucky it is for Marston and myself that you two fellows did not meet sooner. We should have a greater stock of dead bodies on hand than we would like to carry. Heaven, whose favorites we must be, has spared us the very disagreeable task of bothering ourselves to know what to do with them. But now all danger is over, for you two must likewise have been Heaven's favorites. When one terrible duellist forgets his hatred so much that he risks his life for the sake of an algebraic equation, and when the other renounces every chance of killing his enemy for the sake of delivering a little bird from the claws of a spider, the thirst of vengeance that influences their hearts cannot be called exceedingly insatiable ! I'll tell you all about it, Barbican.''

Having sketched rapidly, and with a good deal of humorous exaggeration Marston's and his own adventures from the moment he had been so unceremoniously aroused from his slumbers to the present instant, he added a few words in a voice full of feeling :

'' And now I'll just ask yourselves, if two such good natured, tender hearted, whole souled fellows as you, have been intended by Heaven to blow each others' skulls to pieces with rifle balls ?''

The two rivals were gradually discovering that there was ˙something so comical and at the same time so unexpected and strange in their respective positions, that they felt the anger rapidly oozing away at their finger ends, and they hardly knew what decision to come to. Ardan, conscious of his advantage, pressed it home.

"My dear friends," he continued, his lips wreathed in his sweetest smile, "my dear and respected friends, nothing more has ever existed between you than a little misunderstanding. Now, as you don't know what such a thing as bodily fear is, to show that all ill feeling between you is at an end forever, I want you to accept the proposal I am going to make."

"Speak," said the Captain, "let us hear it first."

"My friend Barbican," said Ardan, "you believe your projectile will go straight to the Moon?"

"Certainly, I do."

"My friend Mac, you believe it will fall back to the earth?"

"Not a doubt of it."

"Very good," continued Ardan. "Now I don't pretend to be able to make you agree. So I simply say: Come both of you along with me, and then you will find out who is right!"

"What's that?" cried Marston, not believing his ears.

The proposal was hardly announced when the rivals found themselves looking at each other very keenly. Neither spoke. Barbican was waiting to hear McNicholl. The Captain wanted to know what the President had to say.

" Well, dear boys," resumed the Frenchman, in a tone that would coax a bird off a tree, " as there is no longer any danger from the concussion————"

" Accepted !" }
" Accepted !" } cried the rivals with one voice,

" Hurrah ! Bravo ! Three cheers !" cried Ardan, shaking the opponents warmly by the hands, while he executed a series of *entrechats* and other fancy steps in a style that would have made a *Black Crook* dancer's fortune.

" And now, my dear boys," he added when he had come to himself, " let me remind you of a very important fact. I am as hungry as an ostrich ! I have had no breakfast to-day and took no dinner yesterday. I don't think you have been a bit more fortunate. I have therefore the honor to invite you to join me, and, to celebrate this happy occasion, we must get the very best that the Tampa market affords. Hang the expense !"

Marston did not utter a word all the way

back to town. He was the whole time engaged
in solving a very difficult problem : What had
he gained by the morning's labors ? Does it
make much difference, whether your friend is
killed in a duel or blown to pieces from a
projectile ?

CHAPTER XXII.

POPULARITY IN AMERICA.

The friends had not finished their *déjeuner à la fourchette* before all America was ringing with the details of the duel and its singular termination. The distinguished part played in the drama by the gallant Frenchman, the unexpected proposition with which he had put an end to the difficulty, its simultaneous acceptance by the two rivals, the contemplated conquest of the Lunar Continent by the allied forces of France and America—everything, in short, conspired to raise Ardan's already great popularity to the highest possible pitch.

Most people in Europe know how madly the Americans run after every "distinguished foreigner," as soon as he lands on their shores. It makes no difference from what country he comes, why he comes, what claim he has on America, or if he has any claim at all ! Dickens, Kossuth, the Prince of Wales, the Grand Duke, etc., etc., had assuredly done very little to excite the crazy enthusiasm of the United States, yet they were honored with receptions worthy of the greatest benefactors of the earth, almost of a divine visitant from heaven. Do you happen, my excellent European reader, for any reason whatsoever, at the present moment to be as the saying is, " in every body's mouth ?" Then go to America at once ; nothing more is necessary to insure you a brilliant reception. Will your popularity last ? Ah ! *mon ami,* that's another pair of sleeves, as we say in France. The fiercest flame is not always the longest or the steadiest, and the Great Republic has not yet freed herself from all the little infirmities incident to our common human nature.

For the time being, certainly Ardan's popularity was absolutely unbounded. Deputations from all parts of the country never gave him a moment's repose. He could not avoid receiving them. How can you refuse seeing a man who has come a thousand miles to shake your hand ? Worse than that. In America you insult a man if you refuse a drink at his invitation. Ardan would not insult anybody, and consequently every resource of his fertile imagination was taxed to the utmost strain in trying to reconcile two ideas diametrically opposite : to avoid giving offence, and at the same time never get tight. How he always struck the golden mean so successfully, how in the hardest bouts his head always kept " level," and his tongue still continued to flow on with the light airy graceful humor that made him such a charming companion, is a problem beyond my powers of solution. Most assuredly his task was not any easy one, for the Americans, though they are never drunk, can put away a good deal of liquor.

Of course, every now and then, Ardan would experience some of the inconveniences to which even greatness is liable. For instance, he was pounced on four or five times every twenty-four hours by the agent of a Boston company called the *Astrocheutic*, or star-diffusing society, who offered him a thousand dollars for every lecture he would deliver in each of the great chief cities of the Union. To get rid of such a leech required the display of patience, perseverance and force of character of a very high order, but every new visit left Ardan considerably weaker than before. He was hesitating what to do, when relief came from an unexpected quarter. The agent of a rival company of New York, the *Utile-cum-Dulci Society*, offered the distinguished Frenchman six thousand dollars a week for five weeks with all expenses paid, for a short lecture every day in whatever part of the country the association might think proper to send him to. This was enough for Ardan. He instantly accepted the offers of both, throwing on the agents the task of settling their conflicting claims to mutual satisfaction. This of course they could never do ; and the result was the famous law suit between the two great societies, which, though the best lawyers of the land were engaged on each side, is still dragging its slow length along in the Supreme Court of the United States.

Another thorn in his side for a while was the famous P. T. Barnum. This distinguished gentleman waited on him in person and offered him a million of dollars for the privilege of exhibiting him for a month, at fifty cents a head, with the Woolly Horse, the Feejee Mermaid, the Giant Quakeress, the Talking Fish, the Living Ichthyosaurus, the Sea Serpent, and the other wonders of his Great Moral Show. The Prince of Humbugs was withal so genial, so plausible, so insinuating that Ardan, finding it impossible to get angry with him, promised to accede to his demands on the return of the party from the Moon, if he, Barnum, would only join them in the trip. But the genial showman, knowing what a serious loss even his temporary absence would prove to the progress of the great Temperance movement in the United States, hastily declined the offer with many thanks, and started that very night for New York.

Need I say that " interviewing reporters " waited on the daring Frenchman by the thousand ? or that they were dismissed as wise as they came ? or that this prevented · their letters from being quite as long and just as veracious as usual ?

I must hurry through a few more instances, introduced simply to give my French readers an idea of their countryman's extraordinary popularity in the Great Republic.

For three Sundays in succession, the sensation preachers of the fashionable churches of New York took his name for their text, and, if they did not handle their subject with much piety, they at least displayed extraordinary ingenuity and learning in giving it a meaning of deeper significance than his parents had ever thought of at his baptism. Some quoted Nineveh inscriptions to prove it to be Aryan ; some by means of cuneiform characters showed beyond all doubt that it was Semitic ; certain passages in Zoroaster convinced some that it was Zend ; Grimm's Rule left no doubt on the minds of others that

it was High German ; whilst others, Max Müller
in the right hand and the Bible in the left,
demonstrated by the strictest adherence to the
laws of language that it was veritable Celtic.
These edifying sermons, so refreshing in their
light, culture and sweetness, were all published
in Monday's *Herald*, and had, it is needless to
say, an enormous sale.

Then his portraits—how could I describe the
endless trouble to which he was subject in pre-
venting deadly conflicts between the rival pho-
tographers ?   Could I even enumerate the
styles in which he was taken ?   Or the sizes,
from that of life down to the little micro-
scopic charms to hang on a watch chain ? or
the position, head, bust, whole figure, vignette,
full, profile, half, three-quarters ?   Even photographs of the back of his head found a ready
sale.   More than fifteen hundred thousand were
sold, and in every album he shared the post
of honor with General Washington.

With all its drawbacks, Ardan hardly found
his wonderful popularity displeasing.   He even
liked it, and readily yielded to its demands.   Unless when engaged writing replies to his thousand and one correspondents, he was always to
be found in some public place — the " Plaza,"

for instance, a beautiful open square in Tampa, not yet quite finished, but already a pleasant place with flower plats, fountains, statues, and shady walks under old trees of the original forest. Here he could be found every evening, or else on the deep verandah of his hotel, surrounded by an eager crowd of admirers. His style of dress became the rage—the " Ardan " is still a favorite name with paper collar manufacturers—his jokes, especially those he never made, were extremely quoted—his " little stories " filled several volumes which formed almost the sole reading of the railroad travellers—and the great " story newspapers " sent him blank checks in return for any article bearing his name on any subject at all. An unfortunate bookseller, nearly ruined by publishing the *Rig Veda*, of which he had sold exactly eleven copies, expressed his perfect willingness to publish all the other *Vedas*, if Ardan would only write a general preface to the work. That would be enough, as he expressed it, " to send them all off like hot cakes."

Need I say that he was even more popular with the fairer portion of humanity than with his own sex ? No good-looking tenor ever emptied into the stove the hundredth part of the *billets doux* he found every morning lying on his breakfast table. If he would only marry and settle, what splendid opportunities he might have by just saying the word ! The rich old maids were continually writing to him for his autograph, but the buxom widows would not be put off with anything short of a regular letter. He was so beset with offers of matrimony that at first he thought of trying the " Moon-dodge," so successfully employed against Barnum, but he soon found it would not work. The old philosopher who, when writing about woman, defines her as *quiddam timidum et se retrahens,* " a timid and shrinking creature," assuredly knew more about his books than his subject. When a woman once makes up her mind, she is the bravest of the brave. In support of this remark we need only state that whereas in the whole United States, after Barbican, McNicholl and one more, not a single man or boy could be induced to go to the Moon on any consideration, letters appeared in the papers every day from women expressing themselves perfectly willing to start on a trip to the Moon, and even to Neptune if any body would take them. But it is needless to say that neither Ardan, Barbican nor McNicholl, all unmitigated old bachelors of the worst kind, " dyed

in the wool," was the man to entertain any such
foolish idea for a single instant.

The first favorable opportunity Ardan had of
tearing himself away for awhile from his courtier
throng in Tampa, he thought the least he could
do was to pay a visit of respect to the Columbiad. The odd moments that he could devote
to the company of Barbican and his other
friends, he generally employed in talking Ballistics with the Club men, whom he often called,
half joke whole earnest, amiable murderers and
scientific life-shorteners. His remarks when visiting the Columbiad for the first time, were somewhat of the same nature. Having descended to
the bottom of the gigantic engine that was so
soon to launch them towards the Starry Queen,
he professed his profound admiration for the excellence of the magnificent piece of work, and
then went on moralizing.

" Now here is a cannon that I like, that I can
recommend, that can do no harm to anybody,
which is more than I ever said before, or ever expected to say, for a cannon in all my life. The
cannon a civilizer! Heartless, heathenish idea!
I differ from my friend Barbican *in toto*—though
I believe that at heart he agrees with me. I
never could bear the sight of your monstrous

engines for burning, crushing, killing, mangling wretched human beings by the score ! I hated the men that served them, and even the horses that dragged them !''

Whilst they were all down there by themselves, sheltered for a moment from the importunities of the public, Marston took advantage of the occasion to broach a project that he had been entertaining for some time, namely to join the Moon party —" it would be so handy,'' as he said, " to have a fourth man for a little game of euchre.'' The poor fellow's real reason was, of course, his despair at the idea of being separated from his friend Barbican, whom he almost worshipped. The President of the Gun Club knew this very well, but he was compelled to refuse positively on the ground of the absolute inability of the projectile to carry any more passengers. Marston, deeply distressed, turned to Ardan for intercession, but the Frenchman shook his head.

" Look here, old fellow,'' he said quietly, " you must not take offence at my words, you know ; but really and truly you are not the style of man that I should like to take with me to the Moon. You are incomplete, you know.''

" Incomplete !'' cried Marston. " What do you mean ?''

" I mean you are an incomplete, mutilated, garbled, truncated man ! Look at your artificial arms ! Imagine our embarrassment on meeting the Selenites. How could we explain away your mutilation ? What an exalted idea they should conceive of us Terrestrians when we told them that we spend a great part of our time fighting each other, breaking each other's limbs, slaughtering each other, and that the most civilized nations train their best men to be nothing better than accomplished murderers—and all this on a globe that could easily sustain a hundred billions of inhabitants, and where there is not at present the eightieth part of that number ! No, no, my dear boy, the very sight of you would get us kicked out of Luna's dominions in double quick time !''

Marston, having no reply ready for language of this kind, was forced to keep silence ; as the days passed on, he became more and more melancholy, falling into a kind of stupor from which even the great preparations made on all sides could hardly arouse him.

A preparatory experiment, made on October 18th, gave the best results and excited the most promising hopes. Barbican, desirous to ascertain the effect of the concussion occurring at the instant of a projectile's departure, had a 32 inch mortar brought from Pensacola. It was placed on the shore so that the shell might descend on the water, and thereby the violence of its fall be diminished—the question being, not to test the effect of the concussion at the end of the course, but at the beginning.

Accordingly a hollow shell was most carefully prepared. Its interior walls were lined with a soft thick padding, firmly kept in its place by a net work formed of the finest steel springs. It was, in fact, a regular bird's nest, artistically made and most comfortably wadded.

Into this harmless bombshell, which could be firmly closed by means of a screw fastened lid, they introduced first a large cat, then a very pretty squirrel belonging to Marston, who had made it quite a pet. The object of introducing the second animal was to ascertain how a living thing so slightly affected with vertigo as a squirrel, could endure the experimental trip.

The mortar was loaded with a charge of powder, the shell put in its place, and the piece fired off. The projectile shot up rapidly, describing its majestic parabola, reached a height of about a thousand feet, and then fell with a graceful curve into the midst of the waves.

Without a moment's delay, a boat started for the spot ; skilful divers plunging into the water and fastening cords to the ears of the shell, it was soon hauled aboard. Five minutes had not elapsed from the moment at which the animals had been fastened up, to that when the lid of their prison was unscrewed.

Ardan, Barbican, Marston, and McNicholl were all in the boat, and you can easily comprehend with what interest they watched the experiment. Scarcely was the lid opened, when out jumped the cat, a little scared and towzled, but as lively as ever, and evidently not a particle the worse for her äerial flight.

But no squirrel made his appearance. They waited for him. They looked for him. They shook the shell, and turned it upside down. No squirrel. There was no mincing the matter. The cat had eaten up her fellow traveller.

It is surprising how deeply this incident affected Marston. Not so much on account of the loss of his squirrel—though the lively little animal had been a great favorite—as from a superstitious idea to which his brooding and unhappy mind now easily became a prey. The little experiment was clearly the type of the great one, and foreshadowed its fate. The

THE CAT TAKEN OUT OF THE SHELL.

cat, of course, was Ardan, who would return safe and sound. But Marston could not shake off the notion that the squirrel's doom was ominous of his friend Barbican's destruction. That the squirrel, indeed, might prefigure Mc-Nicholl was barely possible; yet this was the only straw to which the drowning man now clung for consolation.

The experiment having put an end to all doubt, hesitation and fear, and as Barbican's plans were certain to render the projectile more perfect and to reduce to little or nothing the terrible effects of the concussion, little more now remained to be done than to make immediate preparations for starting. We shall close this chapter with one more instance of Ardan's decided popularity in America.

A morning or two after the experiment, Barbican met Ardan, and, remarking that his friend's countenance always radiant was now resplendent, asked the reason.

" I heard from Ulysse to-day," was the reply, delivered in a tone that betrayed considerable self satisfaction.

" From whom ?" asked Barbican, slightly interested.

" Ulysse."

" Who is Ulysse ?"

" *Ma foi*, Ulysse — my   friend—the   President
of the United States !"

" Oh !   General Grant !   Well, what did he
write about ?"

" He writes to inform me that the House
and the Senate, assembled in an extra session
called for the purpose, have unanimously decided to confer on me, as once before on
my illustrious countryman, Lafayette, the right
to call myself a citizen of the great United
States of America.   And I tell you I am proud
of the honor !"

CHAPTER XXIII.

AN IMPROVEMENT ON PULLMAN.

The Columbiad once finished, examined, criticised and talked about, the public interest naturally passed on to the projectile—the new palace car for what Ardan had called the great Air Line Railroad.

Nobody forgot that the Frenchman in his dispatch had demanded an important modification of the shape adopted by the Committee at its first session. On that occasion Barbican had not troubled himself about any particular form of the bullet, for the atmosphere once passed, the projectile was thenceforth to wing its way through the regions of eternal void. The Committee had therefore adopted the spherical shape, principally on account of its simplicity, as spinning on its axis would do it no harm as it went along. But the matter evidently became quite serious, the moment the projectile was transformed into a vehicle. Ardan had no desire to travel, like a squirrel, head over heels; he wanted to perform his journey like a man, head

(349)

always above, feet always below, and his general
position much more comfortable than in the car
of a balloon, where, though moving far less
rapidly, you are subject to a constant succession
of somersets anything but dignified.

A new draft had accordingly been sent to Meneely & Co., Albany, with directions to have it
attended to with all possible speed. The projectile, thus finally modified, was cast on November 2d ; a few days afterwards, taken charge of
by Adams Express Company, it was moving south-
wardly on its way to Florida.

Its progress was rather slow. In every city
and even village through which it passed, it was
stopped *vi et armis* long enough for all the inhabitants to see it. In some places they even
celebrated its arrival as a holiday, appointed
an orator to address it with an eloquent speech,
and escorted it with a guard of honor as far as
the next large town.

Towards the middle of the month, it arrived
safe and sound at Stony Hill, and you may be
sure it was an object of profound interest to
Ardan, Barbican and McNicholl, whose stout
ship—or as Marston phrased it—" whose adamantine ark it was to be, sailing over the ethereal
billows of the astral deep !"

THE ARRIVAL OF THE PROJECTILE AT STONY HILL.

It must be acknowledged that it was a magnificent piece of workmanship, displaying considerable metallurgic skill, and highly creditable every way to American industry. It was the first time that aluminium had ever been obtained in such an immense mass—which alone was something to be justly proud of. It glittered in the sun like a silver mountain. It reminded Ardan's excited imagination of one of those conical little turrets so often seen on the corners of the great fortified castles of the middle ages. To complete the picture, it wanted only loop holes and a weathercock.

"Yes," he exclaimed with a laugh, "there we shall be quite at our ease, like a feudal lord perfectly safe in his donjon-keep. With a little artillery we might bid defiance to a whole Selenite army, supposing they are foolish enough to have anything of the kind in the Moon."

"You like the projectile, then?" asked Barbican, with a gratified air.

"Very much indeed," was the reply—"only that it does not completely satisfy my æsthetic craving. I should wish its hard lines to be a little more shapely, and its cone to be a little more graceful. And it might be surmounted with some pretty metal ornament—a dragon, for instance, or rather, a phœnix rising from the flames, wings outspread, beak open——"

" *Cui bono ?* What's the good of all that ?" interrupted the matter-of-fact Barbican.

" You ask ? I'm surprised at you ! Remember that whatever you may be at, it is never the worse for a little touch of art. Did you ever hear of an Indian play called the *Baby Coach ?*"

" Never," answered Barbican, looking as slightly interested as politeness would allow.

" In that play," continued Ardan, " a burglar is introduced, who is going to break into a house by boring through the door. Only he cannot make up his mind what shape to give the hole, whether that of a lyre, or a flower, or a bird, or a water pitcher. While he is hesitating, the patrol comes along and takes him prisoner. Now, Barbican, if you were on that burglar's jury, would you have the heart to find him guilty ?"

" Most undoubtedly," exclaimed Barbican, " and if I only had the fellow in Delaware, I should award him an extra amount of lashes on the bare back !"

" Ah ! Barbarian ! Savage ! Steel heart !" cried Ardan, horrified. " I am ashamed of you. Scratch a Russian and you come on a Tartar.

Scratch Barbican and you find nothing but cast iron !''

"They call me old Pig Iron," said Barbican with a grim smile.

"Talking art to you," said Ardan, "is like teaching music to a deaf mute, or explaining the spectroscope to a man blind from his birth. But I give you fair warning. You may keep the outside of the projectile as tasteless and ugly as you like ; I shall take my revenge by furnishing the inside as artistically and as luxuriously as becomes the ambassadors of our most illustrious and majestic planet !''

To this Barbican made no objection, more particularly as he had not an instant himself to spare for the agreeable, every moment being devoted entirely to the useful. In other words, he had been trying to bring to perfection his arrangements for overcoming the tremendous effects of the first concussion.

Here was the trouble. Supposing you are seated in a railroad car moving fifty miles an hour, what would happen if the train suddenly stopped ? You would be shot with frightful rapidity against the front part of the car. Why ? Because, though the car was stopped, *your body was not stopped*, and it therefore continued its

23

motion until it encountered some obstacle strong
enough to arrest it.   A danger of this nature,
though proceeding from a cause precisely the
reverse, threatened our travellers in the interior
of the projectile.   Before their bodies could
possibly have time to partake of the motion,
they would be struck a tremendous blow by
the floor rising up against them with the enormous velocity of 12,000 yards a second.   The
consequence, if not provided against, would be
of course precisely as fatal as if their bodies
had been hurled against the floor with a force
capable of producing the same annihilating
swiftness.   It was while lost in the problem of
how to counteract the effect of this terrible
concussion, that Barbican had forgotten all about
his duel in the St. Helena Woods.   But he
had contrived to solve the difficulty in a very
ingenious manner.

Careful experiments had convinced him that
no combination of metallic springs would be
strong enough to deaden the violence of such
a shock ; at last it occurred to him that water
could be employed for the purpose with perfect success.   This is the way in which he proposed to manage.   The floor of the projectile was
to be overflowed with a bed of water to the

height of three feet. This bed was to support a
circular disc, like the piston of a cylinder, water-
tight, but moving readily up or down. On this
false bottom the travellers would take their
stand. The liquid mass below did not form
one solid body ; it was separated by several
horizontal partitions, to be broken in succession
by the violence of the shock. Each sheet of
water forced up through escapement pipes, by the
sudden rising of the bottom, towards the upper
portion of the projectile, would thus form a
kind of spring equally advantageous to ceiling
and floor ; whilst the floor itself—which stout
pillars, provided with an extremely strong buff-
ing apparatus, prevented from flying to the roof
—could not strike the bottom until after the
successive destruction of the different partitions.
Undoubtedly the travellers would still experience
a very violent concussion the moment the liquid
mass would have escaped, still the first shock,
the most to be dreaded, would be almost completely deadened by this water spring, whose
force was almost beyond calculation.

Such a mass of water, three feet in depth and
nine in diameter, would, it is true, increase the
weight of the projectile by at least two thousand
pounds, but the elastic force of the accumulated

gases, Barbican was confident, would easily overcome the additional burden ; besides, as all
this water would be driven out in less than a
second through holes especially drilled for the
purpose, the projectile would resume its normal
weight almost instantaneously.

This was Barbican's plan for resolving what
we call in France the *contre coup*, and for which
I don't know any English term but *concussion*.
It was an exceedingly clever contrivance, and
the idea was just as cleverly carried out, and
even improved upon, by the intelligent machinists to whose care the whole operation had been
entrusted by Meneely & Co. The shock once
successfully resisted and the water driven out,
the travellers could easily get rid of the broken
partitions, of the pillars which had done their
duty as buffers, and even of the disc itself, if
they should find it in their way.

The ceiling of the projectile chamber was
lined with a thick leather padding hanging
from spirals of the best steel, elastic as watch
springs. The pipes for the escape of the water
were so completely hidden by this thick leather
padding that their existence could not even be
suspected.

(I must, however, acknowledge that in this

contrivance one thing has always puzzled me. How was the water to be got rid of? At the bottom or by the sides? Either supposition lies open to serious objections. How could the padding at the ceiling escape destruction from the dreadful recoil? When the famous Club conferred on me the unspeakable honor of entrusting me with their archives, in order that the admiring people of Europe might have a detailed account of their wonderful transactions, every operation described by Barbican was given in such clear and precise language that I understood it without difficulty, and wrote it out for my readers almost *verbatim*. But this *contre-coup* arrangement proves an exception to the general rule. At the first glance I thought I understood it completely. I now see I don't. Perhaps my readers have more perspicacity. I wrote to Barbican some time ago, stating my difficulties, but have received no reply. He is, I understand, at present deeply engaged in experiments with the spectroscope, and trying to establish a new idea regarding fluorescence. He has, in fact, given up Ballistics altogether, and I see by the papers that he gave a lecture some time ago before the Franklin Institute, in which he advocated the startling notion that the Sun is nothing but a great electric battery, without either light or heat in itself, and that light and heat existed only where the currents came in contact with a planet or its atmosphere. If I ever hear from him again, I shall give my readers the benefit of the correspondence.)

The projectile measured externally nine feet in width and fifteen in height. Not to exceed the assigned weight, the walls had been reduced to about a foot in thickness, but the lower part, having to resist the first terrific shock of the gases developed by the gun cotton, had been considerably strengthened.

This metallic tower was entered by a narrow opening in the upper part, somewhat like the man-hole of a steam boiler. It was closed hermetically by means of an aluminium door turning on a hinge and fastened inside by a powerful screw. Through this the travellers could leave their flying prison as soon as they would have reached the Lunar surface.

Such a trip would evidently afford very little pleasure unless the travellers could look about them while on their way. The contrivance enabling them to do so was simple enough. Four holes, concealed by the leather padding, contained circular lights of plate glass of the best quality and of great thickness. Two of these holes had been drilled through the side walls, one through the bottom, and one through the conical point. By means of these lights, the travel·lers could easily see not only what was going on around them, but also the earth that they were leaving and the Moon that they were approaching. Of course these plates were solidly protected from the shock of the start by strong deadlights, fitted into their places with perfect joints, but easily opened outwards by means of screws worked from the inside. In this way, the air could not escape, and taking observations was an easy matter.

It is almost needless to say that all these appliances and contrivances, subjected to the most rigid tests and working with the greatest facility, were as creditable to the mechanics now at work on the projectile as its casting and finishing had been to the firm of Meneely & Co.

Receptacles, solidly fastened down, contained water and provisions for the travellers, who were also furnished with light and heat by means of a supply of gas kept in a tank under the strong pressure of several atmospheres. All they need do was turn on the cock, and for six days they had gas enough to light and heat the whole cosy vehicle. Nothing, in fact, was wanting in the essential requisites of life and comfort. Even the agreeable united with the useful, thanks to Ardan's artistic eye, who would have turned the chamber into a veritable boudoir if there was only room enough. The travellers, however, were not so closely packed together as you might imagine. They had about fifty square feet to move about in, and as soon as they got rid of the water, their ceiling would be nine feet high. Ardan had by no means exaggerated when asserting that even the Pullman cars on the Pacific Railroad could not surpass the projectile vehicle in solid comfort.

The questions regarding provisions and light being thus satisfactorily disposed of, the next to be considered was how to obtain a supply of air. As a healthy man consumes in an hour all the oxygen contained in 22 gallons of air, it is evident that the slight supply enclosed in the projectile would be soon exhausted. A simple calculation showed that Barbican, his two companions, and two dogs that they intended to take along with them, would consume in twenty four hours at least 540 gallons of oxygen, about seven pounds in weight. Evidently the air had to be renewed ; but how ?

By a very simple plan, called Reiset and Regnault's Process, alluded to already, as the reader may remember, by Ardan, during the progress of his discussion with Captain McNicholl.

Air, as is well known, consists principally of two gases, oxygen and nitrogen, in the proportion of about 20 of the former to 80 of the latter, or as one is to four. What takes place when we breathe? A simple operation. We absorb much of the oxygen of the air, because it is absolutely necessary for our existence, whereas we exhale the nitrogen unchanged. The expired air, having lost nearly five per cent. of its oxygen, contains in place of it about the same volume of carbonic acid, produced by the union of the blood with the exhaled oxygen. It is therefore evident that in a closed apartment, after a certain time, the whole oxygen of the air is replaced by carbonic acid, a gas essentially injurious to human life.

The nitrogen question presenting no difficulty, two things were clearly to be done : 1, to renew the absorbed oxygen ; 2, to destroy the exhaled carbonic acid. Both these objects could be readily attained by means of potassium chlorate and caustic potash.

Potassium chlorate, the well known salt from

which oxygen is most readily obtained for experimental purposes, crystallizes in large six-sided plates, and, when heated to about 800° Fahrenheit, readily parts with its oxygen, chloride of potash being the residue. As eighteen pounds of this salt yield seven pounds of oxygen, two hundred pounds would evidently be more than even twice the quantity required before the travellers got to the Moon.

Oxygen being thus supplied, carbonic acid could be readily destroyed by potassium hydrate, commonly called caustic potash. This white crystalline substance is well known for its powerful affinity for water and carbonic acid, both of which it immediately absorbs from the air, and, uniting readily with them, becomes a moist carbonate of potash.

By combining these two operations, the distinguished French chemists, Reiset and Regnault, had succeeded in purifying polluted air and restoring its life-sustaining properties. Their experiments, however, having been made only on animals, it was still questionable how this artificial air would affect human beings. Such a question evidently requiring an answer of the most satisfactory kind, Ardan professed his willingness to try the effect on himself. But this Marston would not hear of.

" Since I cannot have the pleasure of going with you, my friends," he said in a tone that brooked no contradiction, " you must not refuse me the gratification of making myself useful by keeping watch and ward in the projectile for a week at least."

All objections being useless, particularly as somebody *had* to make the experiment, a sufficient quantity of potassium chlorate and caustic potash being given to him, together with provisions for eight days, he shook hands with all his friends on the morning of November the twelfth. Ordering them not to open his prison until the evening of that day week, he ascended the ladder with a bold heart, let himself into the trap door with some difficulty, pulled the cover after him, which was then hermetically sealed by a temporary arrangement especially contrived for the purpose.

Night and day all that week, watchmen patrolled around the projectile, carefully listening and ready to sound an alarm at the least noise. But they heard absolutely nothing. The great projectile was as silent as the sarcophagus in the heart of an Egyptian pyramid.

On the evening of November 19th, at four o'clock, in the presence of a prodigious multitude, the cover was lifted up. For a moment or two nobody appeared, and the silence of death pervaded the vast assembly. For an instant the spectators felt a cold pang seize their hearts. But they were soon reassured by hearing Marston's well known basso profundo lustily trolling out *Yankee Doodle*, and a tremendous yell rent the air at the sight of Marston's well known bust projecting from the trap door, his face smiling, his arms waving, and his eyes blinking from having been so long deprived of daylight, and probably also from his having been suddenly awakened from a profound slumber.

Far from being injured by the artificial air, he had even grown fat under the treatment!

J. T. MARSTON HAD GROWN FAT.

CHAPTER XXIV.

About a year before this time, just after the close of the great subscription, Barbican, as the gentle reader no doubt remembers, had placed in the hands of Professor Belfast, the Director of Cambridge Observatory, a fund sufficiently great to pay for the construction of a vast optical instrument. This was to be a telescope of power strong enough to render visible any object on the Moon's surface that reached nine feet in diameter.

Telescopes are divided into two classes, the refractors and the reflectors; and it is as well to know the difference between them. A refracting telescope has at its upper and larger end a convex lens called the *object glass*, and at its lower and smaller end another convex lens called the *eye glass* or the *eye piece*, because it is through it that the observer first looks. The rays emanating from a luminous body, converged into a focus by the object glass, there form an image which is magnified by the eye

(365)

glass.   A refracting telescope therefore is closed at each end by the lenses.

The reflecting telescope, on the contrary—invented by Father Zucchi, a Jesuit, in 1652—is open above so as to admit freely the rays proceeding from the object under observation. These rays are reflected by a concave mirror situated at the lower end, towards a looking-glass placed on one side, whence they are again reflected to the eye-piece, which is so disposed as to receive and magnify the image. But whether a refractor or a reflector, the value of the telescope evidently depends altogether on the perfection attained by the *objective*, whether this be a lens or a concave mirror.

Within the last quarter century, these instruments have reached such a high degree of power as to give very astonishing results. We are far removed now from the era, when the " Starry " Galileo watched the heavenly bodies with his poor little telescope, magnifying only seven times. For the last three hundred years, optical instruments have been steadily undergoing considerable enlargement, so that we are now able to sound the heavens to depths formerly never dreamt of.

At the period of the Gun Club's operations,

the most remarkable of the world-famous refractors were : 1, one belonging to the Pulkova
Observatory, a little south of St. Petersburg, the
object-glass of which was 15 inches in diameter ; 2, one belonging to M. Lerebours, the famous optician of the Paris Observatory, with
an object-glass of the same size ; and 3, the
telescope belonging to Cambridge Observatory,
Boston, U. S., with a magnificent objective
reaching a diameter of 19 inches !

Among the reflectors, two in particular, were
famous for remarkable power and gigantic size.
The first, constructed by the elder Herschel, at
Slough near Windsor, in 1789, was forty feet
long with a speculum of highly polished metal,
four feet in diameter. It had a magnifying
power of six thousand, but, unfortunately being
exposed a little too much to the weather, one
night of damp atmosphere dimmed its speculum
so much as to destroy its usefulness forever. The
second, certainly the finest reflecting telescope in
the world, was to be found in Ireland, in the
County of Tipperary, not far from Birr, and belonged to Lord Rosse. It is over fifty-six feet
long, and has a speculum six feet in diameter
and weighing at least three tons. Its reflecting
surface, more than twice as great as Herschel's,

and always attended to with the utmost care, exhibits objects with remarkable clearness and brilliancy. Strong chains, flying pullies, heavy counterpoises attached to walls of solid masonry, are required to move the enormous mass ; the expense of its construction could not have fallen short of 150,000 dollars, yet its magnifying power, under the most favorable circumstances, never exceeded 6,400.

Such an enlargement, no doubt very great, by bringing the Moon within forty miles distance from the naked eye, enables us to see any object on her surface that reaches sixty feet in extent. But our projectile being only nine feet in diameter, in order to be rendered visible, evidently required a telescope possessing seven times the power of Lord Rosse's instrument, that is, one which would magnify at least 48 thousand times.

This hasty *resumé* gives the substance of the problem to be solved by the Cambridge Observatory. There was no trouble in the financial aspect of the question. The difficulties were altogether material and practical.

The first thing to be done was evidently to decide between refractors and reflectors. In one sense, the former presented decided advantages. With objectives of an equal size, they furnish clearer and brighter images, as rays refracted through a lens suffer less absorption than when reflected from a speculum. On the other hand, lenses are limited to a certain thickness ; if this be exceeded, the luminous rays are so much obstructed that precision and definiteness immediately disappear. Besides, when made on a large scale, their construction is extremely difficult, and requires several years of the most patient labor. A reflector was therefore preferred, both as affording greater amplification, and requiring less time for construction.

Only, as luminous rays—especially when reflected, like those coming from the Moon—lose much of their intensity while traversing our atmosphere, the Gun Club had decided on erecting their instrument on one of the highest summits of the Rocky Mountains. There the great relative clearness of the atmosphere should of course allow a superior brightness of the image.

Still, in order to magnify this image 48 thousand times, Lord Rosse's speculum should evidently be considerably surpassed in size, and this was a matter of exceedingly great difficulty. To give the reader an idea of the extraordinary delicacy of touch required to produce the true parabolic curve—without which it is impossible to obtain

24

a correct image—it will be enough to state that, towards the edge of the speculum, a film of metal must be removed about 100 times thinner than the paper on which this page is printed!

Fortunately, a few years before this, Foucault, the famous savant of the Paris Observatory whose pendulum experiment gave a physical demonstration of the earth's rotary motion, had discovered a simple and expeditious process for polishing specula, by substituting silvered glass for the ordinary metal. Nothing more was required than to cast a mass of molten glass of the required size and shape—a task comparatively easy—and then to cover its surface with an exceedingly fine film of silver. By careful polishing, this could be rendered highly reflective, and—most important consideration in the present instance—when, from any cause, the silvered surface of the glass should lose its brightness, the speculum, instead of being irretrievably ruined, could be readily covered with another coating and made as brilliant as ever. It was this suggestion of Foucault's that the Cambridge men had followed out in constructing their speculum. They also adopted Herschel's idea in devising what he called his *Front View Telescope.* Instead of having the plane of the speculum perpendicular to the axis of the tube, it was inclined a little, so that the image was formed just at the edge of the upper end, where it could be viewed directly by the observer by means of his eyepiece. Thus the small mirror being entirely dispensed with, not only more rays were allowed to enter the tube but also less were absorbed, and consequently the image was much brighter and more distinct.

With such ideas determined upon, the necessary work at once began. According to the Observatory calculations, the tube of the new reflector should be 280 feet long, and its speculum 16 feet in diameter ! Yet even this colossal instrument could hardly be compared in size with the two mile long telescope proposed by Hooke, a distinguished English astronomer, who shares with Huygens of Holland the honor of inventing the hair spring of watches, and with Cassini of Italy that of discovering the rotation of Jupiter upon his axis. Nevertheless, the construction of such a mammoth telescope evidently should be attended with extraordinary difficulties.

The question as to its position was soon decided. It was to be located on the summit of a very high mountain, and very high mountains are not readily found in the United States. Indeed the whole oreographic system of that great country is very simple, being mainly confined to two distinct ranges—one on the east, the other on the west. They include between them the immense valley drained by the famous Mississippi, surnamed by the Americans the King of Rivers—the only kind of king these fierce republicans will allow among them.

The eastern range, first called the Appalachian by De Soto from the Indians that he found inhabiting its southern end, follows the general direction of the coast ; it is about 1300 miles long, and its middle portion, in Maryland and Pennsylvania, is about 100 miles wide. Its highest group is in North Carolina ; but even here the Black Hills, so named from the dark foliage of their pine clad sides, reach an average altitude of only 4500 feet, their highest summit, the Black Dome, being no more than 6,760 feet above the level of the sea. Still less elevated is the New Hampshire group, called the White Mountains, on account of their bare, precipitous, granite sides. Its highest peak, Mt. Washington, is 500 feet lower than the Black Dome, though, as it rests on a lower platform, it looks far more towering by the contrast.

The western range comprises the famous Rocky Mountains, which, starting from the Isthmus of Darien, follow the general direction of the coast for about 4,000 miles, and finally lose themselves in the ice-bound swamps bordering on the Arctic Ocean. Their height, however, is far from corresponding with their length, the general altitude in the United States being only about 5 thousand, while that of the Alps is 8 and that of the Himalayas is about 15 thousand feet. Even the highest peaks of these great mountain systems preserve nearly the same relative proportions, Long's Peak being about 14, Mt. Blanc about 16, and Mt. Everest about 29 thousand feet above the level of the sea.

Higher peaks indeed than Long's were to be found on the North American continent—Mt. Hooker and Mt. Brown exceeding it in British America, and Popocatapetl and Orizaba far surpassing it in Mexico, but the Gun Club, for very wise and sufficient reasons, had determined to confine the operations both of the Columbiad and the telescope to the territory of the United States. Therefore, long before the period to which our history is now arrived, the young professors of Cambridge, to whom the erection of the great telescope was confided, had dispatched all the necessary materials to the snowy summit of Long's Peak, in the far off Territory of Colorado.

Their task was a modern labor of Hercules. To-day, thanks to the completion of the Pacific Railroad, a trip to Long's Peak is only a pleasant promenade. You leave New York on Monday and arrive in Chicago on Tuesday. Next day you cross the Missouri at Omaha, and on Thursday you enter Cheyenne, 6,000 feet above the level of the sea. Here you take the Denver branch, and on Friday afternoon you find yourself revel-ling in the heart of the Rocky Mountains. Denver, a thriving city of 10,000 souls, the capital of Colorado, receives you hospitably. Though only settled in '58, the year of the capture of Lucknow, she can already show you her hotels, her banks, her churches, her theatres, her school houses and her tasty residences. Around you can see her gold, silver, coal, and copper mines; her plains often alive with antelopes, buffaloes, and prairie dogs; her wonderful fossil forests; her stony castellations; her deep cut gorges, and her rugged, brawny, amber-colored scenery. Farther off, through the moun-

tain atmosphere, rendered transparent by an altitude of nearly 6,000 feet above the level of
the sea, you can easily follow the Rocky Mountain range for a distance of 200 miles. A delicate haze softens the rich purple and the dazzling
whiteness of its outline. Its serrated edge, piercing the cloudless azure with a thousand snowy pin-
nacles, culminates to the north in Long's Peak,
to the west in Gray's Peak, and to the south
in Pike's Peak, all apparently only a few miles
distant, yet each requiring a good day's journey
to reach even their bases.

But at the period of our history, the Cambridge men had no Pacific Railroad to help
them beyond Julesburg. Cheyenne consisted of
only one house, and Denver was nothing but
a "Roaring Camp," inhabited by gamblers and
miners armed to the teeth, Mexicans, Indians, half
breeds, and desperadoes, generally of the worst
kind. The Colorado gold fever was still pretty
high. In fact, from the moment that the
Cambridge party left the main stream of the
Platte to follow the South Fork, they could
hardly have made any headway at all but for
the aid generously afforded them by the numerous emigrants struggling on towards Pike's Peak.

It was, however, at *Cache la poudre Creek*, a

stream washing the base of the mountains, that their real difficulties commenced, and these now became so great that our pen absolutely shrinks from the task of detailing them. To erect a telescope on the summit of Long's Peak, was a feat of gigantic labor, requiring energy the most daring, skill the most practical, patience the most enduring, and pluck the most persevering. Yet it was not too much for these wonderful Americans.

A railroad had to be built to the mountain top, over yawning ravines, through primeval forests, around dizzy precipices, across lake-like glaciers, and up grades so steep that the cars had to be pushed by a locomotive whose central cogwheel played in the broad, heavy, notched centre rail. This was the first railroad of the kind ever constructed, but since that time the same daring American genius has made itself felt in Europe. The engineer who sent the famous railroad up the sides of the Rigi in Switzerland, first learned to overcome nature by coping with the mountain difficulties of the United States.

Up this railroad had to be carried enormous piles of stone, heavy masses of wrought iron, corner clamps of prodigious weight, detached

THE TELESCOPE OF THE ROCKY MOUNTAINS.

pieces of the immense cylinder, the speculum itself weighing 50 tons—up into regions of perpetual snow, seventy miles from Denver the nearest settlement, in the savagest of savage regions, where, on account of the rarity of the air, even the simple act of breathing is painful and difficult, and the strongest constitutions are soon prostrated by the terrible " mountain fever."

The energy of these indomitable Americans overcame everything. Towards the end of September, less than a year after the beginning of the work, the gigantic reflector pointed towards the stars it monstrous tube 280 feet in length. The enormous cylinder was held in its place by immense chains and counterpoises of vast weight. Ingenious machinery kept it in such complete control, that in spite of its prodigious weight and colossal size, it could be directed at will to any portion of the sky, and being equatorially mounted, it could easily follow the track of any star in its endless march from horizon to horizon. It was a splendid triumph of science, enthusiasm, industry and even honest economy, for, notwithstanding all the time, labor, and genius lavished upon it, its total cost amounted to a little less than 400 thousand dollars in greenbacks. Lord Rosse's, though constructed under his own eye and within his own park and nearly six times smaller, had cost him more than the one-third of that sum in gold.

The first time the observers directed this magnificent structure towards the Moon, they felt themselves moved by a feeling at once of curiosity and indefinable uneasiness. Like Herschel with his four foot reflector just completed, 'or Columbus on the deck of the *Santa Maria*, they almost trembled at the vastness of the wonders to be revealed to them. Were they to discover lunar animals, cities, lakes, fields and oceans ? A few moments' observation, however, told them that though the volcanic nature of every portion of the Moon's surface stood revealed before them with absolute precision, yet they saw positively nothing that science had not disclosed to them before.

Still the great telescope of the Rocky Mountains, before serving the purposes of the Gun Club, rendered immense services to Astronomy. Thanks to its tremendous power of penetration, the depths of the heavens were sounded with a success never reached before, and results were obtained which the learned societies all over the world hailed with delight. *Eta Argus*, for instance, was resolved into a triple star, and thus easily accounted for its puzzling variations in brightness. *Alpha Centauri,* 61 *Cygni,* and Sirius, instead of the luminous pin-points that they show to the ordinary observer, presented a slight angle, like little planets. In the matter of Nebulæ, the great telescope demolished Lord Rosse as effectually as Lord Rosse's discoveries had demolished Sir William Herschel and the Nebular Hypothesis. For instance, the *Dumb Bell,* shown by Lord Rosse to be no Dumb Bell at all, but two unconnected streaks of star clusters, was resolved by the new telescope into three separate stars only, forming an isosceles triangle. *Mu Ursæ Majoris,* appearing to Herschel like a circular cloud, and to Lord Rosse like a halo surrounding a death's head with two ghastly eyes, was now shown to consist of a number of little stars apparently revolving around a centre, like the diagram of a solar system in our school books.

Nevertheless, in spite of its immense power, some of the Great Nebulæ remained apparently as irresolvable as ever. Like misty ghosts they still seemed to flutter on vaporous wings over the outer verge of creation, furnishing endless food for the weirdest fancy. Central nuclei could still be seen with arms radiating like a star fish, or like the fire sparks of a revolving pin wheel. The great Nebula of Orion still looked, according to the mood of the observer, like the head and jaws of some monstrous animal, or like a human being with the lower limbs torn off and the breast mangled with gashes. Not far from the *trapezium* you could still discover the scarred surface of a cloud continent, rent with volcanoes, or the distorted face of some monstrous lion struggling in the last agonies of death. Some few, however, of the Great Nebulæ, under the vast illuminating and magnifying power of the great instrument, changed their appearance so much that the Cambridge men, whom their magnificent achromatic had rendered as familiar with them as with the streets of Boston, often failed to recognize them at all, even after their well trained eyes had been gazing at them long and carefully.

They could see no trace of the planets said to be revolving around Sirius, Arcturus, Aldebaran and other bright stars ; and it is needless to say that they saw no sign whatever of the Great Central Sun, around whose mysterious focus our own Sun with his retinue of planets is rapidly travelling, but travelling in a circle so vast that the period of the duration of the whole human race will be hardly long enough to show even the curvature of its arc ! Nor did the star in Hercules, towards which our universe is moving, appear to be more clearly defined by the great telescope, than when it is viewed with a common opera glass. No wonder. Had our common ancestor, Adam, seen Lambda Herculis the first night he spent in paradise, it would not have appeared to him a particle less remote, than it will to the last of his descendants !

CHAPTER XXV.

CLOSING DETAILS.

Leaving the Rocky Mountains, we return to Stony Hill, the spot on which the eyes of the world were now fixed with interest the most intent. It was November 22d, and in nine days more the final *dénouement* of the wonderful drama was to take place. One single operation yet remained to be performed, but that one was of a nature so extremely delicate and perilous as to demand infinite precautions in order to ensure success. The Columbiad was to be loaded, that is, charged with 400 thousand pounds of gun cotton.

The reader probably remembers that it was against the success of this operation that McNicholl had laid his third wager. The Captain had concluded naturally enough that such a formidable quantity of pyroxyline could hardly be even handled without entailing the most serious consequences, and that in any case, the very pressure of the projectile would be enough to explode a mass of material so exceedingly inflammatble. He also counted on the well known recklessness and imprudence of the Americans, who during the great Civil War, were often seen puffing away at their cigars whilst in the very act of loading mortars with the terrible 30 pounders.

But Barbican, thus far perfectly successful, was determined not to be wrecked within sight of port. Picking out the very best men with his own hand, he made them work under his own eye ; he never left them for an instant as long as they were engaged in the dangerous task ; and by his combined prudence, precaution, and ability to command, he secured in his favor all the chances of success.

First of all, he took very good care not to bring to Stony Hill the whole charge at once. The 400 thousand pounds of gun cotton, divided into portions of 500 pounds each, were carefully wrapped up in cartridges, manufactured by the best hands in Fort Brooke. These were to be carefully put in powder wagons especially built for the purpose, and rendered almost airtight. Each wagon was to contain only ten cartridges ; one by one they were to leave Tampa, and in this way there was never more than 5,000 pounds of gun cotton at one time in the depot at Stony Hill. As soon as the wagon arrived, it was carefully unloaded by workmen walking in slippers, and each cartridge was carried in a hand-barrow to the mouth of the Columbiad. There it was quietly let down by machinery worked altogether by human power. Every steam engine had been removed, and even every fire had been extinguished within a circle of two miles in diameter.

It was, in fact, an exceedingly difficult matter to guard these masses of gun cotton against the heat of the sun, even in November. Accordingly, the men worked at night, which, however, an electric light, obtained by the Ruhmkorff apparatus, rendered as brilliant as day, down even to the very bottom of the Columbiad. There the cartridges were carefully deposited with perfect regularity, their centres being connected by fine wires which were to send the electric spark simultaneously through the entire mass.

All these wires, protected by an isolating material, were to meet together and form a single wire at the point where the projectile was to rest upon its bed of gun cotton. There they left the Columbiad through a hole drilled for the purpose, and ascended to the surface through one of these vents or chimneys left in the stone

facing for the escape of the gases at the casting.
From the summit of Stony Hill, the wire was
then carried on telegraph poles for a distance of
two miles to a Bunsen battery, which, replacing
platinum by carbon, obtained great power at
slight expense. This battery was connected with
the wire by means of a little apparatus resembling Morse's " Key " for transmitting. By simply
touching the button with your finger, the current was established, and fire instantaneously com-
municated through every particle of the 400
thousand pounds of gun cotton. It is hardly
necessary to say that it was only at the last moment that the battery was to be got ready.

The last of the 800 cartridges was stowed
away safely in the depths of the Columbiad on
the evening of November 28th. The operation had therefore completely succeeded ; but
how ? Barbican himself would be puzzled to
tell. Never before had he engaged in anything
that was at the same time so difficult, troublesome and vexatious. It was in vain that he
had announced by great posters that there was
" positively no admittance on any account "
within the board fence enclosing the summit.
The curious crowds pushed in at the gates ;
when the gates were closed they climbed over

25

the fence ; when the fence was made too high,
they broke it down. That was not the worst.
Many were found crazy enough to smoke cigars
and throw burning matches about in the midst
of bales of gun cotton, which, in case of an
explosion, would have sent them sky high by
thousands off the face of the earth ! Poor
Barbican's state of mind I shall not attempt to
describe. Marston was just as much to be pitied.
His impetuous sympathy, combined with his stout
frame and short neck, brought on even an ugly
attack or two, from which he was recovered only
by timely and copious drenchings of cold water.
The other Club men likewise aided their President bravely, unflinchingly ; but what could
forty or fifty do in a crowd consisting of
several hundred thousand sharp, peering, prying
inquisitive Yankees, who smoked as naturally as
they drew breath, and many of whom had never
been without a cigar in their mouths from the
time their teeth were able to hold one ! Even
Ardan, who had volunteered to " boss " one of
the squads that unloaded the wagons, was de-
tected smoking a magnificent *Imperador*, presented
to him the previous evening by a Cuban friend.
As may be readily conjectured, his further " boss-
ing " was immediately dispensed with, and, as

he could not be kept out of the enclosure very well, Barbican had him put under the constant surveillance of a private watchman.

However, through the special providence that watches over, not only little children, but also drunkards, artillerymen and other varieties of the insane, there was no explosion. The loading was a perfect success, and the Captain's third bet was lost. Nothing more was now to be done than to introduce the projectile, and allow it to rest on its soft, tender, downy, but decidedly dangerous couch.

But before proceeding to this last operation, all the objects necessary for the trip were to be stored away carefully and systematically in the vehicle-projectile. These were pretty numerous, and if Ardan only had his way, there would have been no room left at all for the travellers. You can hardly imagine all the articles that this gay and festive artistic Frenchman wanted to take along. A Steinway piano, masks and foils, a violincello, boxing gloves, portfolios of rare prints, birds in cages, a dozen or two pairs of boots, a set of Dumas' novels in 117 vols., a painter's portable easel complete, three cases of *Chambertin*, a few barrels of Florida oranges, six volumes of the Patent Office Re-

ports, presented to him as a great compliment by
an admiring Senator from Pennsylvania — these
articles, taken at random from his list, may give
you an idea of the nature of the inutilities with
which he thought of encumbering the projectile.
But Barbican returned him his list, with a line
penciled at the foot, saying that nothing would
be admitted except what was *absolutely and indis-
pensably necessary*.

Besides the usual supply of mathematical instruments, carefully packed away in a conveniently
fitted chest, the travellers took some extra ba-
rometers, thermometers and telescopes. One of
the indispensables was Beer and Mædler's *Mappa
Selenographica*, the Map of the Moon to which
some allusion has been made in an earlier chapter of our history. This famous chart, published
in four separate sheets, possesses every claim to
be considered a perfect masterpiece of patient
and intelligent observation. It gives with scrupulous accuracy, the smallest details of the
Moon's surface that is turned towards the earth.
On it you can easily trace the mountains, val-
leys, circular cavities, craters, peaks, grooves,
etc., with their exact dimensions, correct bearings and latest nomenclature, from the *Mare
Australe*, on the southwesternmost edge of the

disc, to the *Mare Frigoris*, that is so plainly seen extending itself over the circum-polar regions of the north. Ardan acknowledged that, under the circumstances, such a map was better than the best Steinway, or even his favorite instrument the violincello.

They also provided themselves with three Spencer rifles and three fowling pieces, with powder, shot and patent cartridges in great abundance. " Nobody knows what we may have to deal with," said Ardan. " Men or animals, they may not possiby relish our visit ; we must therefore prepare ourselves for the worst."

Besides weapons of defence, they took also a good supply of picks, spades, handsaws and other necessary implements ; and, as a matter of course, plenty of clothing suitable for all temperatures, from the icy chill of the polar regions, to the burning heat of the Torrid Zone.

Ardan, by no means discouraged at the ill success of his first list, proposed taking along a certain number of animals, useful ones of course, as he saw no great necessity for acclimatizing serpents, tigers, alligators or other noxious creatures in the Lunar regions. " A few beasts of burden, you know," he observed to Barbican, " the horse for instance, and even cows and

sheep would be found exceedingly useful."
" Granted, my dear Ardan," replied Barbican,
" but once more I must remind you that our
projectile is not Noah's Ark. It has neither
its capacity nor its design. Let us once in a
while, by way of change, try to content ourselves within the limits of the possible." But
Ardan persisting, the Captain was appealed to,
and the contest was finally ended by a compromise allowing two beautiful dogs to accompany the travellers. One was a favorite
pointer of McNicholl's, that had helped him to
kill many a fat partridge in Maryland. The other,
a splendid Newfoundlander belonging to a Boston gentleman, had already made himself famous
by saving three lives on the melancholy occasion
of the wreck of the *St. Lawrence* off Cape Sable.
His master, though much attached to him, readily
presented him to Ardan, for whom the animal
had taken a sudden and strong liking.

Several packages of the most useful seeds were
added to the list of the needful articles. Ardan
would have liked to accompany them with a few
sackfuls of earth to sow them in, and he insisted on taking along a dozen or two of young
saplings of different species, carefully wrapped
up in straw.

The necessity for provisions sufficient to last for several months, was evident at the first glance, for, likely as not, the travellers might land in a region of the Moon as bare as the desert of Sahara. Barbican easily succeeded in laying in enough for a year, by reducing to a very small bulk by hydraulic pressure a variety of meats, fruits and vegetables. These had been prepared expressly for the journey, and presented gratuitously by the *American Dessiccating Company* of New York, and the *Liebig Extract of Meat Company* of England. Gail Borden, of Texas, who had invented meat biscuits before Liebig, sent the travellers more of his famous condensed milk than ten times their number would require. They also supplied themselves with a small cask of the best Cognac, a ten gallon demijohn of Gibson's old Monogram—the Captain who was a good judge insisted on this—but they took no more water than would last them for two months, for Barbican, in accordance with the latest astronomical discoveries, had no doubt that they should find a certain quantity of water on the surface of the Moon. Ardan even thought that they were needlessly particular regarding provisions. He was quite confident that the Moon was pretty nearly as well supplied as the Earth. In fact, if he had entertained strong doubts regarding such a subject, he would have never dreamed of taking such a trip at all.

" Besides," said he, one day while talking with his companions, " we shall not be completely lost to our friends on the Earth, and they will be careful not to forget us."

" Forget you ! Never !" cried Marston suddenly, and gazing mournfully at Barbican, he continued in a voice of doleful pitch :

> " Never, Oh never, while life's in this heart,
>   Shall I cease to contemplate the Moon where thou art;
>   Most dear to mine eye shall her ' bulwark plains ' be,
>   And in every ' ring mountain ' a loved face I'll see !"

" Not lost to our friends on the Earth ! What do you mean, Ardan ?" asked the Captain, who had no more poetry in his soul than an old boot.

But Ardan, taking off his hat, saluted Marston with a bow that he would scorn to give an emperor, and shook him warmly by the hand several times before he replied to McNicholl.

" Nothing simpler, Captain. The Columbiad will be always here, ready at hand. What's to hinder our friends from sending us a few shell-loads of provisions whenever the Moon presents herself under circumstances favorable for the purpose ? This being only once or twice a year, it would be easy for us to know when we might expect an arrival, and accordingly hold ourselves in readiness to receive it."

" Good ! Good ! Bully for you, Ardan !" cried Marston like a man struck with a sudden idea. " Well thought of ! No, my brave boys, you shall never be forgotten. Rely upon me for that !"

" Exactly what I do, Marston. I have no doubt that we shall hear from you regularly ; and certainly we must prove to be most unaccountably stupid if we can't hit upon some means of enabling you to hear from us !"

These expressions and more in the same strain, inspired such general confidence that the whole Gun Club demanded with one voice to be allowed to accompany him to the Moon. As this, of course, could not be done, a Projectile Company was formed on the spot, and empowered to construct even a new Columbiad if deemed necessary. Nothing, in fact, could be simpler, clearer, easier, more obvious, more axiomatic than Ardan's idea, delivered, as it was, with a resolution and self-confidence inimitable in their sublimity. Even you yourself, my dear reader, should have had an exceptionally strong attachment for this miserable globe of ours, if you could listen to him for a few minutes without being seized with an uncontrollable desire to join the three heroes in their glorious trip to the Moon.

The different articles enumerated having been all carefully packed and put away in their various receptacles, the water intended to resist the concussion was admitted into its several compartments, and the gas was compressed into a strong reservoir. Of the potassium chlorate and the caustic potash, Barbican, apprehensive of possible delays in the route, took a sufficient supply to furnish oxygen and to absorb carbonic acid for at least two months. An apparatus, self-acting and extremely ingenious, invented by a member of the Franklin Institute of Philadelphia, was relied upon for restoring to the air perfect purity and all its sanitary conditions.

Nothing more now remained to be done with the projectile than to deposit it safely in the chamber of the Columbiad—an operation exceedingly perilous and requiring the most careful precautions. It was carried to the summit of Stony Hill; there powerful cranes, taking hold of it, held it suspended for some time in mid

air over the mouth of the yawning pit. It was
a ticklish moment.· Would the chains hold out
under the enormous weight ? Even the breaking of as much as a single link would cost at
least a hundred thousand people their lives !

Happily everything worked well ; in the course
of a few hours the projectile was quietly repos-
ing on its terrible bed, where its pressure had
no worse effect than to render the charge still
more compact.

" I've lost," said McNicholl to Barbican,
handing him a check on Drexel & Co. for
three thousand dollars. Barbican was naturally
unwilling to accept the money, circumstances
having altered so completely since the time
when the bets had been made ; but McNicholl
insisted, as he wished to leave all his accounts
in proper trim before starting on such a serious
journey.

" You're right, Mac, my boy," said Ardan,
" I like to see a man so conscientious ; only
while your hand is in, you might as well pay
the other two wagers."

" Why so ?" asked McNicholl, somewhat surprised.

" Because it's the only way to be on the
safe side. You either lose or win. You lose,

you pay ; you win, nobody pays ! Besides you
would not be there to take the money !"

"Oh ! We'll see about that," quietly observed the matter of fact Captain.

CHAPTER XXVI.

FIRE !

The first of December, so long expected, at last arrived. On the evening of that day, at precisely 46 minutes and 40 seconds after 10, the projectile was to take its departure ; otherwise, it would have to wait at least eighteen years before the Moon presented the same favorable conditions of zenith and perigee simultaneously.

The weather was magnificent ; the woods revealed the last splendors of the " Indian Summer," and an effulgent sun bathed in floods of dazzling light the beautiful world that its three inhabitants were on the point of leaving, of their own free will and accord, probably forever.

As may be readily imagined, very few people enjoyed their slumbers the previous night, either at Tampa, Stony Hill, or any place within twenty miles around. The weight of protracted suspense many a breast felt to be rather an unpleasant burden, which became only more irksome as the last moment approached. All hearts—

(397)

not excepting the iron organ that swung in Barbican's breast—throbbed with uneasy emotion —all but Ardan's.

Cool as a cucumber, lively as a lark, the unruffled Frenchman came and went, nodding and smiling, chatting and bowing as usual, and never showing the slightest pre-occupation, or even more than ordinary excitement. His slumbers had never been less disturbed. He slept as soundly as Turenne often did on a gun carriage the night before a battle.

From an early hour in the morning, a countless multitude covered the vast plains extending all around Stony Hill as far as the eye could reach. A double track had been laid long since on the little Tampa Railroad, but though long trains, consisting mainly of cars and locomotives borrowed for the occasion from the northern cities, started every quarter of an hour, they could not accommodate half the number of travellers who had come from a long distance, and were arriving at the last moment, to witness the great discharge. In fact, the arrivals at Tampa latterly, by land and water, by horse, steam, and human power, had been so enormous that the *Daily Truth Teller* estimated the number actually present within a two mile radius of Stony Hill, to be very little short of five million souls.

The latest arrivals could not get even within sight of Stony Hill, and, of course, were rather inclined to grumble at such a state of things. Was it for this that they had been for months on the way ?—for some had just arrived from Alaska, some from Chili, some from the Cape of Good Hope, and one had come all the way from Iceland. This was a schoolmaster named Thorvold, sent to Florida by a learned society of Reikiavig, not only to witness and report in full the world famous event, but also to settle, if possible, a point which at that time engaged the learned Scandinavians in a pretty lively controversy. He was to ascertain, by well authenticated historical remains, whether Florida was really and truly the country west of the Atlantic, spoken of in their ancient *Sagas* as having been discovered a thousand years ago not only by Norwegians, who called it *Hwittramannland*, the land of the White Men—but also by Irish sailors, who called it *Irland it Mikla*, or Great Ireland. As the learned gentleman spoke only Danish or Latin, with a strong guttural accent, his investigations, for a while at least, were not very successful. He was beset for two days by

a *New York Herald* reporter, who at first took
him for a regular diamond mine, but, not being
able to manufacture a single item out of him,
had at last to abandon him in despair.

The late arrivals were obliged to suit themselves to circumstances. If they could not get
as near the hill as they wished, they had to
be contented with getting as near as they could.
Otherwise they had not much to complain of.
They found themselves in the midst of a vast
hive of human beings, well supplied with all
the necessities of life, and even not a few of
its luxuries. Tents, blockhouses, frame buildings,
log huts, wigwams, *adobe* cabins, swarmed over
the plains ; with little attention to picturesque
effect, it is true, but all were arranged so as to
form broad streets, giving ready access to sun
and air, and admitting of the freest circulation.

Even solidly constructed houses of brick and
stone could be seen here and there, built by
the learned societies for their commissioners, or
by the rich men of the North, who, for one
year at least, found greater attractions in science
than in the seductions of Saratoga, New York,
Cape May or Washington. These houses were
so well finished, and the site in general was
so well chosen, that *Ardanstown* has now become

a favorite resort .of the fashionable Southerners, and to have a neat villa there is at present one of the surest tests of a wealthy Tampa man's claim to respectability.

We mentioned a few of the countries that had sent some late arrivals. But, in fact, every known country on the face of the earth had its representative at Stony Hill. Every language of the Five Continents resounded there at the same time. The top of the Rigi at sunrise in August—California Street in San Francisco about noon—the Tower of Babel half finished, was only a whist party in comparison to Stony Hill that morning.

" *Comment ça va ?*" cries a lively Frenchman.

" *Muy bien, muchas gracias,*" answers a polite Spaniard.

" *Go de mar tha thu !*" exclaims, smilingly a northern Celt.

" *Hà go magra guth !*" replies a southern ditto.

" *Guten Morgen, schöne Frau,*" says a gallant German from Frankfort.

" *Hur stär det till ?*" asks a Copenhagener, of a friend in the crowd.

" *Questa sera, mio caro,*" answers a Roman.

" *Puri mometz,*" says an Armenian from Bagdad, busy at breakfast.

" *Rax me o'er the pourrie !* " cries an Edinburgher, just commencing.

" *Nánu yénu kodabékee ?* " asks a Hindoo from Arcot, just finished.

" *Mashallah !* " cries a pious Turk from Smyrna, sipping a cobbler.

" *Haidi git !* " roars a choleric one from Constantinople, at an importunate beggar.

" *Khayrak ! Moosh owes hágeh,* " smiles a moon-eyed Egyptian from Cairo.

" *Mooi weertje, Meeheer !* " observes a stolid Hollander to his neighbor for the twentieth time that day.

" *Vervlœkt warm, echter bœs !* " is the Antwerper's invariable reply.

" *Ho dromos einai pleres lēstōn !* " swears an Athenian, whose pocket has been picked twice.

" *O yeou git äout !* " cries an angry Vermonter, whose toes have been just trodden on.

" *My heyes ! such 'eat ! such hair ! such a hatmosphere ! What a hox and a hass I was ever to leave Hingland !* " mourns a fat Londoner with a blue veil over his face.

" *O pueri Americani ! Gens infanda ! En unquam meam dulcem Islandiam iterum videbo ?* " sighs the poor Iceland Schoolmaster, very much

annoyed by some little urchins who are making
fun of his long hair and uncouth garments.

" *Ich hab kein Stück seit gestern Abend geges-
sen !*" roars a hungry Pennsylvania Dutchman.

" *Chin chin bow wow Ah Sin bittee !*" (Try
my nice pork pie !) warbles a Chinese cake
vender.

The cries resounding that morning in Russian,
Persian, Hebrew, Malayan, Servian, Thibetian,
Timbuctooan, Feejeean and other interesting foreign tongues we do not give at present, simply
because our printer's stock of type is not yet quite
as complete as those of the *Imprimerie Nationale*
in Paris, or of the *Armenian Convent* in San
Lazaro.

But to an eye or an ear in search of variety,
the presence of foreigners in Stony Hill was by
no means indispensable. The United States alone
the " new country," furnished out of its own
vast territory, peculiarities sufficiently numerous
and striking to attract the attention even of a
European. The keen Bostonian, the rollicking
New Yorker, the prim Philadelphian, the genial
Baltimorian, the courtly Charlestonian, the gay
Louisianian, the reckless Texan, the dashing Cali-
fornian, with the refined St. Louis man, the self-
satisfied Cincinnati man, the spry Chicago man,

the gloomy looking Salt Lake City man—not to speak of the lawyers and the bankers, the doctors and the professors, the sailors and the fishermen, the hunters and the backwoodsmen, the trappers and the lumbermen, the miners and the steamboatmen, the Canadians, the Mexicans, the Newfoundlanders, the Indians—though mostly clad in the same monotonous black, so characteristic of American male attire, yet each revealing some distinctive mark to announce his race, or district, or city, or calling—all formed a scene endless in variety as a kaleidoscope, and extremely interesting to the student of humanity.

The feature, however, that would most especially astonish our European, was the total absence of soldiers. In Europe, we resemble mischievous schoolboys that the master cannot trust out of sight, and we cannot hold a large open air meeting without feeling instinctively that at any moment we are liable to be trampled to death by cavalry, or blown to atoms by cannon. It is not so in America. There they can meet by the millions, and never catch the first glimpse of a soldier. Whose fault is this ? Our rulers' or our own ?

But it was in the restaurants and the bar rooms that the wonderful variety of American life and

its essential difference from ours, could be seen
in all their perfection. In the first place,
America is the blessed land of abundance ! No
danger of a single individual, out of so many
millions, dying of hunger at Stony Hill. At the
" Free lunches " given every day in every respectable bar room, all were welcome and the
more the merrier ! These lunches outstripped
even the famous wedding feast of Gamacho. The
side tables groaned beneath delicious oysters in
every style, fried, steamed, roasted, and on the
shell ; terrapins rich and racy ; aldermanic turtles ; not to speak of such delicacies as soft
shell crabs, " black fish," " white fish," " hog
fish," caught in the neighboring creeks abundantly and almost without trouble ; canvas-back
ducks, partridges, rail, mallards, shot almost without taking aim ; and oranges, figs, bananas,
citrons, olives, grapes, pomegranates, watermelons,
peaches, cantelopes, etc., all indigenous to the
soil, and flourishing with tropical luxuriance !

The drinks would also excite our surprise
by their variety, and especially by their nomenclature often strange but not always quite mean-
ingless. Besides all the ordinary liquors with
which we Frenchmen are well acquainted, these
Americans had drinks of their own, the exact

composition of which, however, I must acknowledge, I could never learn. To study up the subject was so vast an undertaking that I confined my ambition to learning only some of their names.

" What'll you have, gentlemen ?" cries a smart bar tender, to a party of five collected at the counter.

" A whiskey straight !" " A ginsling !" " Benzine for me !" " For me a sherry cobbler !" " I'll take a julep, if you have any fresh mint !" they all reply together, but the smart bar tender never misses an order or makes a single mistake.

" Look here, old man !" roar some noisy fellows playing cards in a corner, " we want a bottle of strychnine !" " Pass the bug-juice this way !" " Let's see your aqua fortis." " Send your red-eye along !" cry others in the neighborhood.

" I'll take my morning regulator, if you please," quietly observes a nice looking old gentleman with rosy gills.

" We want two brandy-smashes, one porter sangaree, one moral suasion, one phlegm-cutter, and one Tom and Jerry !" sing out some fast youths, laughing and smoking in the middle of the room.

" Here you are, stone fence !" cry the busy waiters running around, " one chain lightning ! Two stock ale ! Tanglefoot ? — Oh ! yes, sir ; all right ! one soda cock-tail with a stick !"

" Lemonade and sarsaparilla for ten !" cries a temperance party from Massachusetts.

" A bottle of Gibson's Monogram !" cries a couple of comfortable merchants from Pittsburg.

" Old Rye !" " Bourbon !" " Soda water and Catawba !" " Scuppernong !" resound from various parts of the room.

" Here you are, ginger pop !" the waiters go on, as they hurry from table to table ; " who said a Rocky Mountain sneezer ? All right, sir. Root beer ? No, sirree. White beer ? Coffee ? No such stuff here ! Get them in the temperance house around the corner. Eye-opener ? Yes, sir. Rum punch for two ! One glass Plantation Bitters ! California champagne ! who said California champagne ?" Etc., etc., etc.

Cries of this kind, however, were exceedingly rare on the morning of the first of December. Even at Delmonico's restaurant, a branch of the famous New York house, and the resort of all gourmands affecting an æsthetic taste, not a single guest could be found after ten o'clock. At four in the afternoon, among the millions of as-

sembled spectators, not a single one thought of
going to dinner, though they had taken nothing
since an early breakfast, except the bread, cheese,
and crackers, sold at the stands ; or sausages and
pies of dubious composition, furnished by peripa-
tetic venders.

It was just the same with the drinking. The
bar rooms were as silent as the grave. They reminded you a little of Philadelphia on election
day, or Massachusetts under the Maine Liquor
Law, where, if you want a drink, you have to
slip in by the back door and sneak down a cel-
lar. Even this resource you would not have in
Stony Hill after twelve o'clock. The colic
might twist you into a corkscrew, you might be
getting livid from the bite of ten rattlesnakes—no
help but to grin and bear it. Landlords, barkeep-
ers, waiters, even the drug clerks had all shut
up shop and run off to see the " big shoot."

Even the gambling rooms were abandoned.
For the last month or two, the " Casinos," the
" Crockfords," and the " Tattersalls" had never
been closed night or day. Not for one hour out
of the twenty-four had the billiard balls ceased
clicking, the ten pins getting knocked over, or
the bells stopped ringing in the shooting gal-
leries. In every tent, hotel, restaurant, " club

house," "casino" or "sample room," where gambling went on, you could find all the rooms full of parties deeply immersed in the mysteries of "old sledge," "high low jack," "poker," "bluff," "euchre," "pharaoh," "monte," "keno," and the other well known games. But now the cards lay idly in confused piles, the dice rested innocently in the casters, the counters in their drawers, the roulette balls in their holes, the rakes raked in no greenbacks, and the seductive voice of the *Croupier*, "Make your game, gentlemen," was heard no more. Croupier, dealer, stool pigeon, victim, professional, amateur, decoyer, decoyed—all suddenly discovered that even the goddess of gambling could lose her fascinations, and after several ineffectual attempts to proceed, they had concluded to suspend their game until the conclusion of the overpowering catastrophe that was now so close at hand.

All through and all over the feverishly excited multitude, standing quietly on the vast plain surrounding Stony Hill, a kind of confused humming murmur had been heard rising and sinking all day long, like the fitful sound of a distant waterfall when a soft wind is blowing. There is something mysterious about this humming murmur. It is said that you can always tell when you are in the immediate neighborhood of a great assemblage of human beings by a peculiar sound emitted by the mass, though individually they all keep perfect silence. In the Virginia campaigns, bodies of Northern troops, marching at midnight, readily *felt* that a certain wood was full of Confederates, though they all lay as still there as so many dead logs. Their very thoughts, as it were, rose in the air and rendered it vocal, as with the hum of disembodied spirits. The sentinels, it is even said, could always tell when the next day's battle was to be an unusually bloody one, by the peculiar noises heard only the previous night, and plainly distinguishable in both camps.

A feeling like this, or rather such a sensation as we can easily imagine the Pompeians to have experienced a few hours before the eruption of Vesuvius overwhelmed their beautiful city in irremediable ruin, now pervaded the countless multitudes around Stony Hill. An indefinable emotion of awe and terror oppressed every heart. The boldest held their breath and silently wished it was all over.

By seven o'clock this feeling had grown to such an intensity, that it could not possibly last any longer. It had to change or people would sink under its effects. Fortunately, just at this moment, the sight of the full Moon rising in the purpling eastern sky, large, silvery, serene, brought about the most welcome and needed reaction. She was hailed with the most enthusiastic cheers. Never before had the " Lady Moon" looked so beautiful. Never on her great festivals amidst the hills of Hindostan had she witnessed more enthusiasm among her countless worshippers. Never even had a grander choral hymn risen from the host of white robed priests moving solemnly around the wondrous temple of Ephesus, chanting the glories of the Crescent goddess !

Higher and higher she ascended, brighter and brighter she beamed, beautiful and more beautiful she looked ; whilst louder, fiercer, wilder, more passionate, more delirious rose the majestic diapason of the myriad voiced army, that stretched away for miles around the base of Stony Hill ! The women, children, and old men left behind in Tampa, twenty miles distant, heard the roaring distinctly, and said it resembled the singing of the telegraph wires on a keen windy day in winter.

A high platform—" shaped like a gallows,"

as somebody said—had been erected beside the mouth of the pit. It was reached by a long straight ladder, and up this ladder, at eight o'clock precisely, the three intrepid travellers were seen ascending. Their appearance was the signal for cheers fully as loud as ever, though by this time lungs were becoming exhausted and throats husky. The three black forms stood for a while calmly gazing around them, apparently taking a last farewell of the faces of their kind, and of the fields of their dear sweet old mother Earth. Happy were the spectators that stood on the southwest side ! Being in a line with the full Moon and the platform, they could easily follow every movement of the dauntless men, thus thrown in the strongest relief on the brilliant background.

By degrees all sounds ceased ; everybody, as if by mutual consent, wanted to hear the last words uttered by such men. Nobody seemed to be aware that the lungs even of a Stentor could not make a voice audible to the tenth part of such a mass. Nevertheless, all shouting ceased, and the roar of many voices was suddenly succeeded by the silence of an Arctic midnight.

Just then, a young German poet, assisted by

the Mannerchor of Philadelphia, commenced to
sing a hymn of his own composition, entitled
Arion's 𝔏𝔢𝔟𝔢𝔴𝔬𝔥𝔩 𝔷𝔲𝔯 𝔈𝔯𝔡𝔢 !—*Farewell to Earth !—*
It was a very beautiful composition, exceedingly
appropriate, and the Mannerchor men never sang
more sweetly or with better expression. But
the Americans, not understanding either the
words or the air, naturally concluded that the
Germans were singing a Dutch version of the
Star Spangled Banner, especially as that majestic air serves themselves admirably on all occasions when they wish to express musically high-
wrought intensity of feeling.

What more natural, therefore, than that the
Sons of Columbia should suddenly break out into
that song, that it should be caught up by the
next circle, and the next, and the next, till it
reached the outermost verge of the vast multitude two miles off ! Even the men on the
platform took their part in singing the mighty
chorus, and Ardan could be distinctly seen
beating time with both arms, and displaying all
the grace, masterliness, and power of a Jullien.
His happy thought added immensely to the
effect of the refrain, the two lines of which
require very considerable variation in the movement, the first being rather quick, and the

second not only very slow but demanding nicely graduated shades of retardation :

" And the Star-spangled Banner in triumph shall wave,
  O'er the Land of the Free and the Home of the Brave !"

At the word *Free !* the voice was the roar of a mighty people rising against the insolence of a haughty tyrant ; at the word *Brave !* the same voice, whilst proclaiming its satisfaction with the turn that things had taken, hinted plainly undying readiness to fight the same battles over again. Such feelings were, of course, rather out of place in the present instance, but in moments of intense excitement our judgments are not very discriminating, and when a fierce fever burns our hearts, it is not very particular as to the manner in which it may find vent.

With the last words of the hymn, the three travellers disappeared from the platform ; the fatal moment was approaching, an uneasy sense of terror once more took possession of all hearts and silence reigned supreme.

The heroes of the evening were immediately surrounded by the members of the Gun Club and by the representatives of many learned societies from various parts of the world. Barbican received them all with perfect politeness, and gave his last directions as coolly as he would order a cab. McNicholl, with calm countenance, eyes resigned, lips closed, and hands clenched behind his back, walked towards the mouth of the pit almost as tranquilly as a Christian martyr ever approached the Coliseum, where he heard the lions roaring and the mob yelling. As for Ardan, gay and happy as ever, you would think he was going to a friend's wedding, or rather, starting on a pleasant excursion to the mountains. Dressed in a tourist's suit of tweed, a satchel slung under one arm, a telescope under the other, in his left hand he held a dressing case, and with his right he distributed the warmest *Good Bye !'s* to the thousands thronging around him. Lively and buoyant as usual, he was in the best possible spirits, laughing, cracking jokes, punching Marston in the ribs and tipping his hat over his eyes, " to cheer him up," as he said, " and to make him look like himself." But poor Marston could not see the point of his jokes, and was more inclined to cry than to laugh.

The great bell now struck ten o'clock.

In the ears of many, it sounded with a melancholy wail, as if tolling the funeral knell of those who were never again to hear a bell's sweet chime in this world. In less than three-quarters of an hour they were to be flying like meteors through the boundless regions of space !

As some time would be required for getting the hoisting apparatus ready, clearing away the scaffolding from the mouth of the pit, and also for screwing down tightly the plate that covered the trap hole, the moment had now come for the travellers to take their places in the Columbiad. Murphy having had the charge of firing off the gun by means of the electric spark, Barbican very carefully regulated his watch to the tenth part of a second by the engineer's chronometer, in order that the travellers, when shut up in the projectile, might be able to follow with their eyes the movements of the second-hand as it marched impassively over the dial to the terrible instant of departure.

The touching moment for the last farewell was now come, and the bravest felt their eyes moisten. Even Ardan's *mot* was a failure, and his laugh hysterical. Poor Marston was quite overcome, and wept like a child while he held his dear friend's hand in both his own. " Let me go with you ! " he whispered hoarsely ; " it is not yet too late ! " " Impossible ! my dear old boy ! " said Barbican, shaking his friend's artificial hands most heartily, but with a voice firm as chilled steel, and eyes dry as unslaked lime.

In a few minutes more, the three companions, lowered into the projectile through the trap hole, have closed the door after them, and fastened it on the inside by means of a screw of immense power.

The workmen cleared away the scaffolding rapidly from the mouth of the Columbiad, and the black chasm was soon able to look with unobstructed range directly into the Zenith.

The three daring men are now walled up irrevocably, hermetically sealed in their awful but self-chosen mausoleum !

It is a moment of profound emotion, rapidly approaching its climax.

All those who had been privileged to come within the enclosure, now, according to a preconcerted arrangement, withdraw, rapidly and noiselessly, to a circle drawn around the pit at a distance of six hundred and sixty feet. No inducement can compel them to go further back.

Death like stillness within the enclosure, death-like stillness without. Every man among the millions is silent as yonder Moon, now treading her peaceful way through the hushed hosts of solemn stars ; every man is quieting even the uneasy fluttering of his heart.

Yet those inside the enclosure easily *hear* the presence of the myriads outside ; it floats on their ears like the mysterious murmurings of a smooth-lipped shell, or like the far-off echo of a storm raging in

" The wild woods of Broceliande !"

Or rather, Life reveals itself unto Life by means independent of our ordinary senses, and never dreamt of in our philosophy.

Higher and higher rises the Moon, occulting some stars, extinguishing others by the splendor of her beams. She has just left the constellation *Cancer*, and is now rapidly approaching *Pollux*, the less brilliant of the *Twins*. Consequently, though she is only half way on her journey to the Zenith, the bullet destined to hit her is to be discharged in a minute or two, as the sports-man always aims a little ahead of the bird that he intends to kill.

The death-like universal hush stills prevails. Not even a breath of wind steals through the leaves of the forest. No sound is heard, except the indescribable voice of

" Life speaking unto Life,'

like the whisper of the snowy avalanche echoing from the distant peaks of the Jungfrau.

All eyes are turned in one direction, the central focus of thousands of concentric circles.

Murphy never takes his eye off the hands of his chronometer. Of the forty seconds still to elapse, each one seems a century.

His voice can be heard counting " one," " two," " three," etc., with the regularity of a great pendulum beating seconds in a cathedral tower.

At " twenty " a universal thrill darts through the thousands that are within earshot. The same idea flashes on them simultaneously. With what anxiety are the travellers, shut up in the projectile, also counting those terrible seconds ! A few suppressed cries are heard, as several fall over in a fainting fit.

" Thirty-five !" " Thirty-six !" " Thirty-seven !" " Thirty-eight !" " Thirty-nine !" " Forty !"

" FIRE ! !"

Touching the button, Murphy closes the connection, and sends the electric current into the heart of the Columbiad.

The unearthly, ear-piercing, drum-rending, brain-shattering roar that follows his words we must not attempt to describe.

Everybody instantly feels as if struck on the head by a hundred pound weight, or, still more agonizingly, as if his heart was torn asunder by blunt nippers. Many faint from the pain, and they are the fortunate ones. Most of them have never quite recovered from the shock, and are troubled ever since by a distressful singing in the ears. Those who have heard the explosion of a powder magazine, or of a mine blowing up a bastion, or of an earthquake swallowing up a great city, may form some idea of the nature of the terrific noise. None else need try ; nor should they be sorry ; there is a kind of experience of which the less you know the better.

Instantaneously with the report, a pillar of flame darts up into the sky, half a mile in height. The earth shakes with appalling violence, and very few indeed of the countless spectators have sense enough left to catch the slightest glimpse of the projectile as it shoots rapidly upwards amidst the dazzling, blinding, blasting glare !

FIRE.

CHAPTER XXVII.

CLOUDY WEATHER.

The crowds of women, children, old men, and others belonging to the " can't get away club," who lined the streets of Tampa that night, thronged its housetops, and filled the decks and yards of every vessel in the harbor, though twenty miles distant from the scene of action, heard the great explosion distinctly and felt the earth quiver beneath their feet. But a minute or so before the arrival either of sound or shock, the red blaze of the flash had burst on their eyes with a suddenness that was painfully appalling. For an instant everything shone as bright as under a blinding sun ; then immediate darkness, black, pitchy, profound, cavernous. While still lost in wonder and trying to recover their dazzled sight, they suddenly heard the crashing sound of the explosion roaring all around them, and at the same instant a frightful tempest swept over their heads, shrieking like a typhoon. The children screamed, the women fainted, the men alternately prayed and

(421)

swore, while the earth heaved like a ship at sea. Many high houses visibly nodded. Several gas chimneys toppled over. St. Mary's Church, a new building not quite finished, on the corner of Washington and St. Augustine streets, fell in, and of the new Bonded Warehouse with the French roof, nothing but a shapeless mass of ruins could be seen next morning. You could have easily imagined yourself at Lisbon in 1755 or at San Salvador in 1854.

Even the vessels in the harbor did not all escape serious damage. Some of them, driven together, shipped water and sunk ; more that were anchored further out, snapped their cables like pack-thread and were tossed up high and dry on the western shore.

But the flash, the shock and the storm attendant on the explosion revealed themselves far beyond Tampa.

Far out at sea, both in the Atlantic and the Gulf, the resplendent coruscation of the blaze was distinctly seen, and more than one captain, forgetful of the Columbiad, marked on his log book the sudden appearance of a gigantic meteor.

The earthquake made itself felt in every part

of Florida; but, as may be readily supposed, it was of the storm that most notice was taken and by it most damage was done. The gases, liberated from the powder and rarefied still more by the heat, struck with instant and terrific violence the surrounding volume of the atmosphere, and sent it roaring in all directions, almost as destructive in its course as the dreaded cyclone of the West Indies.

The worst effects of this sudden concussion were felt, of course, at Stony Hill. Not a man had been able to maintain his footing. All had fallen before the blast, like a field of wheat beaten down by a storm. The fright and confusion were terrible, and many were seriously hurt. Those in the front rank, having to bear the first brunt of the shock, naturally suffered most. Unlucky Marston, as usual nearer to danger than anybody else, had been caught up like a straw and whirled violently, head over heels, for twenty yards or so above the heads of the crowd behind him. For a few minutes, almost all were completely deprived of sight as well as hearing, and to this day many have never quite recovered from the terrible shock that at once affected their eyes, their ears, and their nervous system in general.

The hurricane, having prostrated everybody at Stony Hill, overthrowing some of the most solid edifices, uprooting the forest trees, strewing with desolation everything within a radius of twenty miles, sending the trains flying back to Tampa in better time than they had ever made before, and bursting on that town with the results already given, had extended its circle still further, far beyond the limits of the United States. The terrible atmospheric commotion, aided by a west wind blowing at the time on the Atlantic, gave rise even to a sudden and therefore unforeseen storm at sea. It burst with extreme violence on a number of vessels that happened to be sailing a little north of the Bahama Islands. Some of them lost their masts, more had their captains washed overboard, and one in particular, a fine English merchant vessel, the *Montezuma*, Fitzroy master, engaged in the cochineal and mahogany trade between Balize and Liverpool, was so seriously injured as to founder and prove a total wreck, though fortunately the crew was saved.

It was the loss of this vessel, as my readers no doubt remember, that for a long time presented such a serious obstacle to the settlement of the *Alabama Claims*. England insisted that the American Government was responsible on account of having allowed the explosion to take place ; the Americans grounded their resistance on England's own favorite strong point : *No indirect damages !*

For the next and last instance that I shall give to show the prodigious effects of the great catastrophe in Florida, I cannot vouch, as I have no better authority for the story than the testimony of two colored natives of Sierra Leone, in Africa. According to their statement, which I take from a letter in the *Times*—addressed to the editor by the Mayor of Sierra Leone—the inhabitants of that country and the neighboring regions of Liberia, on the night of the first of December—probably about half an hour after the departure of the projectile—heard distinctly a faint rumbling like distant thunder in the west, though the night was exceedingly calm and the sky clear. This must have been the last reverberation of the sound waves, which crossing the Atlantic, thus broke on the African shore.

Let us return to Stony Hill. The first moment of awful terror and appalling confusion over, the deafened, the dazzled, the thunder struck—the whole mass, in fact—recovering their senses and rising to their feet, rent the heavens with one shout :

" Hurrah ! Hurrah for Ardan, Barbican and McNicholl ! Hurrah !"

Then all who had already provided themselves, whipped out their telescopes, opera glasses, spy-glasses, or spectacles — every pain, trouble and emotion completely forgotten for the moment in the all-absorbing, all-embracing desire to reconnoitre the sky in search of the projectile. But they searched in vain. Not the slightest glimpse of it could they perceive, and they were beginning to reconcile themselves to the idea of waiting for an early telegram from Long's Peak, where Professor Belfast, of Cambridge Observatory, had previously taken his post, attended by a staff ordered to make the most diligent and persevering observations.

But a phenomenon, totally unexpected — yet natural enough when people began to reflect about it—suddenly came to try their patience in a most tantalizing manner. The weather, hitherto superb, all at once changed ; the clouds began to collect on the darkened sky ; the stars disappeared ; and even the Moon could not send her light through the dense mist. How could it be otherwise ? Should not the instantaneous deflagration of 400 thousand pounds of gun cotton have produced a terrific displacement of the atmospheric strata, and the liberation of an enormous mass of vapor ? The whole order of nature had been thrown into confusion. The Americans themselves should have been the first to expect the sudden change. Had they not learned by the bitter experience of several years, that great battles are always followed by violent atmospheric disturbances ?

The darkness soon became so great that neither Moon nor star was visible, and the millions of observers, considering it useless to struggle any longer against what was evidently beyond their control, shut up their telescopes, and retired to take what rest they could after a day and a night of such unparalleled excitement.

Next day the state of things was no better. The Sun even did not show himself. Thick, heavy, dusky clouds formed an impenetrable screen between earth and sky, and, unfortunately, the hazy weather, borne on the wings of a north-easter, soon overspread the whole continent, reaching even the summits of the Rocky Mountains. What a fatality ! The only interesting news in the papers that day—after the telegraphic summary of the proceedings—was the weather report, and even that soon lost its attraction by its unvarying monotony. In the north, cloudy ; in the east, hazy ; in the south, misty ; in the west foggy. " Dire was the tossing, deep the groans." All over the land, the voice of the grumbler was heard to complain. All the Mrs. Partingtons of the country exclaimed bitterly against " Old Probs," the weather man in Washington, and demanded his instant removal. He was not, however, without friends who readily took his part. Had not the great explosion, they asked, for the time being put the weather altogether beyond his control ? If Nature was indignant at the unwarrantable liberties taken with her orderly and in general smooth-working operations, what else could be expected ? Besides, they added very sensibly, supposing the day were one of the finest that ever gladdened the earth, where would be the advantage ? The projectile could not possibly be seen, as, in consequence of the earth's rotation, it was by that time vertical to their Antipodes in Western Australia, or somewhere in the South Sea.

In this unsatisfactory manner the first day ended, and the night brought no improvement. The clouds were denser and darker than ever, and the Moon never showed herself even once. Many people said, half in earnest, that she was angry at being shot at, and that they had seen the last of her. Not a single observation was possible, and the dispatches from Long's Peak, still the melancholy burden bore of :

" Altitude of Station, 14,000 feet. Thermometer 40. Barometer falling. Weather threatening. Wind E. N. E."

Next day, the appearance of some thoughtful, well written articles in the *Boston Post*, the *New York World*, the *Philadelphia Ledger*, and other leading papers in the country, had a very tranquillizing effect. They showed very conclusively that, so far, there was no reason for dissatisfaction ; the experiment might have possibly succeeded ; the probabilities, even, were decidedly on the affirmative side ; it would be time to despair only when positive proof was furnished to the contrary ; the projectile could not possibly reach the Moon until the 5th at midnight ; on account of the small size of the shell it was impossible to follow its track ; in two days more it would show itself on the surface of the Moon, like a little black spot ; and in the meantime their readers should keep themselves as cool and as patient as possible.

This advice was generally followed, and public impatience kept itself within reasonable bounds for the next two days; but when the midnight of the 5th showed itself as cloudy as ever, and obstinately refused to let even a star be seen, the general exasperation reached a very dangerous pitch. "Old Probs" was bitterly denounced as the worst kind of a "fraud," so that even his warmest defenders had not a word to say for him.

The Moon herself came in for as good a share of defamation and scurrility as if she had been an unpopular General, or a President unable to command a majority in Congress. A catching, but not over decent, lampoon on the subject, published the very next morning by a New York journal of civilization, had an enormous success, and the clever artist, who dashed it off in five minutes, was at once pronounced to be beyond all odds the greatest caricaturist of the nineteenth century.

Alas, poor human nature ! In the first moments of our dissatisfaction, how often do we madly smash to pieces to-day the gods we worshipped yesterday with so much fear and trembling ! Only a week ago, five minutes after the appearance of such a cartoon, the great caricaturist would be dangling from the nearest lamp post.

Marston was by this time more than half way to Long's Peak, for which point he had started at an early hour on December 2d, though considerably bruised and shaken by the terrible explosion. He wished to make his own observations. On the road he heard all kinds of rumors, but his brave heart never despaired. He believed too firmly in Barbican to harbor for an instant a doubt regarding his success. Besides, amidst all the startling rumors that, as usual in times of uncertainty, were flying about by the thousand, no report had as yet come of the projectile having fallen back on any of the continents or islands of our globe. The worthy fellow would not admit for an instant the possibility of its having fallen into the ocean, notwithstanding the fact that the surface of the water is three times greater than that of the land.

December 6th. Weather still cloudy. The morning papers announced among the other cable news, that the great telescopes of the old world, Lord Rosse's in Ireland, Sir John Herschel's in England, Foucault's in France, Father Secchi's in Rome, that of Königsberg in Prussia, and that of Pulkova near St. Petersburg, were continually directed day and night on the surface of the Moon when visible. This was almost continuously from her rising to her setting, for, contrary to the state of things in America, the weather throughout Europe was magnificent and highly favorable for observation. However, from the comparatively small size of those instruments, no satisfactory result could as yet be positively reported.

December 7th. No change. Europe, even Asia and Africa, began to share in the impatience of the United States. In spite of the action of the Greenwich Observatory, the English people had become intensely interested in the subject, and the *Times* was flooded with the wildest projects, gratuitously offered to the Americans, for dispersing the clouds accumulated over the surface of the United States.

December 8th. The wind having changed a little, the sky seemed disposed to break, but in a few hours all hopes were again mercilessly dashed to earth by another change in the wind, and the night that followed was no improvement whatever on the previous week.

Matters were now beginning to look serious. The Moon was to enter her last quarter on the 12th; thenceforward her light would go on declining so considerably that even the clearest sky would afford little opportunity for observation. In fact, a week later, she would set and rise with the sun, in whose rays she would become for some time absolutely invisible. In such a case, the only possible resource left would be to wait till the beginning of January, when, being once more at her full, she could be observed with some advantage.

Consoling reflections of this nature began to appear in the morning papers, who, moreover, preached eloquent sermons on patience, easily proving it to be the greatest of all Christian virtues.

December 9th. " Falling barometer, cloudy weather, with areas of light rain, turning to snow in the Northern and Middle States." *Old Probs.*

December 10th. The sun showed himself occasionally, but at short intervals and among watery clouds, as if to tantalize folks ; besides the east and southeast winds still prevalent were charged with too much moisture to allow the telescopes to be used.

December 11th. No change. " All quiet along the Potomac !" as the *Herald* expressed it, alluding to a stereotyped phrase often heard in the early years of the great Civil War.

The *Herald's* little joke fell on deaf ears ; or rather it caused some irritation ; an impatient man cannot relish jokes, and the impatience of the public at large had by this time exceeded all bounds.

At last, on the 12th, one of those frightful storms that are seldom witnessed out of tropical regions, burst on the United States. It came from the southwest and blew all day with fearful violence, turning quite cold towards evening. Every cloud vanished from the blue sky ; the stars came out in all their splendor ; and the Moon, with only half her disc visible, but still as bright, beautiful, and glorious as ever, made her appearance about two hours after midnight, and moved serenely once more through the glittering constellations that spangled the face of heaven.

CHAPTER XXVIII.

A NEW STAR.

On that very night, or rather morning, though long before daylight, bells, guns, cannons, and " extras" roused up people suddenly from their slumbers, and an astounding piece of intelligence burst like a thunderbolt on every part of the Union.

THE PROJECTILE HAD BEEN SEEN !!

It is needless to say that the Atlantic Cable instantly flashed the news to all parts of Europe, in fact to all parts of the world within reach of ·legraphic communication.

The morning papers having made up their forms before the arrival of the telegram, not one of them contained it. The "extras," therefore, went off by millions, but the public had been too often victimized by bogus dispatches during the war to trust implicitly to anything short of the official announcement. Here it is word for word, forwarded a few hours later by Professor Belfast. As will be

(435)

seen, it contains the learned gentleman's final conclusions regarding the ultimate issue of the Gun Club's famous experiment.

LONG'S PEAK, C. T., *D.c.* 13.

" To the Regents of the Smithsonian
Institute, Washington, D. C.:

" GENTLEMEN :

" I have the honor to inform you that the projectile, discharged by the Columbiad at Stony Hill, has been perceived this morning at three (3) hours, twenty-seven (27) minutes, and thirty-six (36) seconds after midnight, by Messrs. McConnel and Belfast, of the Cambridge Astronomical staff, at present on active but temporary service at this Observatory.

" The projectile has not reached its destination. It is passing on one side, near enough however to be affected by the Lunar attraction.

" Its rectilinear motion having become circular in obedience to the two forces by which it is actuated, it has been compelled to follow an elliptical orbit around the Moon, thereby becoming substantially her satellite.

" The elements of this new heavenly body we have not as yet succeeded in determining, as neither her actual velocity nor the precise amount of the Moon's attraction has been sufficiently calculated. Her mean distance, however, from the Lunar surface may be roughly estimated at 2,333 miles.

" Now, in this state of things, two different results

may occur, each of which would produce a very considerable modification.

" 1. Either the Lunar attraction will finally prevail, in which case the travellers will effect their purpose ;

" 2. Or, kept continually whirling in the immutable path of its orbit, the projectile will go on revolving for ever around the Moon until the end of time.

" Which of these two hypotheses, the only ones possible, will prove the true one, observations alone can and will determine, but, so far, the Gun Club's experiment has been attended with no other result, than presenting our Solar system with one more heavenly body

" All of which is respectfully submitted.

" J. M. BELFAST,
" *Director.*"

With what breathless eagerness this dispatch was read in the evening papers ! What an infinite number of startling questions was called forth by this totally unexpected *dénouement !* What investigations of a palpitating interest should henceforth await the watchful eye of science ! A great problem had been resolved, marking a new era in the world's annals, and, like the discovery of America, destined to modify our history forever. Thanks to the courage and the sublime devotion of three men, the enterprise of sending a bullet to the Moon, instead of being put off to future ages, like other so called Quixotic projects, was now a living, accomplished fact. Its consequences defied all human calculation. The travellers, shut up in the new satellite, might perhaps never exactly attain their purpose, but at least they would form part of the Lunar world. They would gravitate around the mysterious Queen of the Night, and, for the first time direct the unaided eye of man into the dark mysteries of her surface. The names of Barbican, McNicholl and Ardan should be henceforth and forever written in letters of living light on the brightest pages of astronomical research. In the far off ages of the future, when so many other illustrious names shall be extinguished in the black waters of oblivion, these three men shall stand forth as the representatives of an age of profound investigation, most pains-taking industry, and unparalleled audacity. It was only such an age that could have given birth to explorers so daring, engineers so accomplished, and lovers of abstract science so singularly pure and unselfish !

It must be acknowledged, however, that lofty sentiments of this kind were confined to the scientific, the learned, the æsthetic, the cultured classes—in other words, to the few. The world at large heard the result with a cry of horror, surprise, and profound sorrow. Could not something be done to deliver those dauntless heroes from their appalling situation? Come to the rescue, scientific men! Now is the time to show the value of your boasted knowledge! Do something for the bravest hearts that ever beat within your ranks! But the scientific men shook their heads hopelessly. Nothing could be done. These daring spirits had, of their own free will, transgressed a great law of nature and nature's God, and therefore should abide by the consequences of putting themselves out of humanity's reach. They had air enough for two months. They had provisions enough for a year. " And after that?" shrieked the sorrowing world, wringing its hands in despair. " Oh! what after that?"

But to this terrible question, the most scientific of the scientific men gave no more satisfactory answer than an ominous shake of the head.

One man alone never lost courage, one man alone never considered the situation desperate. By the force of his intense friendship for Barbican, and profound admiration for Ardan, he had come to partake of the force of character of both. *Nil desperandum !*—Never give up the ship !—*Quand même !*—What of it ?—the deathless mottoes of his vanished friends had now become completely and inseparably his own. Need I say that this man was Marston?

As said before, he had started on the 2d, but though he travelled day and night and performed miracles of locomotion, he could not accomplish a journey of considerably more than two thousand miles in less than ten days. Not arriving at Long's Peak until the morning after the reported discovery, he had consequently suffered the profound grief of being too late to catch a glimpse of the projectile.

But his resolution was immediately taken. Until that projectile would again become visible, and as long as it would continue visible on the Lunar disc, so long would he continue solid and determined, at his post beside the great telescope of the Rocky Mountains. All other thoughts, hopes and emotions were to be henceforth concentrated into one single uninterrupted operation : to watch for the projectile that contained his three friends. The instant the Moon again appeared, he framed her in the mirror of his great reflector, and never lost sight of her from the moment she rose in the eastern sky until she sank behind the snowy peaks in the west. It need hardly be

MARSTON AT HIS POST.

said that his eye sought continually the little black spot that Belfast had reported as seen crossing her silvery disc. Sometimes he imagined he saw it, but in an instant it would completely disappear. This he naturally attributed to his want of experience in taking observations with large telescopes, though Belfast seemed to consider it to be owing to the diminished size of the Moon's surface. He saw enough, however, to convince him that his friends were still safe, and, although Belfast soon began to entertain serious doubts on the matter, he would never admit the remotest possibility of losing them.

" No, no," he would soliloquize, when Belfast had retired after a hot discussion regarding the identity of the black spot and the projectile. " No danger of the Boys ! Their heads are too level ! Correspond with them ? Of course we shall. It's only a question of time. And they will correspond with us. Won't you, Boys ? How are you up there ? Do you ever think of old Marston ? Of course you do ! Belfast says you will never come back ! Can he be right ? The thought gives me a pain in the heart ! But I don't believe him ! He does'nt know what you are made of ! *I* know you like a book ! You are the three blossoms of our wonderful nineteenth century. Two of you are the embodiments of practical *Science* and practical *Industry,* as developed in my own great country, the young Queen of the New World ! The other of you is the embodiment of practical *Art,* as fostered in his own fair land, the graceful Queen of the Old ! You to fail ! I can't believe it. Science is immortal. Its votaries are indestructible ! To quote lines of my own composition, written a few years ago for an address to the *Polytechnic College* of Philadelphia :

> " Empires the proudest vanish in a day,
>   The rock-ribbed Pyramids confess decay ;
>   But what of those hearts that lofty Science trains
>   *Man* to value, not sordid Mammon's gains ?—
>   Radiant as yon Stars, they shine while Time remains !"

Thus did the faithful friend, alternately hoping and fearing, patiently watch at his post on the lonely peak of the mountains.

END OF FROM THE EARTH TO THE MOON.

PERFECT END

A RINEHART SUSPENSE NOVEL

Other Yellowthread Street Mysteries

YELLOWTHREAD STREET
THE HATCHET MAN
GELIGNITE
THIN AIR
SKULDUGGERY
SCI FI

Also by William Marshall

SHANGHAI